Bean Counter

a novel of murder, malfeasance, and mayhem

T. A. Clark

Bean Counter Mystery Book 1

This is a work of fiction. Names, characters, places and incidents either are the product of the author's imagination or are used fictitiously, and any resemblance to any actual persons, living or dead, events, or locales is entirely coincidental.

ISBN-13: 978-1523731886

For Nga

Thank you for your patience.

ONE

There's no such thing as a stranger. A stranger is just a business opportunity you haven't figured out yet.

From – *Talk Your Way to the Top*

The plaza in front of the Boca Cheeca Key ferry terminal was nearly deserted. The sun had set over an hour ago, and with it, the last mainland-bound ferry of the day had left the dock. One man waited under the eaves of the terminal roof, seated at a sticky table in front of the shuttered snack bar. He slouched in the plastic chair. His forearms, tattooed in a red and orange flame pattern from wrist to elbow, rested on the edge of the table. He scanned the dark waters of the bay for signs of the returning ferry, methodically tearing open sugar packets and pouring the contents into his mouth. The only sounds were the lapping of the water around the pilings, and the echoes of his right heel tapping on the concrete.

Just as he finished the last of the sugar and was thinking about moving on to the Sweet-N-Low, he spotted the ferry as a dark blotch against the bright lights of Miami. He wiped his hands on his jeans, leaving stray granules of sugar stuck to the denim, then finished his grooming by running his fingers through his greasy hair. As the ship turned into the channel, he stood and walked into the shadows of the parking area.

After the ferry nuzzled into its slip, it disgorged only three passengers. An elderly couple stepped carefully down the ramp, each struggling under the weight of several large shopping bags. Behind them, clearly impatient with their slow progress, was a paunchy fifty-five-year-old businessman wearing a blue sports coat and tan pants, his shirt open at the collar. He carried a well-worn brown briefcase stuffed near to bursting.

As soon as propriety allowed, he scooted past the slow-moving couple ahead of him, mumbling an insincere "Have a nice evening." He walked into the parking lot and sat heavily in the seat of his custom electric cart. As he inserted his key, the man with the tattooed flames on his arms and the sugar on his pants sat down in the passenger seat and extended a hand, saying, "You must be Dick."

With cat-like reflexes honed by years of doing business in South Florida, the older man automatically took the extended hand and shook it. "It's Richard," he said. "Richard Golden."

"I'm gonna call you 'Dick.'"

Affecting calm, Richard Golden asked, "And you are?"

"I'm Scorch."

"Scorch?" He tried to extricate himself from the handshake but found he was firmly in Scorch's grasp. "Like a small burn?"

Scorch's face went taut. "No, goddammit!" he sneered. "Like a bad burn. Like the serious, fucking burn I'm gonna put on your ass in about five minutes." He pulled Richard Golden toward him with his right hand and revealed a large knife in his left.

Richard Golden's already pallid complexion turned even more ashen at the sight of the blade. Struggling to retain some composure, he asked in a voice that sounded small even to him, "What is it you want, Mr. Scorch?"

"It's just Scorch, Dick," he said, friendly again, "and what I want is for you to drive."

The Village of Boca Cheeca Key was billed as "Your Haven in Paradise," with the slogan, "Who says money can't buy happiness?" The residents referred to it as "the island," but it was actually three small islands on the eastern edge of Biscayne Bay, directly abutting the Biscayne Bay Marine Sanctuary. It had caused an uproar among environmentalists when it was first proposed, and sparked strong opposition from numerous groups, but money can buy more than happiness in South Florida, and eventually the permits were issued and dredging and blasting and the construction of seawalls started.

The construction was completed in phases. Phase One had been the "town center," consisting of the marina, a clubhouse, and a few small shops, surrounded by fifteen hundred condominium units. Phase Two had added eight hundred town homes. Phase Three was just now under construction on the southernmost of the three islands. It would soon offer twenty-five waterfront mansions, each completely filling its postage-stamp-sized lot and surrounded by its own eight-foot concrete wall. The roads had only recently been completed, and several of the homes were under construction.

Scorch directed Richard Golden to drive over the bridge, past the "Coming Soon, Phase III" sign. There were no lights yet, and Richard Golden had to proceed slowly in the profound blackness of the moonless Florida night. The electric cart's one headlight glowed feebly, unable to penetrate the darkness more than a few feet ahead.

As he carefully picked his way around the construction debris in the road, he glanced at his captor. In the dim reflected glow of the headlight, he could not read any expression.

He quietly cleared his throat and hoped his voice would

come out sounding calm as he asked, "What is it exactly that you want from me?"

In response, Scorch just said, "Keep driving. I'll tell you when to stop."

Richard Golden persevered. "I mean, if there is something you need, money, for instance, I would be happy to cooperate. There's no need for violence."

Scorch laughed. "Of course there is, Dick. Violence is what it's all about. I'm being paid for violence."

"Someone is paying you to beat me up?"

Scorch nodded in the darkness. "They sure are."

"But why?"

"Apparently, they ain't happy with you, Dick."

Richard Golden saw a ray of hope. "Look," he said, "I'm a businessman. You're clearly in this for the money. Whatever they're paying you, I'll double it. I can wear some fake bandages for a few days, and you can get paid by both of us. That's a good deal. Triple pay, and no effort."

Scorch ran a hand through his hair as he considered for a moment, then shook his head. "It's tempting, Dick. Really. It's a good offer, but I have a reputation, you know? Besides, my employers aren't the kind of people you want to piss off. You're about to find that out."

"Who are your employers? Who wants me hurt?"

Scorch ignored the question and pointed to a cleared lot ahead. "You can pull it over there."

Richard Golden had been too young for the military draft, and in the thirty years he'd lived in and around Miami, he had always succeeded in avoiding violence. He feared pain, and his whole life had been spent accumulating the kind of wealth and power that would allow him to avoid situations where he might have pain inflicted on him. He was completely unprepared, mentally and physically, for what lay ahead, and he was determined to avoid it.

As directed, he turned into the empty lot. Though it

would soon be a ten-million dollar bayside mansion, it was now just a plot of roughly graded sand and coral running from the road to the seawall. As the cart bounced over the uneven ground, Richard Golden hatched a plan.

"Stop here," Scorch said.

Richard ignored him and pressed the accelerator to the floor. He steered directly for the seawall, as fast as his little electric cart would go. Unfortunately, that was not very fast. Under the best of conditions, it had a top speed of only about twenty-five miles per hour, but loaded with two full-sized adults, bouncing over rough terrain, it didn't even get close to that.

Scorch had to hold on with both hands to keep from being thrown from the bucking cart. "Hey!" he shouted. His head bounced off the roof. "Stop this thing, now!" He tried to threaten with the knife, but could only raise it briefly before having to grab the seat again.

Richard Golden pressed on with grim determination, keeping his seat with a white-knuckled grip on the steering wheel. His plan was to jump from the vehicle just before it careened over the seawall and plunged the five feet to the beach below, hopefully exploding in a ball of fire as so often happens in movies.

Unfortunately, before Richard could execute a graceful exit, Scorch pushed him from the driver's seat with a violent shove, sending him tumbling to the ground. The electric cart was designed to lose speed quickly once the accelerator was lifted, and that's precisely what it did.

As the cart drifted to a stop, Scorch turned the wheel, easily avoiding the seawall. He jumped to the ground, swearing. "Goddamn it, Dick! Now you're really pissing me off! You don't want to piss off the guy who is about to kick your ass. That ain't a good idea, Dick."

Scorch looked back toward the road, but in the undiluted darkness, could see nothing. "Shit!" he said, spitting the word out like a bad taste. He climbed into the driver's seat and turned the cart around. The headlight swept the ground with its meager beam and quickly fell on Golden's body, lying in the gravel near the spot where he had landed.

"Now that didn't get you too far, did it Dick?" he said as he pulled up beside the crumpled form. He stepped out of the cart and stood over Richard Golden. "That was a stupid thing to do," he said, and then gave him a vicious kick in the ribs.

When that got no reaction, he knelt beside the body and rolled it over. Richard Golden's head lolled at a disturbingly unnatural angle. Scorch pressed his ear to his victim's chest and listened for a heartbeat that wasn't there. "I don't fucking believe this!" he shouted at the night. "You stupid piece of shit!" Scorch stood and began kicking the body again, and if Richard Golden wasn't already dead from a broken neck, the wild beating he received at the hands and feet of Scorch would have finished him off.

***

Earl "Buddy" Grinnell was Chief of Police for the Village of Boca Cheeca Key. At six feet three and 250 pounds, his qualifications for the job were an imposing physical presence, and three years working as a night watchman for Miami Security Consultants. His other major qualification was that he had been a high school football teammate and friend of Andrew Keene, Jr., son of the developer. He had proven a good choice so far. His deep voice was soothing to the residents when they called with their problems, and he was liked and respected by the other former security guards who made up the police force for the island.

Buddy Grinnell's biggest shortcoming as a police officer was that he had begun to think that he really was a police officer. When the call came in from the construction company offices about the body of Richard

Golden, rather than call the real police, Buddy grabbed a camera and a couple of rolls of crime scene tape, rounded up several of his men, and headed out to the construction site in the green and white electric carts that served as the island's police cars.

By the time Buddy and his men arrived at the scene, curious construction workers had been milling about the site for over an hour. They were immediately shooed away, and they shuffled back to work, their dozens of feet helping to obscure the tire tracks and footprints of the previous evening.

While Buddy surveyed the scene and took notes, his men quickly began stringing the police tape they rarely got to use, managing to empty both rolls. They then took pictures of the body, and the abandoned cart, and then of each other standing over the body, until Buddy finally yelled at them to cut it out.

When Buddy eventually thought of it, he sent someone to fetch Ed Folger. Edmund Folger was a retired obstetrician who received a break on his monthly condo fees in return for making himself available to the village government as a consultant on all things medical. His knowledge of forensic medicine was about as extensive as Buddy Grinnell's knowledge of police procedure, but he was not a stupid man. He immediately questioned Buddy's conclusion.

"How do you think this was an accident, Chief?" Ed Folger always referred to Buddy Grinnell as "Chief," partly out of respect for the man's imposing bulk, and partly because it secretly amused him to do so.

"Here's what I think happened." Buddy pointed up the road toward the bridge that connected Phase II to Phase III. "He got lost and took a wrong turn over the bridge." He traced the imaginary path of the cart with his arm as he spoke. "He drove into this construction area, and in the dark, he went off the road. He hit a bump and pitched head first out of his cart, breaking his neck. Accident."

The doctor nodded. "My guess is you're right about the broken neck. But the rest of it?" He shook his head. "How do you get lost on this island? And why is the cart facing one way, and the body the other? And did you notice, Chief, there are no keys? Someone parked this cart."

Buddy Grinnell peered into the vehicle and confirmed the doctor's observation. He considered the implications of a non-accidental death: the involvement of outside investigators, the inquiries, questions about his handling of the evidence, panic among the residents, and an angry boss.

"Those construction workers were all over the place when we got here. One of them probably moved the cart and accidentally pocketed the keys." Buddy turned back to his notes and wrote "Accidental" in large block letters. "Unless you want to say otherwise, I say this was an accident. Case closed."

Ed Folger was old and he was uncomfortably hot under the early Florida sun. He also didn't receive a big enough discount to fight with the police chief. He nodded. "Of course, Chief, that's probably what it was."

"An accident, pure and simple.

"A tragic accident." Ed Folger looked again at the body of Richard Golden, limbs askew and head at an impossible angle. "I mean, what else could it be, right Chief?"

Buddy Grinnell shuddered. He didn't even want to think about that possibility.

TWO

There are no problems in life, only opportunities.

From – *The Sixty Minute Miracle*

Nick Rohmer slipped into his cubicle ten minutes late again. He checked his voice mail to make sure he hadn't missed any early morning calls that he should have been there for. He sighed when he heard the first message was from Richard Golden at 4:48 the previous afternoon.

"Nick. Make sure you come to see me before you leave today."

The second message was also from Richard, left fifteen minutes later.

"Nick, this is Richard. I certainly hope you haven't left already. I need to see you before you go home today."

Nick swore. The third message from Richard finally got to the point.

"Nick! I just stopped by your cubicle and it is obvious that you're gone. We're going to have to have a little heart-to-heart tomorrow. Either you got my messages and ignored them, or you didn't get them because you left early. We'll speak about this tomorrow."

The message went on. "I'm going to be out of the office in the morning, and, God help me, you will be the only account manager in the office. You need to be here, so no long lunch tomorrow. Stay in the office until I get in. Also, Dorothy is down again. See if you can get it working."

Dorothy was the electronic document retrieval system that had recently been mandated by the head office. Nick seemed to be the only one who could keep it up and running, and sometimes he thought that his computer skills were the only reasons he had not been canned yet.

Nick glanced at the clock over the door. 8:15. He figured he had at least four hours before Golden showed up. Plenty of time to fix Dorothy and get a little reading in. He booted up his computer, started streaming his favorite station, and sat back in his chair with one of the many self-help books given to him by his fiancée. He chose The Sixty Minute Miracle, because he figured he could use one, and he had the sixty minutes to spare right now.

***

"Hi, Nick."

Nick looked up from his book to find the troll-like face of Lydia Martinez poking into his cubicle. He tried not to sigh as he set down his sandwich. He mumbled around a mouthful of meatball sub, "Hello, Lydia."

Lydia interpreted the lack of outward hostility as a warm greeting and swung her pear-shaped bulk around the partition into one of Nick's guest chairs. She was positively beaming. "What's up?"

Nick felt the key to conversations with Lydia was to keep the answers as short as possible. "Lunch."

"Why don't you ever eat with us in the lunchroom? You either go out by yourself or you eat at your desk. If I didn't know you better, I'd think you were antisocial."

Nick reached over and turned up his speakers. "I like a

A gift for you

Greetings from Charleston SC! Enjoy one of my favorite books- hope you like it too. Stay well! From Megan Click

little music while I eat."

"We've got the Muzak in the lunchroom."

"It isn't really my kind of music."

"We could get a radio."

"I'm fine here. Really."

Lydia shook her head sadly. "It's not good for you to be alone all the time."

Nick glanced at his clock. "Was there something you wanted to tell me?"

Lydia's face lit up again as she leaned forward like a conspirator. In a stage whisper, she asked, "Did you hear the news?"

Nick was always the last to hear any gossip, probably because he didn't eat in the lunchroom. Lydia's job on the switchboard put her in an ideal position to be the first. She was the most dedicated gossipmonger Nick had ever encountered. "Is this real news, Lydia, or rumor? Because, I really don't want to hear any gossip."

Lydia's face fell at the suggestion. She thrust out her lower lip in an exaggerated pout that might have been cute on a six-year-old but was disturbing in someone as homely as Lydia. "You know I would never spread rumors, Nick. I have real news. Terrible news."

That explained her excitement. Terrible news was the most fun for Lydia to share. "Okay, Lydia, what is it?"

Lydia Martinez continued to pout. "I can't believe you think I would be here just to gossip."

"I'm sorry, Lydia. But you know how some people in the office like to talk."

"I know! You should have heard Joanna this morning. My God! That girl likes to poke her nose in everybody's business."

"But what is it you wanted to tell me?"

Lydia's face assumed a look of solemnity. "It is so sad." She leaned forward and in a real whisper this time, said, "Mr. Richard Golden is dead."

"What?"

She nodded slowly. "It is true. He was killed last night in a freak golfing accident."

"Dead? A golfing accident? How do you have a golfing accident? And no one plays golf at night. Where did you hear this?"

"From the police. They called for Mr. Golden's boss."

"But Richard is the boss."

"I know! So I asked if I could take a message. That's what they told me, that he died in an accident with a golf cart. Weird, huh?"

Nick knew about the electric-car-only policy on Boca Cheeca, so it now made a little more sense to him.

"You know," Lydia said, "I think he may have had a premonition or something."

"What?"

She leaned forward and whispered loudly again. "Just yesterday he was cleaning out old files and things from his office. He said he was spring-cleaning. In August!" She shook her head at the absurdity. "He left a ton of shredded paper for the cleaning crew. They were pissed. I think they're going to complain."

"And you think that constitutes a premonition?"

"Sure! It is like he knew he wouldn't be back and didn't want to leave a mess for the next person. I've read about that. It's like when sick dogs wander off to die."

Nick didn't think that Richard would have appreciated the comparison to a sick dog. "Who have you told about Richard's death?"

Lydia suddenly looked defensive. "No one. Just you. And a couple of people who were eating lunch."

"Has anyone called Chicago?"

"Not yet, I think. We just found out."

Nick thought for a moment. "Joanna should call. As Richard's secretary, she knows those people up there already."

Lydia shook her head. "She can't. She's hysterical. She can't stop crying."

Nick was beginning to see why Lydia had come to him. Richard Golden's longtime second-in-command, Alberto Herrera, had resigned recently, taking two senior accountants and a large portion of the client base with him. The new number-two man in the office, Steven Weiner, was on a cruise in the Mediterranean. And Nick's immediate boss had not yet returned from triple bypass surgery.

"So who's going to call?" Nick asked.

Lydia reached across the desk and handed Nick a pink "While You Were Out" slip. "Here's the main number in Chicago. Joanna says you should ask for Mr. McCall."

***

Scorch parked his 1995 Impala in a patch of shade across from the trailer. His shirt was unbuttoned to his navel, his back was soaked with sweat, and his jeans were sticking to his legs. He would have been much more comfortable in shorts, but only jocks and wimps wore short pants. Real men wore jeans, even in ninety-four-degree heat.

As he crossed the dirt road, he spotted Donna sitting in a beach chair as close to the trailer as she could get, trying to squeeze into its minimal shade. She was wearing a bikini top and running shorts and was fanning herself with one of his recent Maxim magazines. Her long, unnaturally blond hair was pulled back in a ponytail. She looked beautiful but pissed.

Scorch had been through this before. "Hey baby," he said. As he bent down to kiss her, she turned her head, so instead of lip, all his kiss caught was a little bit of her sweat-moistened cheek. She tasted good. "What's the matter, baby?"

"You been gone all night, Scorch. Again. What do you think's the matter?"

"Ah, don't be like that, Donna. I told you, I had a job."

She squinted up at his face, silhouetted against the

bright sky. "Oh yeah? Well, where's the money?"

He ran his fingers through his hair. "Shit, you think they're gonna give me a check for the kind of work I did for them? I gotta collect the cash, I ain't got it yet. Let me make a few phone calls. Shit," he said and laughed. "They'll probably give me a bonus, I did such a good job."

She went back to fanning herself. "You better make those phone calls, then, because we need the money."

"As soon as I cool off and get a cold brew. I'm dyin' from that piece-of-shit Impala. That thing is like an oven."

"Yeah? Well, I know the feeling."

He started for the door. "You comin' in?"

She laughed. "Naw. You go on and cool off. I'm just gonna enjoy some more fresh air."

Scorch climbed the two steps to the door, and even before he opened it, he could feel the heat drifting through the screen. He stepped inside, and it was even hotter than his car. He opened the refrigerator, and there was no refreshing blast of cool air, and no light, just the stale smell of food going bad. He grabbed a warm beer and went back outside.

"When the hell did that happen?"

Donna's eyes were closed as she spoke. "Last night, while you were 'working.'"

"Goddamn FP&L," he muttered.

"Goddamn you!" she yelled and hurled his magazine at him.

"Hey, that's the new issue." He picked it up and tried to knock the dirt off it.

"I felt like a fool last night, Scorch. When the power went out, I waited a while, thinking it was just temporary. When I finally called to report it, they said we'd been disconnected for non-payment. You told me you paid the bill."

"I was gonna, but did you see how much it was? It's robbery what they charge us. I wasn't gonna let them rob me like that."

"You didn't pay it because you didn't have the money."

"Hey! I could get the money. It's the principle of the thing."

"You don't stand on principle with the electric company, Scorch. They turn your power off."

"Yeah? We'll see about that." Scorch fished his phone out of his pocket. "Shit. It's dead!" He set his beer in the shade and climbed back into the sunbaked trailer. He connected his charger and then remembered the power was off.

He shouted through the screen door. "Donna, I need your phone!"

"Fuck you, Scorch," was her response.

Scorch spotted her pink phone on the counter and grabbed it. He fished a limp piece of paper from his pocket and dialed the number that was written on it in faded pencil.

It was answered on the second ring. "Hello?"

"This is Scorch," he said, then listened as the other end disconnected. "Goddamnit!" He hit redial.

This time, the phone rang ten times before it was answered. Before Scorch could say anything, the voice on the other end said, "Do not call here again," and hung up a second time.

"Bastard!" Scorch hit redial again and waited. After another ten rings, it was picked up and Scorch said, "If you won't talk to me on the phone, I'll come find you in person. Is that what you want?"

There was a heavy sigh from the other end, followed by a pause. "Very well. What do you wish to say to me?"

"What do you think? When do I get my money?"

There was a dry rattle from the other end of the phone that might have been a laugh. "You were contracted to do a job. A very specific, and very simple job. You failed to provide the service contracted for, and therefore, you will not get paid."

"What the fuck are you –"

"Please do not use that kind of language with me, or I will hang up."

"Fine!" Scorch took a deep breath and tried it again without the profanity. "What are you talking about? I did exactly what you asked. I scared the shit . . . I mean, I scared the . . ." He tried to think of a non-profane word and failed. "I scared him good."

"I don't want to have this conversation on the telephone, but since you insist, let me enumerate the reasons for non-payment. You were contracted to threaten a man, and, if necessary, use physical means to intimidate him. 'Threaten' and 'intimidate' were the key words here, not kill. Murder was nowhere in your instructions. In fact, this death creates an enormous problem for my client, which may entail the expenditure of substantial funds to correct. You will therefore not be paid, as you failed to fulfill your end of the contract. Is that clear enough?"

"It's not my fault he got so scared that he ended up killing himself."

"Actually, it is."

"So you're not going to pay me anything?"

"Very good! So you do understand! And understand this as well. Do not persist in calling me, and do not try to find me, or I will hire someone far more capable than you to make my point in a more physical manner."

Before Scorch could respond, the line was disconnected again. He stood a moment, looking at the phone in his hand, and then hurled it full force across the trailer. It slammed into a lamp, knocking it off the table. "Shit!" he yelled as he realized it was Donna's phone that he threw. He snatched it up from the floor and put it back on the counter, just as Donna climbed up to the open door.

She stepped inside and got her purse and her phone. "I'm going to the mall to cool off. If the power isn't back on by the time I get back, I'm moving out."

"Aw, baby, don't be like that." Scorch hated the sound of pleading in his voice. "I'll get the power on, you'll see."

The only response was the slam of the trailer's screen door.

***

After calling the Boca Cheeca police to verify the story of Richard Golden's demise, Nick Rohmer picked up the pink note Lydia had handed him and dialed the number in Chicago.

"Burnham & Fields."

Nick glanced at the note again. "May I speak with Gordon McCall, please?"

"One moment."

He listened to the music on hold, the same Muzak tune that was playing in his own office. He tried to remember what he had heard about Mr. McCall. It wasn't much. Nick had nothing at all to do with the main office. His superiors handled all those matters.

"Gordon McCall's office." The voice was deep and rough, and Nick couldn't tell if it was a man or a woman.

Nick cleared his throat in unconscious response to the raspy voice on the other end. "May I speak with Mr. McCall, please?"

"Mr. McCall is not available at the moment. Would you like to leave a message?"

"It's rather urgent."

"He's not available. Would you like to leave a message?

"Sure." Nick left his name and number, and the brief message that Richard Golden was dead. Having done his duty, he hung up with a clear conscience.

Within sixty seconds, his phone rang. It was Gordon McCall.

"What the hell are you thinking, leaving a message like that? If you have news of that magnitude, you talk to me directly."

"Your secretary said you were unavailable, so I left a message."

"Listen to me, son. First of all, Chris is not my secretary, but my executive assistant. Second, I don't care what you're told by anyone up here, if the news is important, you give it to me directly, not to some secretary."

"I thought Chris was your executive assistant."

"Exactly. Now tell me what's going on in that den of sin."

Nick related the details as he had gotten them from the police.

"So Golden is out of the picture." Nick imagined that he could hear Gordon McCall crossing off the name on his office directory. "Where's this other guy," there was a brief pause, "Weiner?"

McCall pronounced it like "whiner." "It's pronounced 'wiener,' like a hot dog."

"Don't correct me, son. Where is he? Why isn't he the one calling me?"

Nick explained about the Mediterranean cruise, the recent defections of several top executives, and his own boss's health problems.

"So are there any partners there at all?"

"No, sir. I'm the only account manager here right now."

"And what is your title, son? I don't see you on my telephone list."

"Account Associate, sir."

"Jesus H. Christ! You're the only management we've got in that office?"

Nick was feeling a little hurt. "At the moment, yes. Mr. Weiner should be back in a week, though."

"A lot can happen in a week, son. Hold on."

Nick listened to muffled talking in the background. Then McCall came back on the line. "We're going to try to get someone senior down there as soon as possible. In the meantime, don't do anything."

"Don't do anything?" This sounded too good to be true.

"Just make sure the telephones are answered and messages are taken, but don't do anything else. If anyone asks, the office is in mourning over the loss of," another pause, "Richard Golden. That ought to hold them for a few days. You think you can handle that, Rohmer?"

"Absolutely. If doing nothing is what you need, I'm your man."

"Don't screw up," McCall said and hung up.

Before Nick could set down the phone on his end, Lydia stuck her head in his cubicle. "There's a call for you on line two."

"No calls, Lydia. Just take a message."

"They say it is urgent."

"Tell them we're in mourning due to Mr. Golden's sudden death."

"It's about Mr. Golden."

"And they won't leave a message?"

"He insists on talking to the person in charge. He sounds upset."

Nick sighed. "Fine. I'll take this one call, but no more. Just take messages."

She pointed to the blinking light on Nick's phone. "Line two."

***

The northernmost of the three islands making up the Village of Boca Cheeca Key was devoted solely to the Keene family's personal residence, and to the executive offices of Keene Construction Co., the developer. In one of those offices, Walter J. Hughes was listening to Muzak being piped over his speakerphone from the Miami office of Burnham & Fields. He glanced at his watch as he heard someone come on the other end of the line.

"This is Nicholas Rohmer. Can I help you?"

"Do you know how long I have been holding?"

"No sir, I do not, but I apologize if you have –"

"Five minutes and ten seconds."

"I'm sorry you had to wait, but we're a little –"

Walter Hughes was not in the mood to waste any more time. "Do you even know to whom you are speaking?"

There was a slight pause, then a hesitant, "Not yet."

"This is Walter J. Hughes. Do you recognize that name?"

"No, sir, I'm sorry. What company are you with?"

"I am a director of Keene Construction, and I am the company's general counsel. Am I correct in assuming that you have heard of Keene Construction Company?"

"Absolutely sir. You're one of our very best clients."

"We are, in fact, your biggest client." Walter Hughes rose from his over-sized solid mahogany desk and walked to the window. He enjoyed his view of the Atlantic Ocean, stretching to the horizon and suggesting unlimited possibilities, but it was not as spectacular as Andrew Keene's view across Biscayne Bay to the Miami city skyline. On calm, sunny days like this, the deep blue of the water helped to soothe him. He turned his back on the window, and addressed his speakerphone again, this time with a little more patience in his voice.

"Are you the most senior person there at the moment, Mr. . . ?

"Rohmer. Nicholas Rohmer. Yes, sir. I'm afraid I am. With Mr. Golden's unexpected death –"

Walter Hughes waved a hand impatiently at the phone. "Yes, yes. We are all sorry to hear about Richard. But when will someone in authority be in the office?"

"It looks like it may be just me for a few days. Steven Weiner is –"

"I'm not going to deal with Mr. Weiner, so pay attention. Effective immediately, Burnham & Fields is no longer our accounting firm of record. We have retained Alberto Herrera as our outside auditor, and I would like you to immediately transfer all of our records to his firm." He listened to the silence for a moment. "I assume you will want confirmation of this in writing."

"Is there something . . .?" Nick stammered. "Is there some way. . ? I mean, how can I . . .?"

"By way of explanation, let me just say that we have been unhappy with your firm for some time, and the only reason we did not move prior to this was Mr. Keene's close personal friendship with Mr. Golden. That no longer appears to be an impediment. Upon receiving the news of Mr. Golden's death, the Audit Committee had a meeting, and it was decided that it was the right time to move, for the good of the business."

"Is there any way that I can –"

Walter Hughes cut him off in mid-sentence for the sixth time. "You will be receiving my facsimile transmission shortly, with the original following by mail. Good day."

Walter Hughes ended the conversation with the press of a button. He then sat in his high-backed leather executive chair, picked up his one hundred and fifty dollar pen, and crossed out the item, "Discharge Burnham & Fields," from his to-do list. He peered at the next item for a moment, then he circled it and wrote a question mark after it. It read, "Recover Golden's personal records."

THREE

Fortune not only favors the bold, it consigns the timid to the dustbin.

From - *CEO by 30*

There were three lounges in the Colonial Pines Psychiatric Hospital. One was for the use of the general visiting public, and another for the use of voluntary patients with acceptable social skills. The third lounge was marked "Restricted Access," and was for use by those patients, who for one reason or another, had their movements within the building and the grounds strictly controlled.

One of these patients was Betty Keene, second wife of Andrew Keene. Five feet tall, and ninety-eight pounds, she was a tiny woman of indeterminate age, but guesses ranged from forty to sixty years old. Other than her diminutive size, Betty Keene would have been physically unremarkable, except for her sense of style. Her hair was currently dyed in stripes of fluorescent green, orange, and blue, a souvenir of her last visit beyond the gates of the hospital. She also had an astonishing number of body piercings for a woman her age. In addition to the multiple rings and studs in each ear, other visible adornments included a ring through her left eyebrow and a silver stud in her tongue.

Betty sat in her favorite chair in the "Restricted" lounge. It was in front of one of the few windows in the room, and commanded a view across the levee into the Everglades, or the "Big Swamp," as she referred to it. Dressed in a cropped T-shirt, running shorts with the waistband turned down, and Tweety-bird slippers, she perused the morning newspaper, which is where she learned about Richard Golden's death.

"I'll be damned," she said, as she scanned the obituary. When she got to the part announcing the funeral service for that afternoon, she set the paper down and scowled at the floor for a moment.

Betty abandoned her cherished seat and took the paper with her. She walked to the nurses' station and addressed the young girl on duty. "I need to make a telephone call, please."

The nurse smiled at her with blindingly white teeth. "You know the rules, Mrs. Keene. No calls before ten o'clock."

Betty allowed her face to crumple as she fought to hold back tears. "But you don't understand," she sobbed. "My friend has died, and they're having the funeral today, and I won't be there." She let a tear roll down her cheek. "I just wanted to call someone to see if they could attend in my place." She held out the newspaper open to the obituary page for the nurse to see.

Though young, the nurse had worked with Betty Keene for several months and knew better than to accept her story at face value. She took the proffered paper and quickly read the obituary. When she saw that Richard Golden was a founding partner of Keene Construction, she began to believe it might be true.

"Very well, Mrs. Keene. But just one call. Any others will have to wait until after ten, like everybody else." The nurse placed the telephone on the desk.

Betty forced a wan smile through her tears. "Thank you, nurse. You're very kind."

The nurse gave an embarrassed smile, as she watched to see that the call was local. Satisfied, she stepped back a foot to give the illusion of privacy.

Hunched over the phone, as though still fighting back tears, Betty waited impatiently for the call to be answered. Eventually, a groggy voice came on the other end.

" 'lo?"

"Hi, honey, it's me."

"Huh?"

"It's me, damn it. Are you awake?"

"Un-uh."

Betty looked up to see if the nurse was still listening. She was. "Richard Golden is dead."

"Uh-huh."

"His funeral is today."

"Yeah?"

"I won't be able to be there, you know?"

"Uh-huh."

"I want to be there, but I can't be. Understand?"

"Huh?"

She tried not to sound frustrated. "I want to go the funeral."

"Oh."

"But you will have to make arrangements for me." She tried to make the emphasis subtle.

"Okay."

A quick glance at the nurse confirmed that she was still paying attention. "I need you to pick up a few things. Can you do that at 10:30? For me?"

"Where?"

"The usual place."

"Okay."

Betty sighed. "Thank you, honey. I'm sure Richard would appreciate it. I know that I do."

"Okay."

"Don't forget. I am counting on you. 10:30."

"Okay."

"Good-bye, dear," she said and hung up without waiting for his monosyllabic response. She slid the telephone back across the desk and thanked the nurse, who looked puzzled.

"He'll know what to do?" the nurse asked. "Those weren't very specific instructions. You didn't even tell him where the funeral was going to be."

"He knows what to do," Betty Keene said. "We've done this before."

***

Nick Rohmer knocked on the door and waited for Victoria Pawlowski to open up and let him in. Even though it was not yet eight o'clock, he was uncomfortably hot in his best dark suit, some kind of wool blend that was not appropriate for South Florida in August. He could have left the jacket in his car, but he wanted to impress her.

As the door opened, he squared his shoulders slightly, and tried to assume a suave, but relaxed demeanor. "Good morning, my love," he said, in a voice an octave below his usual tone.

Victoria stood in the doorway dressed in a red silk robe, her head wrapped in a towel. A few stray wisps of chestnut brown hair had escaped around the base of her neck. "You sound funny. Do you have a cold?"

Water droplets still glistened on her legs, and her long neck beckoned him. "No," Nick said, his voice now unintentionally husky. He tried to kiss her, but she placed a well-manicured hand in the middle of his chest and pushed him away.

"You're all hot and flushed. I think you're sick. Don't kiss me." She backed into the apartment and let Nick past her. "I don't have much time. I have to get ready," she said. "What do you want?"

Nick tried to embrace her again, but she squirmed free.

"I don't have a cold," he said. "A guy can't just drop by to see his fiancée on his way to work?"

"You never do. And what's with the suit?" She stepped into the bedroom.

Nick raised his voice so she could hear him in the next room. "I've got to go to Golden's funeral today."

She called back, "You'll be sweating like a pig in that."

"I know," Nick said, "but it's the darkest suit I own." He stepped up to her bedroom door and watched as she applied her makeup. "You don't need all that junk, you know. You're beautiful without it." And she was. She had creamy ivory skin that looked like it had never seen the sun, and it was so smooth it was like porcelain. Her pale blue eyes were doe-large and shaded by surprisingly long lashes. Her lips were always a warm rosy color, even before she smeared them with lipstick.

"Sure." She leaned toward the mirror to work on her eyes. "You men say that, but you don't really mean it. You always think a girl looks better in makeup, even if you won't admit it."

"Maybe we can have lunch today. Can you get into the city later?"

She never broke stride with the makeup. "No. Paul and I are doing a school board function from eleven to one-thirty. Then we're heading up to Dania for a Chamber of Commerce meeting."

"Nothing before the school board meeting?"

"Just some strategy and planning sessions."

"Then we have a little time," Nick said as he took a step into the bedroom.

"Don't even think it," she said, holding up one hand like a traffic cop. "First of all, I don't have time, and second, you know how I feel about that. Not until after the wedding."

"That's not for another ten months! Are you seriously saying that I can't touch you for another ten months?"

She gave him her coquette smile. "You can touch, but

only if you can control yourself. I've told you how I feel."

"Well I still don't get it." Nick sat on the bed and looked at the tips of his shoes. They needed some polish. "You didn't have any problems about sex before we were engaged."

"Don't talk dirty. I hate that." She turned from the mirror for a moment and graced Nick with her full attention. "I want to be traditional. I want to wait until we're married. That's why I asked you to move back into your apartment until the wedding, remember?"

"I don't get it, Victoria. Most guys, when they propose, that's when they move in with their girlfriends, not the other way around."

"We already had this discussion, Nick. Besides, I have Paul to think about."

"What the hell does Paul have to do with it?"

She returned to her reflection. "Don't start that again, Nick."

"No. Really. I want to know what Paul Smith has to do with our sex life."

"First of all, it's Paul Gonzalez-Smith. Call him by his correct name –"

"Hah! Correct name, my ass. The man has been Paul Smith for 30 years, and the minute he runs for State Rep he discovers his Hispanic roots. That's just hypocrisy."

"Don't make fun of Paul's Hispanic heritage. Your bigotry is not attractive."

"I'm not bigoted. He's an opportunist. One maternal great-grandmother does not make someone Hispanic. I think he made up the story just so he could stick 'Gonzalez' in the middle of his name."

"Don't be ridiculous."

"Let's assume for a minute that we can agree on his name and heritage. How is it that Paul whatever-his-name-is is keeping me out of your bed?"

"Let's not have this argument again."

Nick crossed his arms. He was hot as hell in the wool

suit, but he didn't dare take the jacket off for fear Victoria would think he was making another unwelcome advance. "I just want to be clear on how these items are related."

Victoria sighed heavily, lightly steaming the mirror. "You know his platform of returning to family values, and protecting children from sex and violence. I've told you this before."

"But I don't want to have sex near children."

"How would it look if it became known that Paul Gonzalez-Smith's campaign manager was having pre-marital sex? What kind of message would that send?"

"That his campaign manager loves her fiancé?"

"Don't be glib, Nick. It isn't becoming."

"How about after the election? I think that I could live with that."

"Then who would be the hypocrite, Nick? I've told you how it is. You can either live with it, or we can call the whole thing off." Now nearly finished with the makeup, she stepped into her bathroom. "I'm going to get dressed now. Would you mind waiting in the other room?"

"You know, I get more action than this hanging out in the ladies' department at J.C. Penney."

"The real action is at Neiman Marcus. Those girls are exhibitionists. Now wait in the other room. I don't want to have to fight you off."

"Fine." Nick sulked his way to the kitchen and finally removed his heavy suit coat. His back and underarms were soaked. "Great," he said and turned on the ceiling fan. He poured himself a glass of orange juice, and sat in the artificial breeze, trying to dry off.

When she finally emerged from her bedroom, she looked conservatively beautiful. Her forest green dress was high-necked, but not prudishly so. Her skirt was long enough to cover her knees, and her hair was pulled back in a tight French twist, leaving her elegant neck fully exposed. Despite the conservative cut of her clothes, she could not disguise the length of her legs, or hide the ample size of her bust. The sight of her was driving Nick crazy.

"You look beautiful," he said.

"Thanks. A girl's got to look her best." She bent down and gave Nick a light kiss on his cheek. He resisted the temptation to grab her, figuring that it would get him nowhere.

"I miss you, Vic. I never get to see you anymore."

"Please don't call me 'Vic.' I've told you; I don't want people to start referring to us as 'Nick and Vic.' It's ludicrous."

"Sorry. I just wanted to say that I miss you. When was the last time we spent an evening together?"

"I'm sorry. I've been so busy with the campaign getting crazy and all. And you must be going nuts, too, with Mr. Golden's accident. Your office was already short-staffed."

"Guess who is in charge of the office." He pointed to himself as a hint.

"Really?" She sat and took Nick's hand in hers. "Nick, that's amazing. Did you get a promotion?"

"No. But with everyone else either on vacation, or sick, or dead, I'm the senior person in the office. Probably until next week."

"This is a great opportunity to show what you can do. If you handle this right, it could start you up the ladder."

"Don't get too excited. The guy in Chicago has already told me not to do anything. At all. And, I may already have lost our biggest client." He told her about his telephone conversation with Walter Hughes at Keene Construction.

"That's it!" Victoria jumped up and began pacing the small kitchen. "This could be your big break."

"Well, I'll admit that losing our number one client will get me some name recognition, but I don't think it will be in a positive way."

"Remember that book I gave you? CEO by 30? It says to use any means to get noticed. This is it. This is your chance to get noticed. Does the Chicago office know about your client changing firms?"

"God, I hope not. The last thing I need is McCall all over me. They can find out next week when Weiner's back. He can take the heat. He's paid for that sort of thing."

"That's the wrong attitude, Nick. You need to take charge and let them know."

"That sounds kind of risky to me."

"My God. When are you going to realize that you have to take some risks in life to get anywhere? You're just sitting there and letting everyone pass you by."

"If I wanted to take risks, I'd go skydiving," he said.

"You can't let your childhood traumas stunt your future, Nick."

"Please leave my childhood out of this," Nick said. "I wish I'd never told you about it."

Nick's childhood essentially ended when his father, a beat cop in Dayton, Ohio, was killed. Nick was seven and an only child. His mother was so traumatized by the loss of her husband, that she went to extremes to protect her child from any possible threats. No more bicycles. All contact sports were banned, including baseball (sliding into base looked too dangerous). The only approved athletic endeavors were track (good training if you needed to outrun danger), and swimming (a good precaution against drowning).

She even plotted Nick's career path for minimum risk. Manual labor was out, as was doctor (too many sick people) and lawyer (too many potentially dangerous and unsavory characters). Accounting was the perfect job, as far as Nick's mother was concerned: desk-bound and nothing more perilous than numbers.

When she learned that her life was going to end prematurely due to cancer, she made Nick promise that he would continue to live cautiously and avoid undue risks. Since then, the most dangerous thing that Nick had done was move from Ohio to South Florida, and he still felt guilty about it.

Victoria stepped behind Nick and placed her hands on his shoulders, as though she was pointing him toward a new future. "You have to let those people in Chicago know there's a problem, and then you can show them that you can fix it. It's the kind of thing Paul is doing now with the voters. Point out what's wrong, then give them a solution. That's what gets you elected."

At the mention of Paul Gonzales-Smith's name, Nick gritted his teeth. "I've got a news flash for you: I'm not running for office."

"But you want a promotion."

"Well . . . More money would be nice."

"Then you need your boss's vote. Call it what you like, but we're all always running for something." Victoria let out an excited chirp and held her hand up to her mouth. "I've got it!"

Her excitement was making Nick nervous. "What have you got, exactly?"

"You said this Keene guy was a friend of Golden, right?"

Nick answered hesitantly, fearing some sort of logic trap. "Yeah."

"Then he'll probably be at the funeral, right?"

Nick held up his hands, palms outward. "Whoa. I really don't think a funeral is the appropriate place –"

She was too excited to be slowed by such feeble resistance. "Of course it is! It's the perfect venue. He'll be remembering his friendship with Golden, thinking about old times, blah, blah, blah, and all you have to do is play the loyalty-to-a-dead-friend card. He won't be able to resist. Just get him talking, and I know you'll be able to save the business."

"There's a loyalty-to-a-dead-friend card?"

"This is your big chance, Nick. Don't blow it for yourself. Don't blow it for us."

Nick wasn't sure how, but somehow their future "us-ness" depended on him tactlessly trying to talk business with his dead boss's friend at the funeral. "I'll see if I can subtly introduce myself, but –"

"This is no time for subtlety. Show your killer instinct. Get the job done."

Nick glanced at his watch. He stood and with jacket in hand, gave Victoria a kiss on the cheek. "I'll try."

"Don't let this opportunity pass us by, Nick. You've got to get serious about your career. At some point, you either have to fish, or cut bait."

Nick made his way to the door. "But you know what?" he said, as he stepped outside. "I don't like fishing, and the whole bait thing is gross. I'd really rather just go swimming."

"Don't be glib," she said and closed the door.

***

Colonial Pines Psychiatric Hospital was neither colonial, nor were there any pine trees on the grounds. It was a bare two-story concrete block building erected on former swampland in far western Broward County. At the time of the building's dedication in 1969, the drainage canal on which it sat had been bounded by beautiful, wispy, Australian Pines. The building also had decorative black plastic colonial-style shutters framing each window, slightly relieving the ugliness of the design.

During the first summer following its dedication, the plastic shutters melted in the fierce Florida sun, sagging and drooping on their mounting brackets, giving the whole building a Salvador Dali-like effect. This proved to be very disconcerting to some of the patients, and the shutters were eventually removed. In the fall of that year, a tropical storm swept inland from the Atlantic, dropping twenty-two inches of rain in twenty-four hours. The Australian Pines, with their shallow roots more suited to the soil and climate of the Land Down Under, were quickly uprooted by the storm and fell into the canal, clogged it and prevented it from draining. The whole property was under a foot of water.

Little had changed since the removal of the pine trees. Nothing had been planted in their place, and the squat building sat in the middle of three acres of treeless, flat land, surrounded by a ten-foot tall chain link fence, painted green for aesthetic reasons. Beyond the fence, a retirement community of high-rise condominiums had sprouted, surrounding the hospital in acres and acres of blacktop. By contrast, the bleak hospital grounds seemed like an oasis of green.

On any particular morning in August, the neighborhood was generally quiet. The condominiums were only twenty percent occupied, with most of the residents traveling north for the summer, leaving their apartments shuttered and dark. The hospital was also quiet. Its population was efficiently muffled within the air-conditioned, hermetically sealed building. Even the patients who were allowed to stroll the grounds tended to prefer the climate-controlled interior to the hot and humid exterior.

On this morning, however, the neighborhood peace was disturbed by a blue and white ice-cream truck winding its way between the condominium complexes with its external speaker playing *Candyman* at top volume. The sound from the truck was so loud that the few remaining condo residents could not even hear the Colonial Pines alarm bell as it signaled an unauthorized exit.

Within the hospital, there was a burst of activity as orderlies and nurses rushed to close the breach in their security. With practiced ease they threaded their way through the suddenly-agitated patient population, calming and cooing as they went. Everyone was quickly ushered back to their room and told to wait for the head count, and their doors were discreetly locked. If Colonial Pines had been a prison rather than a hospital, it would have been called a lockdown.

Amid the temporary bedlam, a gaggle of young girls dressed in red and white stripes made their way back to their aid station near the visitors' lounge, fighting against the flow of patients being herded toward their rooms. As volunteers, the candy-stripers had no official duties and had been trained to stay out of the way until the situation was controlled.

Mostly teenage girls in nursing or pre-nursing programs, they tended to gather in groups of two and three as they walked, talking excitedly among themselves. Here and there, a solitary striped figure hurried to catch up or scooted from one group to another.

As they reached the aid station, they all filed in. All except for one girl, who was bringing up the rear, hurrying to catch up. She turned left just before the display of overpriced flowers and headed for the service wing. She waved her security badge in front of the electronic sensor and stepped through the double doors and down the corridor. Wheeled canvas baskets of dirty linen and uniforms lined one side of the hall. The other side was stacked with canned food and bags of flour waiting to be stored in the kitchen. She threaded her way past and then out through the last set of doors into the early morning heat of the employee parking lot.

Crowded around the door were several of the kitchen staff, smoking and talking in a strange mixture of accents. She stepped through them with a muffled, "'Morning," and headed into the parking lot, stepping quickly between the cars.

She stopped at the fence and slipped her card into the slot. The gate began to slowly roll open and she squeezed through as soon as the gap allowed. Listening to the distant strains of *Candyman*, she stood on the side of the road, looking up and down the deserted street.

Behind her, the gate had completed its opening cycle and was closing again when there was a burst of activity at the employee entrance. Two white-jacketed orderlies burst through the door, nearly knocking over one of the smokers. They said something and the kitchen workers all pointed across the parking lot at the little candy-striper waiting for her ride.

The orderlies broke into a run, darting between the cars. One of them yelled out, "Wait right there, Mrs. Keene! There's nowhere you can go."

Betty swore to herself and again scanned the empty street. She turned to face her pursuers. The orderlies were nearly at the gate, which was just closing the last few feet. She looked around for something to jam the mechanism, but the neatly maintained grounds held no promising debris. There were no sticks or rocks or even stray beer cans.

The orderlies both crashed into the gate, just feet from their quarry. One of them shook the fence in frustration, and then said, "Wait there, Mrs. Keene." He turned to his companion. "Open the gate, Frank."

"Right." Frank fumbled in his pocket for his security card.

"Stay right there, Frank. You too, Jose." Betty reached inside her red and white striped uniform, and both Frank and Jose took an involuntary step back. "Don't move."

Jose narrowed his eyes in suspicion. "What are you doing?"

"Just watch." She had to raise her voice slightly to be heard over the increasingly loud music. She finished fishing inside her uniform and pulled out her brassiere.

Both orderlies relaxed a little, and Jose said again, "Open the gate, Frank."

Frank began digging for his security card again while Betty stepped up to the fence. She passed one end of her bra through the steel mesh then looped it around the post and tied it off in a snug square knot.

Too late, Jose realized what she was doing. "Shit! Frank, wait!"

Frank didn't wait. He swiped his card and the gate

started to roll. It met resistance from the bra, and bounced back, jumping in its track, but the motor kept running and it tried to open again, bouncing and bucking like a wild horse.

Jose stepped up to the fence, but was strangely reluctant to touch the lady's undergarment. But it was too late anyway. Beyond the gate, the road was no longer empty as the blue and white ice-cream truck pulled up, its speaker blaring and horn honking.

Betty jumped into the truck and threw her arms around the driver. "Baby, you made it!" She gave him a long kiss on the forehead. "You're late," she said and slapped him. "When I say 10:30, I don't mean 10:35."

The driver shrugged his shoulders but said nothing. He wore an expensive-looking camera around his neck, and as Betty sat back in the passenger seat, he leaned forward and took a quick picture of the orderlies struggling with the gate.

"Stop goofing around and let's get out of here," she said. "I need to get out of this silly dress, and can we please change that music?"

Jose and Frank watched from behind the jammed gate as the truck sped off at a stately twenty-five miles per hour. As it rounded the bend, *Candyman* abruptly stopped, replaced by an all-bell version of *Sunshine, Lollipops, and Rainbows.*

FOUR

Rules are for everyone else.

From – *Surviving the Cubicle*

Scorch had spent a restless night. The aluminum shell of the trailer absorbed heat with such efficiency that even hours after the sun had set, the small amount of breeze that found its way through the undersized windows could not cool it enough to allow him to sleep inside. Around midnight, he finally dragged his mattress outside for some relief. Scorch was eventually able to sleep, until a summer thunderstorm swept through the trailer park around two a.m., drenching him and the mattress.

He spent the rest of the night lying on his soggy bed in his wet clothes, cursing God, the electric company, Donna, and Richard Golden. Between revenge fantasies, he plotted ways to get his power turned on without having to resort to actual payment of the bill. By morning, he had a plan.

At first light, Scorch climbed into his Impala and headed for the local Home Depot. The early morning breeze rushing through the windows helped to revive him, and he became more certain than ever that he was the cleverest man alive. He would never have to pay another electric bill.

At the store, he purchased his supplies with a stolen credit card, then went next door to the Moonlite Diner for breakfast. He scooped up an unattended tip from the next table, left a portion for his waitress, and used the loose change to call Donna from the pay phone.

"Hey, baby."

"What do you want, Scorch?"

"I just thought you might want to come home, that's all."

Her tone brightened perceptibly. "You got the power on?"

"Come by in an hour or so. Everything's going to be fine."

"You paid the bill?"

Scorch chuckled. "Something even better. Come on home, and you'll see." He hung up and then gleefully headed back to the trailer park, already sure of his triumph over Florida Power & Light.

Within an hour, and with no electrical training, Scorch had successfully spliced one end of a fifty-foot, heavy-duty, bright orange extension cord into his mobile home's electrical system. He then took the other end and crawled under the Browns' trailer, next to his. The Browns were both alcoholics, and Scorch doubted that either of them ever took the time to look at their electric bill. If they did, he figured they were probably too drunk to understand it.

Working with the power on, and without insulated tools, Scorch struggled through the pain of near electrocution several times, and used most of a roll of electric tape, before he was through. But eventually, he crawled out from under his neighbor's home and heard the satisfying rattle of his own air-conditioner struggling to defeat the Florida heat. He did a small victory dance.

Scorch stood a moment to savor his triumph, but could not help noticing how conspicuous the orange extension cord appeared. He kicked some dirt and leaves over it, but that wasn't very effective. He swore when he realized he would have to bury it. Digging ditches was a little too much like real work for his taste.

As he was thinking of ways he could convince Donna to bury the cord for him, things inside the trailer were going very wrong. The lamp that he had knocked over the previous day in his fit of anger with the cell phone was still lying on the floor, under the rain-stained and dirty draperies that hung behind the couch. The polyester material was in contact with the light bulb, which with the restoration of power, was now on. As the bulb heated up, a tongue of flame appeared and quickly climbed the drapes to the ceiling. Within moments, the fire had spread to the sofa and the imitation wood paneling.

The first indication that Scorch had of the problem was when the fiberglass screen in the living room window flashed into flame. He watched for a moment in fascinated horror as the flames began to lick the aluminum exterior. Then he sprang into action.

He turned on his garden hose and pointed the feeble spray of water through the window, without noticeable effect. He then ran next door to the Browns, and when no one answered his frantic knocking, he broke in. By the time he called the fire department and stole a few CDs, his trailer was engulfed in flames.

As he stood there watching his meager possessions turn to ash, Donna arrived. She slowly climbed out of her car and stood quietly next to Scorch for a moment, watching the fire.

She then turned to him and slapped him as hard as she could across the face. "You couldn't just pay the electric bill, like a normal person," she said. Without another word, she climbed back in her car and drove away, passing the fire trucks as they arrived.

***

Gordon McCall's office was decorated in dark, subdued tones, as befitted a seat of power. The top of his large oak desk was inlaid with expensive burgundy leather. On the dark-paneled wall behind the desk, where visitors could not miss them, were pictures and memorabilia from his Marine Corps career, the highlight of which was the invasion of the Caribbean island of Grenada.

Gordon McCall sat at his desk, sipping his third cup of coffee of the morning from his Marine Corps mug, which he set in his brass Marine Corps coaster. He scanned the email and faxes that had come in overnight. All the correspondence was screened and sorted by his executive assistant, Chris, with the most pressing issues on top.

As he reached the middle of the pile, Chris knocked and entered. "This just came in from Miami. I thought you should see it right away."

McCall nodded his thanks and accepted the fax. It was a copy of the letter from Keene Construction terminating their relationship and instructing the firm to forward all records. He scanned it once quickly, then again more slowly. "Who is this Keene Construction?" he asked his assistant. "And is this it? No cover letter?"

Chris shrugged. "That's all that came in, sir. No cover letter and no explanation."

"Call Miami. Get that kid, what's-his-name, who called here yesterday. I want to talk to him."

"Yes, sir." Chris turned to leave.

"And find out who this Keene company is. I need to know what the hell is going on down there."

***

Immediately after sending the fax, Nick Rohmer left the office, along with most of the remaining staff, to attend the funeral of Richard Golden. He put Lydia in charge with strict instructions to take messages, and say only that calls would be returned as soon as possible.

The service was held at Temple Beth Am. It was well-attended, but mostly by professionals and business acquaintances. Richard Golden had no children, and his only living relative was his ex-wife, Delores, who delivered a very awkward eulogy. To her credit, she tried to focus on the good things in their life together. She didn't explicitly mention the philandering, the gambling, the verbal and psychological abuse, or the missed alimony payments. And though she tried to stay positive, it was hard not to get the impression from her tone that she believed the bum had finally gotten what he deserved.

After Delores Golden's strained eulogy, an older man stepped up to say a few words. "Good afternoon," he began. "For those of you who don't know me, I'm Andy Keene. I've been a friend and business associate of Richard's for over 30 years."

Nick tried to focus his attention on the speaker. Here was his quarry. For better or worse, here was the man who was going to get him noticed at Burnham & Fields.

From what Nick knew about Andrew Keene, he was immensely wealthy, and just about everything he touched turned into money. Yet to look at him, Nick would never have guessed it. A beefy man in his sixties, he wore what was obviously an expensive suit, but made it look like something he got off the rack at Sears. His full head of white hair crowned a face that appeared to have been ravaged either by too much sun, or too much drink, or possibly both. His nose, in youth probably described as aquiline, was puffy and red and dominated his face. His jaw line was almost lost in the numerous folds of his jowls, which evidently caused him difficulty when shaving. There were several fresh razor nicks around his chin and neck, one of which was still oozing blood.

"But Richard was much more than that," Andrew Keene said. "He was family."

"Is that why you treated him like dirt?" someone shouted from the back of the room. All heads turned to see who it was and a murmur spread through the crowd. When it was not immediately clear who was responsible for the outburst, Andrew Keene hesitantly continued.

"Richard was one of the reasons for the early success of my business. Even though he was very young at the time, he knew his stuff. He became a partner."

"Until you tossed him aside like a used condom!" The voice was shrill and girlish, and loud. "Just like you toss aside everyone else when you're finished with them! You're a user, Keene. It should be you in that box."

The crowd was completely turned around now, and several people stood, trying to spot the culprit. Whoever she was, she was not visible from where Nick stood on his toes, neck craned. There was a small scuffle near the door as several people forced their way out, and Nick could not tell if someone was being thrown out, or trying to escape.

Things calmed after a moment, and Andrew Keene tried to re-engage his audience. "I've been heckled by tree-huggers and hippies, but this is the first time I've ever been heckled at a funeral." That got a small chuckle.

He resumed his eulogy and without further interruption, listed the highlights of a career with Richard Golden at his side. He told how Richard had eventually sold him his share of the business so he could start his highly successful accounting practice, where he was still deeply involved in the success of Keene Construction. Andrew Keene went on to recount how Richard had taken his small firm from nothing to local prominence until he sold it to Burnham & Fields just over a year ago. He concluded with some sort of golfing story about Richard Golden that Nick didn't fully understand because he didn't play the game. But it seemed to involve cheating and elicited another chuckle from the crowd.

He concluded by saying, "Richard was a lot more to me than just a business advisor and a source of good tax advice. He was my loyal friend for thirty-two years, and I will miss him terribly. I only hope that wherever he is right now, they have a thirty-six hole championship golf course, with reasonable greens fees."

Twenty minutes later, after the crowd had relocated to the graveside for a few more words, and Richard Golden was finally lowered into the ground, Nick found himself stalking Andrew Keene as he walked across the parking lot. The old gentleman had a young blond woman on his arm and was accompanied by another couple. Unable to come up with a clever pretext for starting a conversation, and quickly running out of parking lot, Nick opted for the direct approach.

"Excuse me, Mr. Keene," he called, trotting to catch up.

Both men turned around, and it was immediately apparent to Nick that the younger man was Andrew Keene's son. He had the same heavy build, only softer looking. Unlike his father, his hair was cut very short, in almost a military style, and instead of jowls, his face was framed by a series of chins that melded into his neck and hung over the top of his collar, obscuring the knot of his necktie. Despite these differences, the look was the same, only about twenty years younger.

The senior Keene glowered at Nick from beneath bushy white eyebrows but did not say anything.

Nick hesitated under the glare of the four Keene eyes. He glanced quickly at the young woman on the older man's arm, but could absorb little more than the astounding amount of cleavage she displayed in her low-cut black mourning dress before he forced himself to meet the gaze of Andrew Keene.

"Excuse me, sir," he began again and extended a hand with a slightly crumpled business card in it. "My name is Nick Roh—"

"How dare you!" spouted the younger Keene, indignation dripping from his tongue. "How dare you attempt to solicit my father's business at a funeral?" He blustered with such force that his chins jiggled.

The elder Keene held up a hand to his son. "Shut up, Skip. Don't jump to conclusions." He turned his attention to Nick. "This better not be what he thinks it is. Not only would that be unforgivably rude, but it pisses me off when my son is right."

Nick slowly lowered his hand. "No, sir. It's nothing like that." Nick slipped his card back in his pocket. "I worked for Richard Golden. I just wanted to say what a touching eulogy you gave, despite the interruptions. It was very moving."

"Don't waste my time with bullshit. What do you want?"

"I just wanted to introduce myself. With Mr. Golden passing, we may have occasion to be working together. I'm with Burnham & Fields," he added by way of explanation.

"I don't involve myself in that," he said. "I employ people to handle those things for me." He gave Nick a head-to-toe appraisal. "You look a little green to be taking over for Golden."

Nick gave a forced chuckle. "Oh, I'm not taking over for Mr. Golden. I'm just here to pay my respects. And to say 'hello.'"

"Well, you've done that. Was there anything else Mr. Roller?"

"Rohmer, sir. Nick Rohmer." He held out his hand again, and this time, the old man shook it. His grip was vise firm.

"You have a card, Nick? With Richard gone, I guess I'll need to know someone in that office."

Nick fished in his pocket again for his now seriously creased business card and handed it over. "Actually sir," he said, and cleared his throat. "About talking to someone?"

"Yes?"

"I had a call from a Mr. Hughes."

The elder Keene was beginning to glower again. "Yes?"

Nick plunged ahead. "He dismissed the firm, sir. I was just wondering if I could possibly convince you to reconsider, or perhaps just better understand the decision –"

"I knew it!" interjected the younger Keene. "I knew he was soliciting our business, Daddy. Do you believe how rude this is?"

"Shut up, Skip." He looked at Nick again. "I warned you this would piss me off."

Nick nodded. "Yes sir, you did."

Andrew Keene fingered the business card for a moment. "He dismissed the firm? With a telephone call?"

Nick nodded again. "He did follow up with a fax. He said the Audit Committee had met and that their decision was final."

"Before old Richard was even in the ground. Damn! That seems cold, even for Walt. He said the Audit Committee?"

Nick nodded. "Yes, sir."

Andrew turned to his son. "Were you part of this, Skip?"

Skip nodded. "We had a meeting, and the whole committee agreed, didn't we, dear?" he said, turning to the woman at his side.

She nodded vigorously. "We all thought it was time to get a real accounting firm," she said.

"And you my dear?" Andrew said to the chesty blond woman on his arm.

She shrugged. "They all wanted to change, so why not?" she said. "I'm hot. Can we go home now?"

Andrew Keene ignored her and addressed Nick. "I worked with Richard for a long time. Your company knows my business. I don't see why we would want to change. Frankly, the whole thing smells to me." He reached into his pocket and pulled out his cell phone. He tapped the screen a few times, then spoke into the microphone, "Note: Why are we changing accounting firms? Consider scheduling a full audit? Discuss with Walt."

Andrew turned again to Nick. "I want you to come see

me tomorrow and convince me that I should stay with your firm. If nothing else, it will put a bug up Walt's ass." Andrew Keene looked at Nick's card for the first time, then spoke into his phone again, "Note: Invite Nick Rohmer to dinner to discuss decision of the 'Audit Committee.'"

Speaking to Nick again, he said, "My secretary will call you to set up a time."

"Thank you, sir. That's very generous of you."

"Don't make me regret this. Be prepared. I really want to know what's behind this decision. It's time to light a few fires under some asses."

"I'll be happy to help you light them, sir."

Andrew Keene smiled for the first time. "You've got the right attitude. See you tomorrow." He pointed at Nick's suit. "And try to wear something that's not going to act like a sauna. This is Florida, son. It gets hot here in the summer."

This time, Nick grinned.

As the entire Keene party turned to leave, Nick could not help noticing the narrowed eyes and tight lips of Skip and the woman he was escorting. Nick guessed that he had not made a friend of the younger Keene.

Nick watched them walk to their car, a black Mercedes-Benz. As Skip pushed the unlock button on the keychain, and the car emitted a happy chirp, there was a small explosion of white and yellow on the hood. Startled, all four froze where they stood.

Immediately, there was another splat of eggshell and yolk as a second egg landed on the roof. Another egg struck Skip squarely on the head, and he let out a yelp. Suddenly, all four of them were trying to enter the car at the same time and merely succeeded in looking like a scene from a Three Stooges short. As they fought to get into the car, they were fully exposed to the fusillade of eggs that rained down on them. Within moments, they were covered in sticky egg gunk.

Nick looked left, the direction from which the barrage was coming. He spotted a small woman in a headscarf and long black dress, and a young man dressed all in white, a large camera around his neck. In his white suit, he would have looked out of place at the funeral even if he wasn't hurling eggs at the Keenes. The woman held the hem of her dress hitched up in her left hand creating a pocket of material that held their eggs, like a farm wife just back from tending the chickens. With her right hand, she threw with surprising accuracy. The man at her side had a wind-up like a major league pitcher, and now that their quarry was in the car, he was concentrating his fire on the windshield.

The Mercedes' windshield wipers came alive, working in vain against the thick yolk and glutinous whites that were quickly congealing in the fierce heat. As the Keenes' car began to move, the egg snipers finally exhausted their ammunition, and the man in white snapped a few pictures.

With a two-handed shove, the woman started her accomplice moving. They threaded their way through the parked cars, past dozens of amazed and bemused mourners, then cut across the cemetery, running as they hit open ground.

Nick watched as they disappeared into the maze of grave markers, then chuckled to himself as he went to find his own car, parked next to a blue and white ice-cream truck.

FIVE

You need to evolve with the changing environment. If you fail to adapt, you fail.

From - *The Darwinian Executive*

"There are a ton of messages for you."

Nick accepted the stack of pink notes from Lydia's outstretched hand. "Thanks," he said, "but keep telling people I'm not here. I have a special project I have to work on."

"Most of those are from Mr. McCall. He seemed anxious to talk to you." She whispered conspiratorially so that everyone nearby could hear. "Do you want me to lie to him, too?"

"No. I'll call him. Is Joanna back from the service yet?"

Lydia shook her head. "It's in one of the messages. She's too upset and won't be back today. Are you going to fire her?"

"No, of course not. I'm not her boss, and she has a right to be upset. She was Richard's secretary for, what, five years?"

"Six." She slipped into her stage whisper again. "But she never really liked him."

"Nobody did, but that doesn't mean she isn't entitled to a little grief."

Nick took his messages and headed for his cubicle. As he sat down, the phone rang. It was Lydia.

"I have Gordon McCall on the line."

Nick sighed.

"You told me not to lie to him."

"I know. Put him through. But no more calls after that, okay?"

"Hang up and I'll transfer him."

Nick set the phone in its cradle and waited for two rings before he picked up.

"Where the hell have you been?"

"There was a service –"

"I left five messages there. When I leave five messages, I expect a return call."

"I was at the funeral for Mr. Golden. I only now got back to the office. I haven't even sat down yet."

"The girl on the switchboard wouldn't give me your cell phone number. What the hell is that all about? Does she know who I am?"

"She doesn't have my personal number," Nick said. "But she gave me all your messages. I was about to call you back."

"'About to' doesn't cut it. Tell me what's going on with Keene Construction. Why did they fire you?"

Nick regretted having taken Victoria's advice about sending a fax. "I don't really know, but -"

"Your office can't afford to lose another big account. What is wrong with you people?"

Nick assumed the question was rhetorical. "I spoke with Mr. Keene at the funeral, and I have an appointment to see him tomorrow. I should know more then."

McCall was silent for a moment, then said softly, "You approached a customer about business at a funeral?"

"Not during the funeral itself. It was in the parking lot afterward."

"Bad tactical move, Rohmer, but you got the appointment?"

"Yes, sir. Mr. Keene's secretary is to call with the time."

"As soon as you get that time, you call here, got it? I'm going to fly down tomorrow and meet with these people myself."

"But –"

"Someone will call you with my flight information. Pick me up at the airport. We have to talk before I meet with this Keene fellow."

"But –"

"Keep me posted. And for God's sake, don't do anything else until I get there." There was a click and Gordon McCall was gone.

"Shit!" Nick slammed the telephone down. "Shit!"

"Nick?"

He looked up to see Lydia, her headset wire dangling, hovering in front of his cubicle. "Not now, Lydia, please."

"I thought you might want this message. It's from some guy named Ken, or Kean, or something."

Nick jumped up and practically snatched it from her hand. It read, "Meet tonight. Dinner Key fuel dock, 6:00."

"What does this mean?" Nick asked.

Lydia shrugged. "I don't know. He just said the meeting you discussed is tonight instead of tomorrow. He said someone will meet you at Dinner Key Marina." She affected her loud whisper again. "Are you interviewing for another job?"

"No. He's a client."

She gave Nick an exaggerated wink. "Sure he is."

It was almost three o'clock, which gave Nick just about two hours to become an expert on Keene Construction. "Do you know where the key is for Richard's office? I need to pull a few of his private files."

She held up her hands. "I don't know anything about any keys. You don't pay me enough to have that kind of responsibility."

"Do you at least have Joanna's phone number? She must know where there's a key."

Lydia gave a slow nod. "Sure. I have everyone's number. Except yours, Nick."

"I just need Joanna's."

Lydia tried to look coy. "Well, you might try looking for the key in her bottom right-hand drawer first. She has a little clay pot her daughter made where she keeps important stuff. It is the ugliest thing. I swear, I think that little girl is retarded, but Joanna shows that ugly pot off like it was a Ming vase. I could do better with my eyes closed."

Nick scooted around her. "Thanks, I'll try that. If it isn't there, I'll come get her number from you."

She called after him. "If you need it, I've got it."

***

Richard Golden's office was the largest and most opulent in Nick's limited experience. He had been in that room only once, briefly, on the day he had been hired. He had been told that the second time an associate entered Richard's office, it was either to be made partner or to be fired. Nick had so far avoided that second invitation.

The office was large enough to comfortably accommodate Golden's desk, leather executive chair, and two guest chairs. It also held a full-sized sofa with a coffee table and two overstuffed armchairs, along with a conference table with seats for sixteen. There was also a wet-bar concealed behind a sliding panel in the west wall. The carpeting was so plush Nick found it hard to get his footing. But the highlight of the room was the view.

The entire east wall was glass with an unobstructed view of Biscayne Bay. To the right, he could see the Rickenbacker Causeway swooping over the water to Key Biscayne, and beyond that, the pale blue waters of the upper bay fading into the misty distance. Straight ahead, he could see across the shallows to the old Marine Stadium, derelict now, filled with pleasure boats riding at anchor within its protecting enclosure. Slightly to the left was the port, with huge gleaming cruise ships lined up waiting for their cargo of vacationers. As Nick watched, a seaplane rose from behind the ships and banked, heading east.

Nick pulled himself away from the view and started to search the office. That morning he had already gone through the firm's filing room and signed out the Keene Construction files, but for a thirty-plus year client of its size, the information was surprisingly incomplete. The file clerk, who insisted on the title "archivist," told him that Richard Golden kept much of the more sensitive material locked in his office.

Nick tried the desk, which was locked. Another visit to Joanna's wonderful clay pot yielded the key to that also, but the desk was a washout. He sat in Richard Golden's chair a moment and looked around the office. There was nothing obvious like a filing cabinet, but there were a few promising-looking doors to try.

They turned out to be a private bathroom, a closet filled with spare suits, shirts and shoes, and a second exit. Nick tried the wet-bar and fixed himself a drink.

The bar installation was ingenious. It was built into the wall, and with the front panel closed, it was practically invisible. Nick slid the panel closed and admired the handiwork. It reminded him of the secret passages he used to read about in Hardy Boys mysteries when he was a boy. He moved right and tapped on the wall. It sounded solid. He stepped to the left of the bar and tapped again. This time, the echo was satisfyingly hollow.

It was just another minute's work before he had the panel open to reveal a row of five filing cabinets, the middle one devoted entirely to Keene Construction. Nick was not sure exactly what he was looking for, but he needed to find something to show that his knowledge of Keene's business was unique, and not easily transferred to another firm. He pulled open the top drawer.

It was empty. As was the second drawer. As was the entire cabinet.

***

Betty Keene stood with hands on hips, impatiently tapping her right foot. She was standing toe-to-toe with Roberto Vilaseca and holding her own. At six feet, three inches, Roberto had the size advantage, and his body-builder physique, on full display in nothing but a bathing suit, appeared more than capable of holding his own against anybody. But facing the determined and angry Betty Keene made him feel like a giant, helpless doofus.

She wagged a finger at him. "You've got no right to turn me down, just because I'm a woman."

"Lady, I'm not turning you down because you're a woman. I've got to follow the rules. I just work here, you know?"

"And the rule says you won't rent me a jet-ski?"

"I can't rent to anyone without a driver's license unless you want to put a $5,000 deposit on your credit card."

"That's ridiculous. Besides, I want to pay cash."

"Which is why I have to turn you down."

"We'll see about that." She stomped off toward the street where she had left her accomplice from the morning's breakout and later egg attack. They were both still dressed in their funeral attire. Her dark, conservative dress was bizarre for a renter and was a jarring contrast to her multiple earrings, hoops, and studs. The rainbow-colored hair only added to Roberto's suspicions. The guy she was with was dressed like a milkman.

She returned pushing the milkman ahead of her.

"This is my son," she said. "He's an attorney, and he'll sue your ass, won't you, Nelson?"

Nelson nodded but said nothing until Betty jabbed a finger into his kidney. "Yes," he grunted.

"See? You don't know what you're messing with. He'll sue you for discriminating against women, short people, the elderly, non-drivers, and people with bad credit. Is this public land you're operating on?"

Roberto looked at the strip of beach he stood on between the road and the water. "Yeah, I guess."

"Then you are required by the Americans with Disabilities Act to provide equal access to your facilities to all people, regardless of disability. If you fail to comply, my son will have you kicked off this beach so fast, your head will spin."

Nelson nodded emphatically.

"You've got a disability?

"Apparently, in your eyes, if you refuse to provide a service to me that is available to the rest of the public. You must see a disability of some kind."

"I just need a driver's license, lady. I'm not asking for anything that I don't get from everybody who rents from me."

"Then my lack of a driver's license is a disability, right Nelson?"

Nelson nodded again.

Roberto Vilaseca pointed a thumb at Nelson. "Does he ever speak for himself?"

"You don't want him to speak. Once he starts talking, it costs me $400.00 an hour, and you'll be responsible for attorney's fees, plus court costs and all out-of-pocket expenses. I'm willing to waive all that right now in return for the prepaid rental of two jet-skis for thirty minutes. Is that too much to ask?"

"Yes, but you know what? I'm tired of fighting with you. Pay me for the rentals, and you can take your jet-ski ride. Just don't go outside the area marked by the buoys. Okay? Are you happy now?"

Betty Keene smiled with such sweetness that Roberto thought he was looking at a different person. "Thank you very much. That's all I ask."

Within moments, the cash had changed hands, and Betty and Nelson were mounted on their rented steeds.

As the machines idled in shallow water, Roberto prepared to give them operating instructions. Before he could even open his mouth, both throttles were opened wide, and the machines zoomed away from the shore, shooting rooster tails of water in the air behind them. Roberto stood in knee-deep water and watched in silence as the two jet-skis raced past the artificial boundary set by the buoys and headed directly out to sea, slowly fading in the distance.

***

Nick stepped out of his car, briefcase in hand, and walked into the Dinner Key Marina. As his eyes ran over the millions of dollars floating there in row after row, he realized why Burnham & Fields had wanted to buy Richard Golden's accounting firm. South Florida is where the money is.

He asked for directions to the fuel dock and made his way carefully, stepping between coiled dock lines and ships' power cords. He felt out of place in his suit and tie, moving among the boaters and dockhands dressed in their shorts and T-shirts. He loosened his tie and glanced at his watch. He still had ten minutes before he met Andrew Keene, so he took his time.

The afternoon spent in Richard Golden's office had not been entirely wasted. Despite the surprising lack of documentation, Nick had been able to bone up on Keene Construction by accessing the archived documents available through Dorothy. He did not discover any shocking revelations, but the time and effort had been worthwhile. Nick believed that he now had a good understanding of the company's history, where it stood at present, and some of the challenges it faced for the future as all the desirable undeveloped land was paved over. He had made copious notes and brought along a few documents about which he hoped to ask intelligent-sounding questions.

He thought again about Gordon McCall, and the pink note Lydia had handed him on his way out. It had McCall's flight information for the next day. Nick's step lightened as he thought how he would relish meeting McCall at the airport, casually telling him how he had saved the account.

Nick stood on the fuel dock and looked around. The place was busy, with the smell of diesel strong in the air, making his stomach churn. He glanced at his watch again. Six o'clock had come and gone, and he didn't see anyone who looked like he was there for a business meeting.

Nick stepped up to a dockhand filling the tanks on a gigantic sport-fisherman. "Excuse me?" The young man looked up at Nick through mirrored sunglasses. "Do you work here?"

The sunglasses nodded slowly, once.

"I'm supposed to meet someone from Keene Construction. Do they have an office around here or something?"

The sunglasses moved from side to side, then turned to look out over the water. The dockhand pointed to a fast-moving boat coming in the channel. "That's one of their boats," he said.

Nick looked up and saw a bright green and gold boat charging down the channel at high speed, headed directly at them. As he watched, the engines were throttled back, and the boat settled into the water, quickly losing speed. It coasted toward the dock, and just when it looked like it would ram the pilings, the engines slipped into reverse and the boat turned hard left. The starboard side slid around and gently kissed the bumpers, as a young girl in a faded bikini top and shorts stepped from the deck to the dock.

She handed a rope to Nick and said, "Tie off the bow."

Nick looked at the rope in his hand, then back at the girl.

"Never mind," she said and snatched the rope back

from Nick. "Hey, Jerry!" The fuel attendant looked up. "Tie it off, okay?" She tossed him the line and turned back to Nick. "Wait here. I'll be right back."

Nick watched as she stepped into the small building that sold ice, bait, and snacks to the departing boaters. From what he had seen of her darkly tanned face behind oversized sunglasses, he guessed she was in her mid-twenties or so, and pretty in a surfer-girl kind of way. Her nose was sunburned, and she wore no makeup. She was small, only about five feet two inches, and probably didn't weigh much more than a hundred pounds. Her dark hair was pulled back in a long ponytail that poked out the back of a green baseball cap with the word "Keene" embroidered on the peak.

She emerged from the store in a moment with a stack of packages balanced in her arms. Nick stepped forward to help.

"Just get out of the way," she said and nimbly climbed back up onto the boat and dumped everything behind the captain's seat. She looked back down at Nick. "Well, are you coming?"

Nick hesitated a moment. "Are you the person from Keene Construction?"

She bent over, giving Nick a clear view of her freckled chest, and pointed to her cap. "Just like it says on the hat."

Nick raised his eyes to look her in the face. "And where are you taking me?"

She raised a slender tanned arm and pointed southeast across the bay. "To Boca Cheeca. Where did you think you were going?"

Nick shrugged. "I guess I thought I was going to meet with Mr. Keene somewhere –" he gestured vaguely to the boats in the marina, "around here."

She laughed. "Only drug dealers and yacht brokers do business in marinas. Come on." She extended a hand to help him aboard.

Nick grabbed his briefcase and took her hand. It was

soft and warm, not dry and callused as he had suspected. Before he could finish his appraisal of her grip, he was yanked aboard with surprising strength.

Once on board, Nick immediately lost his footing and crashed to the deck. She looked at his black leather shoes and said, "You're going to have to take those off. And your socks, too, or you're going to be slipping and sliding all over the place."

Without trying to get up, Nick did as she suggested, neatly tucking his socks into the toes of his shoes. When he finally rose, he extended a hand and said, "I'm Nick."

"Yeah?" she said and took his hand to shake. "Then I guess I got the right guy."

"And you are?"

"Jeannie." She pulled her hand away and sat in the captain's seat. "So you're an accountant, huh?"

"Yes. With Burnham & Fields."

"Well, that sounds fascinating," she said, and started the engines, making further conversation impossible.

With Jerry's help, the lines were let go, they pulled smoothly away from the dock, and powered out the channel into the bay. Nick was not a boat person, but he could tell a powerful vessel when he was on it. He guessed that half of the forty or so feet of hull was filled with engine. As they reached the relatively open water of the bay, Jeannie opened the throttles, and they started skipping over the water. The bay was calm, with only a light chop, but they bounced from crest to crest, flying, barely touching the water. Nick felt like he was on one of those amusement park rides he that he avoided. The ones that made him sick. He hoped it wasn't a long trip to Boca Cheeca.

***

Ten miles to the north, two jet-skis slowly motored past the mouth of the Miami River. They threaded their way carefully between the pleasure craft and work boats and headed south toward the bay.

As they passed under the causeway, they picked up speed. They zoomed down the bay, annoying the fishermen and sailors and ignoring the "No Wake" signs.

They passed the barking seals at the Seaquarium and buzzed the expensive houses on the beaches of Key Biscayne. They jumped the wakes of powerboats at Cape Florida, then continued south, toward Boca Cheeca Key.

***

Scorch walked back to the trailer park. During the commotion of the fire, he had casually strolled away, anxious to avoid questions that might have come up about the fire's cause. It was now late afternoon, and the remains of his mobile home still smoldered.

The trailer was a complete loss. The entire center portion was gone. Only the ends were still standing, like twisted and blackened bookends. The only item that was intact was Scorch's mattress, which he had hauled outside the night before. It had been thoroughly soaked, though, and he guessed it might never be the same.

Scorch only paused a moment to view the wreckage, then walked across the dirt lane to his car. He had left the windows down, and it was in the shade, so it was a reasonably comfortable temperature. He drove away from the scene, taking one last glance through the rearview mirror.

He headed east, toward the beach. His lack of sleep the night before, followed by a day of wandering around Dania on foot, had left him physically beat, and the loss of his home had done nothing to improve his mood. All he wanted to do now was sleep.

He drove into the parking lot at John U. Lloyd State Park and pulled the car under a tree. Not many of the locals went to the beach in August, and there were no tourists yet. There were just one or two dog-walkers and evening strollers around. He leaned back in his seat and closed his eyes.

He opened them again and scrunched forward to reach into his back pocket. He removed his wallet. It held almost no money but was surprisingly bulky with a collection of credit cards and driver's licenses in a variety of names. He set it on the passenger seat and closed his eyes again.

Within seconds, he was fiddling with the seat adjustments, trying to recline, but only succeeding in making the seat back even straighter. Finally, he climbed out of the car and slammed the door behind him. Then he gave it a hard kick, adding another dent to the quarter panel.

Scorch opened the door again and climbed into the back seat. He swept the McDonald's and Burger King wrappers and cups onto the floor and uncovered the beat-up old briefcase he had taken from Richard Golden. It took up half the seat, so he shoved it onto the floor, too, and stretched out.

Something was still digging into his side.

He reached under his back and pulled out a ring of keys, the ones that had been in Golden's electric cart.

"Goddamn son-of-a-bitch fucking whore piece of shit bastard keys!" he yelled, and then he hurled them out the window into the underbrush.

He lay down one more time, then sat bolt upright. "Goddamn it!" he said. He scrambled out of the car and started looking through the tangle of vegetation until he found the keys. He held them up in triumph, and shouted to the wind, "Who's the best!"

Scorch pocketed the keys, got back into his car, and headed south. He glanced at his watch. There was a ferry to Boca Cheeca Key in an hour. He had plenty of time.

SIX

The difference between a social occasion and a business one is that some people think there's a difference. There isn't. It's always business. Always.

From - *Get Off Your Ass and Succeed*

Nick had turned a pale gray, and despite the heat, his face was clammy. He took deep breaths, fighting to hang on to his lunch, willing the island to grow closer. He wanted to get there sooner, and he wanted Jeannie to slow down, but mostly, he just wanted to get off.

Jeannie eased the boat into the Boca Cheeca channel. Rather than head south into the town's marina, she turned toward a private harbor on the north island. She slipped between two docked boats, one similar to the monster she was driving, and the other a gleaming white sailboat with two masts. Beyond that, there was a sport fishing boat with a tall tower and a handful of smaller open powerboats and skiffs.

Jeannie shut off the engines as the big boat gently nudged the pilings. Nick immediately scrambled from his seat and jumped barefoot to the dock, where he fought to control his breathing and regain his composure.

She deftly tied off the dock lines and set some bumpers, then tossed Nick's shoes to the ground and handed him his briefcase.

"You look like shit," she said. She jumped down beside him and looked up into his face. "It'll pass in a minute."

If Nick had not been so pale with nausea, he would have blushed under her examination. "I don't get out on boats much . . ."

"Really? Who'd have guessed?" She grabbed a coiled hose from one of the pilings and turned it on. "I'm going to be a few minutes. You can head up to the house."

Nick looked at the enormous two-story yellow structure gleaming in the light of the setting sun. He had assumed it was a hotel or country club, and from where he was standing, it looked like it covered the whole island. "That's a house?"

"And the Bates Motel is just another motel," she said.

Nick tucked his shoes under his left arm. "Well, thanks for the ride."

"It's what I do," she said, without looking up.

Nick started toward the house along the light-colored brick path that snaked through the immaculate lawn, but it burned his bare feet. He walked in the grass until he reached a bench set under some palm trees. The sun was now so low that the trees provided no shade, but he sat anyway to put on his shoes.

Looking northwest across the bay, Nick could clearly see the Miami skyline rising from the water. The distance softened the hard edges of the buildings and gave the city a fairy tale look. If it had been emerald green, he might have thought he was in Oz.

Nick tied up his laces and then sat a moment longer to examine the gigantic Keene homestead. The path led to a set of ten-foot high double doors under a tall portico. Flanking the doors were massive carriage lights, nearly as tall as Nick. To the left and right of the entrance, the building went on for at least a hundred yards in each direction.

The walls were pale yellow stucco, under a red barrel tile roof. The facade was pierced by dozens of windows, open to catch the breezes coming in off the Atlantic. The house was beautiful, and huge, and vaguely Mediterranean-looking, but something about it didn't seem quite right to Nick. He just couldn't put his finger on it.

Nick walked the remaining twenty yards to the imposing front doors. There was a giant brass knocker on each. He grabbed one and banged away.

Nick had lived in Florida long enough to know that when someone opens their front door to you in the summer, the first thing you feel is a blast of air artificially chilled to near arctic temperatures. It was always a welcome feeling after a long walk from your air-conditioned car. Though it was now evening and the temperature was only in the high eighties, Nick had subconsciously been anticipating the cool embrace of refrigerated air after his boat ride and long trudge up the lawn. He was still in his woolen funeral suit, and the beads of sweat on his face had gathered together into little rivulets.

When the door was opened by a small man wearing Bermuda shorts and a golf shirt, and there was no rush of cold air, Nick realized what it was that had bothered him about the house. The windows were open. That meant no air conditioning. That meant no relief.

He felt faint.

"You look like shit," said the little man.

Nick tried to stand more erect and straightened his tie. These comments were making him self-conscious. "I'm just a little warm."

"You'll probably come in here and pass out or throw up. I should have expected it, I suppose. The day has been too pleasant up until now. Just try not to be sick on the rugs."

"I'm not sick."

"Everyone says that, then - wham! - it's 'Philip, get the mop.'"

"Don't worry about me. I'm fine, really. I'm just here to see Mr. Keene."

"Isn't everybody. Do you know which one?

"Senior."

"Lucky you." Philip stepped back from the door. "You may as well come in. Dinner is just about to start."

Nick stepped inside and followed the depressed little man, envious of his shorts. They crossed a marble foyer with a twenty-foot high ceiling. On either side, a curved stairway swept up to the second floor. Large ferny-looking plants stood in heavy ceramic pots along the walls, and the walls themselves were painted a soothing shade of blue.

Philip paused in front of a set of French doors and pointed at Nick's briefcase. "I suppose you'll want me to keep that for you during dinner."

Nick handed it over. "Thanks."

"You may as well give me your jacket and tie, too. Dinner is informal."

"Great." Nick slipped his tie out of its knot and surrendered it too. "I didn't know this was a dinner invitation. Is there a big group?"

"It's always a dinner invitation, though only God and Andrew Keene know why. Tonight it is just the family, plus one or two. It doesn't matter, though. It will still be horrible."

Philip opened the door and stepped back. As Nick passed through, Philip slammed the door behind him without another word, leaving Nick in a small dining room nearly filled by a table already partially occupied.

"What are you doing here?"

Seated on the left side of the table was Andrew Keene's son, still looking unhappy. "Hello, Skip." Nick stepped around to him and extended a hand. "We met at the funeral today, but we weren't formally introduced. I'm Nick Rohmer."

"I know who you are," Skip said, ignoring Nick's attempt to shake hands.

"Nice to see Dad's instincts haven't changed." This was from the woman on Skip's right, the one that had given him the icy stare in the synagogue parking lot. "He practically rewards people for being rude." She spat out the word "rude."

Nick, his hand still extended hopefully, swung slightly to the woman. "I'm Nick," he said. "I didn't get your name."

She crossed her arms and said to Skip, "Some people."

Nick gave up and put his hand in his pocket. The room was smaller than he expected, and given the size of the house, was probably not the main dining room. Opposite the door he had come in was another set of French doors that stood open onto a large courtyard or terrace paved in the same light-colored brick as the path from the dock. Nick could see another building, or perhaps just more of the same building across the terrace.

"This is quite a place," he said. His voice seemed flat and forced in the hostile room. "Do you all live here together?"

No answer.

"Do you mind if I look out here?" Nick asked, indicating the patio area.

Skip's companion answered. "Don't go poking your nose where it doesn't belong, Mr. Neb-nose."

Unsure what that meant, Nick ignored her. He walked toward the open doors but was almost knocked down by a tall, thin man coming in. He was in shorts and a T-shirt and had a large camera slung around his neck. He moved quickly, with a nervous bounce in his walk. His head was down, and Nick had to grab his shoulders with both hands to prevent a collision.

"Whoa. Excuse me," Nick said.

The nervous walker only glanced up and mumbled, "Sorry." He quickly took a seat at the table opposite Skip.

"Well, look who showed up," said Skip. "Where have you been all day?"

The man didn't answer.

"You were supposed to drive us to the funeral," said the woman. "When we couldn't find you, Dad Keene drove. It was awful. You should start showing a little more consideration."

Before he could show any consideration, the door from the hallway opened, and the extremely busty blond woman from the funeral entered. Philip had not exaggerated when he said dinner was informal. She was wearing a cut-off T-shirt with a bikini bottom.

Nick could not help staring. From the waist down, she was a normally proportioned woman. But from the waist up, it looked like someone had applied an air hose. She had the largest breasts Nick had ever seen, including the ones on the woman at Steve Mathews' stag party, who up until now had been the standard for Nick. Her T-shirt was not so much worn as draped over her torso, like a tarp over a large statue. The shirt must have been huge, but was thrust so far forward by her chest, that the hem stood a good foot out from her flat and well-muscled stomach, visible above her tiny bikini bottom.

"I remember you," she said. She extended a hand limply toward Nick. "I'm Charlotte Keene."

Nick shook her hand gently. "I'm Nick."

She sat at the foot of the table, near the hallway. Because of her extraordinary proportions, she could not pull her chair all the way up to the table. She indicated the seat to her right. "Why don't you sit here? I could use a new diversion."

"Don't start with him, Charlotte," said Skip's icy companion, "or I'll tell Dad Keene."

"Ignore her," Charlotte said to Nick. "She's just frustrated."

"At least I don't throw myself at every pair of pants that walks in here."

Charlotte turned her gaze on the other woman. "That's because you're frigid. You couldn't enjoy sex even if Skip knew what he was doing."

Skip blustered. "How dare you suggest . . ."

"I'm telling Dad Keene," Carolyn said.

Ignoring them both, Charlotte turned back to Nick, who was still standing. She patted the table. "Sit down. I won't bite."

Nick hesitated. "I thought I should wait for Mr. Keene."

"Well, I'm Mr. Keene's wife, and I want you to sit here."

Charlotte Keene could not have been much more than thirty. "You're Mrs. Andrew Keene, Senior?"

She smiled, showing her perfectly capped teeth. "For almost five years now."

"I didn't realize . . . I thought . . . I mean . . ."

She patted the table again. "As your hostess, I want you to sit here. You wouldn't want to upset your hostess, would you?"

Nick sat. As he slid his chair up to the table, a soaking wet Andrew Keene entered from the patio. Nick immediately stood up again.

"Well, look at that," Andrew Keene said. "We got a polite one. You kids should all take a lesson from . . . from . . ."

"Nick Rohmer," Nick said.

"Right. From Nick. Sit down, sit down."

Nick sat.

Andrew Keene was wearing only an enormous pair of baggy plaid swim trunks that hung down past his knees in the front and were slipping ominously at the waistband. His barrel chest and ample stomach were covered in curly white hair, plastered down by water. He looked like a polar bear in a swimsuit.

He stepped over to Nick, leaving a trail of water on the floor. He held out a dripping paw. "Glad you made it."

Nick stood slightly to shake his hand. It was cold. "Thanks for having –"

"No time for jawing. Dinner is just about ready. Hope you brought an appetite." He returned to the head of the table and sat.

As Nick sat for the third time, Jeannie, the young woman who had driven the boat, entered from the patio. Nick stood again.

Jeannie had put a shirt on over her swimsuit top, and removed the hat, but was otherwise dressed the same as for the boat ride.

"You're late," Andrew Keene said.

Her only response was to hold up her right hand, middle finger extended.

"Still daddy's sweet little princess," he said as she took the seat between Nick and the nervous walker. Nick sat again.

Andrew Keene addressed Nick. "You know everybody here? Probably not." He pointed to Skip. "This is my oldest son, Andrew Junior. He's the company's General Manager. He runs the day-to-day operations." Skip acknowledged the introduction with a slight nod, setting his chins to jiggling. The finger swung to the left. "Next to him is my lovely daughter-in-law, Carolyn."

She ignored Nick but gave her father-in-law an ingratiating smile.

"Carolyn is also our Vice President of Human Resources, because of her warmth and empathy."

He next pointed at the tall and nervous fellow who had almost knocked Nick over. "This is my other son, Nelson, who is given to disappearing for long periods of time." Nelson responded by leaning forward and snapping a picture of Nick. "What have I told you about that god-damned camera? If you wear it to this table one more time, it will be the last you ever see it." Without a word, Nelson quietly removed the camera and slid it under his seat.

Andrew Keene continued calmly. "And next to you

there is my sweet-natured daughter, Jeannie. Weren't you supposed to be watching your brother today?"

"I am my brother's keeper," she said. "He stayed home."

"Well, he was missing most of the day. You're going to have to do a better job than that if you want to keep him around."

"Next time I'll be sure to chain him to something."

"And on your left is my wife, Charlotte."

Charlotte reached out and laid her hand over Nick's, nearly causing him to jump out of his chair. "We've already met," she said. "I've been trying to make him feel at home."

Nick heard Carolyn make a loud "tschh." He looked up to see Skip and his wife glaring at him.

"Charlotte is the titular president of the company," Andrew said.

"He just loves saying that," Charlotte said to Nick.

"With a woman as president, we get to bid on some contracts reserved for companies that are minority or female owned. Plus, I get to say 'titular' occasionally. And to my wife's left . . . Where the hell is Walt?"

"He's late again," said Skip. "He has no consideration."

"Shut up, Skip."

"I saw him in the hallway," said Charlotte. "He was on his phone."

"Somebody go drag his ass in here."

The ass-dragging proved unnecessary as the door from the hallway opened, and a thin, neatly dressed man in his sixties entered. Perhaps it was the hat, or the trim, white mustache, but the word that immediately came to Nick was "natty." Nick stood again.

"For God's sake!" shouted Andrew Keene, "you're like a fucking jack-in-the-box. Stay in your goddamn chair."

Nick quickly sat again and turned bright red.

"Christ sake, Walt. We're all waiting. Get your ass in that chair."

Walt strolled with unhurried grace and sat at the last seat, opposite Nick and to the left of Charlotte Keene. He removed his hat to reveal a shiny bald pate fringed by short white hair. Nodding toward Nick, he addressed Andrew Keene.

"Who is your new victim, Andrew? Another friend of Jeannie's that you are trying to run off?"

"No, Walt. He's a friend of yours. Nick, let me introduce Walter Hughes, the company's general counsel and the man who canned your ass yesterday."

Normally Nick would have risen to shake hands, but he was terrified to stand again, so he just nodded.

Walter Hughes ignored him. "Your sense of humor leaves much to be desired, Andrew."

"Do I know how to throw a dinner party, or what? The whole Audit Committee's here, along with the guy you just fired. After dinner, we're going to sit down for a little chat."

Walter Hughes turned his full attention to Nick for the first time and was apparently unimpressed. "I don't expect that it will take very long to finish our business."

"I'm real interested to know what prompted that decision, and why you thought I didn't need to know," Andrew Keene said. "I think it's time for us to have a little come-to-Jesus."

Walter Hughes got no further than opening his mouth to reply.

"But let's not spoil the dinner with shop talk. We'll discuss this after we've eaten. Phil!" he bellowed. "Where's the goddamn food?"

SEVEN

Etiquette and manners have their place, but there is no "proper" fork to use when stabbing someone in the back.

From – *Go Ahead, Make My Career*

The people who worked on the ferry knew to report any sightings of Betty Keene immediately. So did security. In fact, just about every employee of Boca Cheeca Key had been trained to report Betty-sightings. When the word went out that she was on the loose again, the island went on heightened alert.

The ferry terminal was off-limits, as was the town harbor and her ex-husband's private marina. Betty knew this and enjoyed the challenge of finding new ways to breach the Keene fortress.

After she and Nelson reached Boca Cheeca, they split up. Since Nelson was not being hunted, he had simply beached his stolen jet-ski on the Atlantic side of the main island and walked over the bridge. He slipped into the house unnoticed and changed clothes for dinner.

Betty headed for the South Island. She ran her jet-ski onto the beach near the construction site, quiet now with the work crews gone for the day. She stripped off her sodden dress and lay in her underwear, catching the last rays of the setting sun.

As the last afterglow of the day was fading over the Everglades, she awoke. It was still warm, with a gentle breeze from the east. Betty stood and brushed the fine sand from her back and legs, then tied her dress around her waist and pushed the jet-ski back into the water. She climbed aboard and headed for the northernmost of the three islands, where the gigantic Keene residence sat.

As part of the security package for the development, surveillance cameras had been mounted strategically around the Keene house to cover all entrances, the private marina, and the bridge from the main island. The monitoring station was in the town center at the police station. There, a bank of monitors showed the view from cameras on all three islands, and anyone interested in watching could have kept good tabs on all the comings and goings. Buddy Grinnell did not run a particularly tight operation, and typically no one paid much attention.

Betty knew this but thought that with the word out about her, someone might be making the effort. Besides, it was so ridiculously easy to disable the system that she couldn't resist.

She motored into the Boca Cheeca channel, zipped right under the nose of the incoming ferry, and under the bridge. The jet-ski lurched as she nudged it onto the sand. She climbed the gentle bank to the northern base of the bridge where it sat on concrete pilings driven deep into the coral rock. Snaking under the bridge's span, tucked neatly out of sight along with the main electrical feed and the telephone lines, was the single cable that carried the signals from all the cameras on the north island to the security office.

Working by touch, Betty separated the video cable from the others. She removed one of the silver studs from her eyebrow and drove it into the hard plastic insulation, through the wiry heart of the cable, and out the other side. She wiped her hands on her dress, still knotted around her waist, then headed up the sandy bank toward the house she used to call home.

***

Nick sat in a large white wicker chair with a floral-patterned seat cushion, facing the mahogany door of Andrew Keene's office, and he was fidgety. He had been in this spot watching the closed door for signs of activity for over half an hour. In that time, he had watched Carolyn and Skip enter in a huff and leave in a huff. He had seen Keene's wife enter, but not leave, and he had witnessed Walter Hughes leave twice, without ever having seen him go in. Nick guessed that, like the dining room, the office also opened out onto the patio. He hoped he would soon get to find out first-hand.

Nick glanced at his watch for the tenth time. He had been kept cooling his heels since dinner, which had been as horrible as Philip had suggested it would be. He had never seen a family as devoid of manners and consideration as the Keenes. The moment Philip placed anything edible on the table, it was attacked by six pairs of hands. Only Walter Hughes and Nick had stayed out of the fray. Some deference was shown to Andrew Keene, Senior, but for the rest, it was a free-for-all. They grabbed and slapped and fought over the food like a pack of feral dogs. Carolyn and Skip added dialogue to the scene, accusing the others of being pigs, and appealing to Andrew Keene to castigate first one person, then another. The scene reminded Nick of something out of the Lord of the Flies. It didn't help that the main course was barbecued spare ribs. The combatants ended up splattered and smeared in blood-red barbecue sauce, adding to the barbaric picture.

Lacking the requisite competitive spirit, Nick got little more than scraps to eat, which was fine with him.

Watching the Keenes attack the food and each other had taken the edge off his appetite.

When the last of the food was gone, the dinner party broke up quickly. Only Skip and Carolyn left together. The rest drifted off in different directions with little more than grunts of acknowledgment to each other. When everyone but Walter Hughes and Nick had left, Andrew Keene pushed his chair back and chuckled. "Quite a show, eh?"

"Disgusting, as usual," said Hughes.

Andrew Keene turned to Nick. "What did you think?"

Nick fought the urge to tug at his collar. "The, um, food was delicious."

"How do you know? Did you even get any?"

"I had plenty, really. I couldn't eat another thing."

"That's because there isn't another thing."

"Allow me to explain," said Walter Hughes. "Andrew intentionally presents meals that are inadequate to feed the entire family, to foster a competitive spirit. Isn't that right, Andrew?"

"I want them to know that you have to fight for what you get in this world. It's not all going to be handed to you on a silver platter."

"Andrew is a firm believer in survival of the fittest."

"I'm not going to live forever. Someday, one of them is going to have to take over this business, and they're going to have to know how to fend for themselves."

"And table manners be damned," said Hughes.

"Manners didn't get me where I am today, Walt."

"They certainly did not, Andrew. Truer words were never spoken."

"Asshole."

Hughes' only reply was an arched eyebrow.

Andrew Keene stood and hitched his bathing suit up. "Enough bullshit. We got some business to talk. Follow me."

Keene left through the door to the hallway and turned left, leading Nick back through the entry foyer and past a few more doors. He indicated a pair a wicker chairs in the hall. "Have a seat for a minute. I got a few things I have to do first." With that he passed through the office door and closed it behind him.

Nick sat, but Walter Hughes remained standing. "I'm going to the loo," he said and walked off down the hall.

That had been forty-five minutes ago, and Nick had twice more seen Hughes as he emerged from Keene's office and walked down the hall, once left and once right. He felt like he was watching a play where the stage direction had been badly written.

Nick glanced at his watch again and sighed. He was going to need to find the bathroom soon, too.

***

The ferry was mostly empty. There were only a handful of residents on board for the trip, distinguishable by their gray hair and expensive clothing, and the way they congregated together in the lounge sipping mixed drinks. The working stiffs usually stayed on deck when the weather was nice, and this evening was beautiful. No domestics or employees of the island were headed out at this time of the day, so Scorch had the deck to himself. He stood in the bow and let the breeze blow his greasy hair around.

The last glow of the sunset had already faded as the ferry entered the Boca Cheeca channel. They were slowing down when something small, dark, and fast flashed in front of them. The captain blew the ship's horn and even Scorch was impressed with the stupidity of someone riding an unlit jet-ski at night and taking on a vessel as big as the ferry. He cupped his hands and shouted, "Moron!" at the receding figure.

After the ferry was safely tied up at the dock, Scorch waited for all the old farts to get off. He didn't want them to see that he didn't know where he was going. He fingered the keys in his pocket, and then pulled out the bill he had found in Richard Golden's briefcase. He was sure it was Golden's home address, but the address was not very helpful. He lived at Number 15 Keene Boulevard. It was a starting place.

When the last of the gray-heads disappeared into the night, Scorch made his way down the gangplank and under the roof of the parking enclosure, hoping to find Richard Golden's electric cart. If he was going to have to wander around looking for a condominium, he didn't want to do it on foot. He swore. The cart was not there.

Scorch walked around to the front of the ferry terminal where there was a large "You Are Here" map under glass. He wasn't much of a map person, but the island was not that complicated. There was only one main road, and it spanned all three islands. It was Keene Boulevard.

"Shit! That son-of-a-bitch would have to live on the longest road."

He looked at the map more closely. The "You Are Here" arrow was very close to the north end of the middle island. The road started just over the bridge in front of a building labeled "Keene Residence." Scorch could see the bridge from where he was standing. It seemed as good a starting place as any. He would begin at one end and work his way south, and this way he was bound to find it. He took one moment to bask in the glow of his cleverness, then set out to cross the bridge to the Keene residence.

***

In the security office, Ernesto Ruiz, who was theoretically watching the video monitors, was in Buddy Grinnell's office eating a TV dinner and watching the Atlanta Braves game with Buddy. He swallowed the last of his beer and looked at the empty bottle dejectedly. He wiggled it in front of Buddy. "I'm dry. You want another one?"

Buddy nodded. "And get some pretzels or something."

After a detour to the bathroom, Ruiz made his way to the lunchroom, where he grabbed two beers from the fridge and a bag of pork rinds from a cupboard. On his way back to Buddy's office, he passed by the video monitor station. Whether it was a pang of guilt over a job neglected or just idle curiosity, he paused to scan the monitors. Three were out, showing nothing but static.

Ruiz set down a beer and tapped one of the screens. When the static didn't change, he whacked it harder. To his surprise, this also had no effect on the picture. After exhausting his repertoire of tricks, Ruiz abandoned his repair effort and returned his focus to the mission at hand. He picked up his beer and rejoined the Chief in his office.

"The Braves just struck out," said Buddy, accepting the beer.

Ruiz sat down and opened the bag of pork rinds. "A couple of the monitors are out," he said.

"Again?"

"Yeah. I tried to fix them, but they're really messed up. I couldn't get them to work."

Buddy seemed absorbed by a beer commercial. "Well, what can you do? Make a note to call the alarm company in the morning."

Ruiz acknowledged this with a nod because the beer in the commercial was now being enjoyed by beautiful women in tiny bathing suits. It required all of his concentration.

***

Scorch stood in front of the Keene house and wondered what the hell it was. It didn't look like an apartment or condo building. There wasn't enough parking, for one thing. And it seemed too big to be a private residence.

Scorch walked around the building, taking care to stay beyond the glow of the spotlights reflected off the pale stucco. The few windows that were lit from the inside revealed the kind of opulence you only expect from the extremely wealthy. Scorch was intrigued.

He worked his way around the building to the end that opened out toward the Atlantic Ocean. He turned the corner and discovered a large courtyard surrounded by building on three sides. It had a screened roof running from one wing of the building to the other, and a two-story high screen wall at the open end. The courtyard was much more dimly lit than the front of the building, with heavy shadows cast by the landscape lighting. In the center was a gigantic swimming pool. To his right and left, French doors lined the first floor, many of them invitingly open onto the night.

Scorch observed the scene, liking his chances. Though it wasn't late, the place seemed quiet. It was an opportunity that he couldn't resist.

He watched the house for a while, memorizing the details of the layout, looking for the comings and goings of the residents. It presented a tempting target to someone with larceny on his mind.

***

Nick counted silently with his eyes closed. When he reached three hundred, he looked at his watch. "Damn!" he said. He thought it would have been at least five minutes since he last looked. It wasn't. He had now been parked in this hallway for over an hour and a half, and he was finally beginning to lose patience. And he really did need to find a bathroom soon.

He stood and scanned the hallway. It had been nearly an hour since he had seen anyone, and he decided it was time to take the initiative. He stepped up to Andrew Keene's office door, raised his hand to knock, then paused. He listened for a moment, leaning close to the door, nearly pressing his ear against the wood. There was no sound. He wasn't sure if that was a good thing or not.

Nick knocked tentatively, then stepped back. There was no response. He waited thirty seconds, and then knocked again, harder.

When there was still no reaction from the quiet office, Nick finally gave in to his impatience. He banged his knuckles hard against the heavy wooden door and shouted, "Mr. Keene? Are you in there?"

After waiting a decent interval, he tried the bright brass doorknob, and it turned in his hand. Slowly he pushed the door open, calling out to Andrew Keene as he did so. The office was empty, and except for the faint hum of the ceiling fan, it was quiet as a tomb.

Nick's first impression was that a small forest had been sacrificed to build this office. Every inch of wall that was not hidden by shelves of expensive leather-bound books was covered in dark mahogany paneling. The French doors, open onto the patio, also looked to be made of mahogany. The floor was parquet, made up of a pattern of dark and darker woods. Even the ceiling was paneled in the same heavy wood as the walls.

There was a brown leather sofa against the wall to Nick's right, and it was nearly invisible among the browns of the floor and wall. Mounted on the wall above the couch was what appeared to be a lifetime of awards, plaques, and various other framed mementos of construction and groundbreakings.

To Nick's left, perpendicular to the French doors, was two tons of dark wood that had been carved into a desk. Behind the desk, empty, was an enormous, brown leather desk chair. In front of the desk were two brown leather armchairs, their backs to Nick.

Though there was a reading light on in the corner, and the desk lamp was lit, the room was still dark. All the available light seemed to have been absorbed by the dark wood of the walls and ceiling, and into the dull browns of the books and furniture.

"Hello," Nick called again. Like the light, his voice was sucked into the room and died without an echo. He stepped inside, but left the door to the hall open.

Nick saw his briefcase on the floor next to the desk. Thrown carelessly onto the sofa was his suit jacket, the one Philip had taken from him before dinner. Nick stepped to the sofa and picked up his jacket, trying to brush the wrinkles out of it. It wasn't an expensive suit, but it was Nick's best. He laid it neatly back on the sofa and turned to get his briefcase. That's when he saw the body.

Not the whole body. From where he stood, he could really only see just the one arm on the floor, sticking out from behind the desk. Nick stared at it a moment, then moved slowly toward it, stepping farther behind the desk, until he could see who it was. Stretched out face up, Andrew Keene's unseeing eyes stared at the expensive ceiling. His head lay in a small pool of blood, and he was naked except for his plaid bathing suit. The only other thing that he was wearing was Nick's red patterned tie, twisted into a grotesque knot around his swollen neck.

Nick's first impulse was to run. He fought it and took a deep breath. His second impulse was to run, too. Before he could take flight, though, his sense of duty took hold. Even though he was pretty confident that he was looking at a corpse, Nick did not have much experience with dead bodies. Maybe Andrew Keene was just unconscious, or catatonic, or something else non-fatal. In which case, he should see if he could help.

Nick knelt beside the body and gingerly laid a hand on Andrew Keene's arm. It was still warm, which Nick took as a hopeful sign. He put his ear to against Keene's chest, hoping to hear a reassuring "lub-dub," but there was no discernible heartbeat. He took this as a bad sign. The only other thing he could think to do was to remove the tie. If there was any chance that Keene was alive, the tie was obviously not helping.

Even at its best, Andrew Keene's neck was a mess of

fleshy folds. In Keene's current condition, all that extra skin lay in a series of layers that made getting at the tie difficult, even for someone less nervous and frightened than Nick. He fumbled at the knot under the layers of skin, trying to figure out how to get it loosened. This was no Windsor knot. Just as he thought he was making progress, he heard the scream.

Nick jumped up so violently that he knocked the desk chair over. He fought to regain his balance, but his heart was pounding so hard from fright that he thought it would explode. And still, the scream was going on, a high-pitched screech so piercing that Nick clamped his hands over his ears.

The screamer was Skip Keene. He stood in the open doorway to the patio, pointing at the body of his father. His eyes were open so wide that Nick could see the whites all the way around his irises. Slowly Skip's gaze shifted focus from Andrew Keene to Nick. He paused in his scream only long enough to take a deep breath, and as the shrieking resumed, he pointed at Nick.

EIGHT

Logic and reason are fine as far as they go, but sometimes an emotional response is what is called for.

From – *The Business Executive's Little Red Book*

Buddy Grinnell sat on the sofa in Andrew Keene's office, observing as one of his men took pictures of the body with a cell phone. Dr. Folger was there, trying to shield his eyes from the flash of the camera, and trying to avoid conversation with Buddy, who was in a foul mood as he faced his second corpse in two days.

Buddy took a sip from a bottle of water he was nervously swirling. "Well, doc?"

"I see you're not using the police camera?"

Buddy Grinnell grunted. "We filled up the chip at Golden's accident scene."

"Hell of a flash."

"Sorry, Doc." He spoke to the man wielding the phone. "You can stop with the photos of Mr. Keene. Start taking pictures of the room. I want every square inch of this place photographed. And be sure you get pictures of this." He pointed to the trophy wall above the sofa. "It looks like a couple of spaces are blank, like maybe something's missing. Might have been used as a weapon."

The officer nodded and headed off to a corner of the room where he resumed his photo duties.

Ed Folger looked at the body between flashes and shook his head. "I'd have to say it sure doesn't appear to be an accident."

"No shit."

"Have you called the Miami-Dade cops yet?"

"Yeah, but it's not their jurisdiction."

Ed Folger arched a bushy white eyebrow. "It's not?"

"It's complicated."

Actually, it was pretty simple. When the Village of Boca Cheeca Key was incorporated, it had the option of buying services from Miami-Dade County. Things like water and sewer, fire and rescue, and police were all available from the county for a price, but Andrew Keene knew the value of a penny, and believed that he could do all of that for a lot less than the county was asking. He built his own water treatment plant, set up a volunteer fire department made up of retired business executives who wanted to play fireman, and paid bottom dollar for Buddy Grinnell and his associates to act as local police. The county cops received no money from the Village and had neither the inclination nor the jurisdiction to help.

"I think I need to call the FDLE," Buddy said.

"The who?"

"You're not from around here, are you doc? The Florida Department of Law Enforcement. It's sort of like Florida's FBI. They step in when crimes overlap jurisdictions, or if the investigation requires resources the local cops lack. That's us right now. But, Skip wants me to hold off." He looked at his watch. "I can't wait too long, though, or it will look like –"

Before Buddy could finish, Skip Keene, with his wife close behind, barged into the room, pushing Ernesto Ruiz ahead of him.

"This is a crime scene," Ruiz was saying. "You can't come in here, Mr. Keene."

Skip puffed and blustered as he pushed Ruiz ahead of him. "Of course I can come in here. This is my house, and that's my father lying there dead. How dare you . . .?"

Buddy waved a hand at Ruiz. "It's okay, Ernie. Just see if you can keep the rest of them out of here. I'll talk to the Keenes."

"Sorry, Chief," Ruiz said and stepped back out onto the patio.

"You shouldn't be in here until we're finished," Buddy said.

"I need to know what you're planning to do about this," Skip indicated the body of his father, still lying on the floor uncovered. "How do you intend to proceed here? Have you arrested anyone yet? Is anyone else coming?"

Buddy shook his head. "I called the Miami-Dade Police, and there isn't going to be any immediate help from them. The doctor and I were just talking, and we think that we need to bring in the FDLE right away."

"You don't call anybody until we tell you to," Carolyn said. "Skip and I are in charge now, and we'll decide who to call and when."

Buddy looked from Carolyn to Skip. Skip looked away and said, "We think we can contain this and not have to let outsiders in here to dig into our business. They don't know the family like you do, and it could get ugly and inconvenient and embarrassing."

Carolyn jumped in. "We think you can get this wrapped up right away. It's pretty clear that awful accountant did this. Why do we need outside help with something so simple?"

Buddy shook his head. "Even if this kid did kill Andrew, which I personally doubt, we still need to bring in the FDLE. We aren't equipped or trained to deal with this kind of situation. For god's sake, we're taking pictures of the crime scene with a cell phone!"

"There's going to have to be an autopsy," Dr. Folger said. "There's no getting around that in a suspicious death, and they don't get much more suspicious than this."

"You shut up," Carolyn snapped. "No one asked you."

"He's right," said Buddy. "We don't really have a choice here."

"I have an idea," said Skip. "Let's call the family together and we'll take a vote."

"This isn't something that you vote on, Skip. As the chief of police, I have to follow the law."

"Chief of Police! Ha!" Carolyn stabbed a finger at him. "You work for my husband now, and you'll be Chief of Nothing if you don't do as he says."

"Actually, I work for the Village of Boca Cheeca Key, and I serve at the pleasure of the town council. As long as I have their confidence, I will continue to do my job to the best of my ability."

"I control the town council, you idiot. You're as good as unemployed."

Skip laid a hand gently on his wife's shoulder. "Now Carolyn . . ."

She shrugged him off roughly. "Don't 'Now Carolyn' me. Tell him, Skip. Tell him we'll fire his unqualified ass if he doesn't do as you say. Tell him who's in charge here. Be a man for once!"

"I'm in charge here," said Buddy. "This is a crime scene, and I'm in charge. I'm calling this in. This is a murder. Someone in this house killed Andrew Keene, and we need this to be properly investigated. If we wait, it's going to look like we're hiding something. You're not hiding something, are you, Carolyn?"

"How dare you suggest . . ."

"How about you, Skip? You got something to hide?"

"Of course not, we just thought . . ."

"Then I'm calling in the professionals. We'll let them put together a proper case that'll hold up in court and see somebody imprisoned for this."

"I'll have your job for this," Carolyn hissed.

"Fine. In the meantime, please clear the room, and no one is to leave the island until they're cleared by the FDLE.

"We're not going to stay here just because you say so," Carolyn said.

"Then I'll have you arrested." Buddy met her glare with a steely look of his own, one he used to use on the football field when staring down an opposing lineman.

They locked eyes for a moment, then Carolyn looked away. "You'll be sorry," she said, with less certainty than before. "You'll all be sorry." With that, she turned and marched out through the open French doors.

Skip hesitated a moment. Before he could say anything, Buddy spoke. "Sorry about that, Skip. She just really gets my dander up, you know?"

Skip slowly nodded his head. "She has that effect on people."

"I'm afraid you're in for a long night."

Skip shrugged. "It won't be the first." He turned to leave, then stopped. "You know she's going to get you fired at the next council meeting."

"I know. I guess I'll be updating my résumé once this is over."

Skip just smiled, nodded and turned to follow his wife.

Buddy turned to Dr. Folger, who was standing quietly, observing the whole scene. "What have I just done, Doc?"

"The right thing," he said.

***

Buddy hung up the phone. "They won't be able to have anybody out here until morning. In the meantime, they want us to bag all the evidence, get Andrew's body on ice, and otherwise not disturb the crime scene."

Dr. Folger nodded. "Well, I guess I should take a look at the body first."

"Not yet, we still have to chalk it. Ernie!" he shouted. "You got the chalk?"

Ernesto Ruiz entered from the patio where most of the cops were hanging around, chatting with the freshly widowed Charlotte Keene. He held up a couple of pieces of chalk in his hand. "Right here, Chief. I got it from the shuffleboard court."

Buddy nodded toward the corpse. "See if you can get a nice outline on the floor, then give the Doc a hand with the body."

Ruiz cringed. "I got to touch it?"

"No. I want you to stand there and applaud. Of course you've got to touch it. He's heavy, and the Doc ain't that young."

Ruiz demonstrated the demeanor of a professional. "Yuck."

"Just start chalking."

***

In the next room, Nick Rohmer stood facing two of Buddy Grinnell's cops. It was overkill; any one of Buddy's men could have done the job alone. But these two were of below average usefulness, even for Boca Cheeca cops, so Buddy had them both keep an eye on the suspect and each other.

This room was a smaller, less opulent version of Andrew Keene's office. It was used during the day by Andrew's executive assistant. There was a connecting door to Andrew's office, now closed, and the usual French doors open onto the patio.

Nick pointed to the telephone on the desk. "Do you gentlemen mind if I make a call?"

The cops looked at each other, and then back at Nick. The one on the right shrugged. "I guess. That's what you get on TV."

His partner nodded. "Yeah. You have the right to one

telephone call, and the right to remain silent."

"But not on the phone," the other cop said. "You don't have to remain silent on the phone. That wouldn't be much of a call, you know?"

"Right. You can talk on the phone, then you can, like, remain silent after."

"Great," said Nick, and he moved toward the desk. They stepped aside for him. "So I'll just make that call now."

Both cops nodded. "Okay," one said, "but no funny stuff."

"You can count on it, officer."

Nick picked up the receiver and dialed Victoria's cell phone. After three rings, she picked up. There was loud party noise in the background."

"Hello?" she said, in a half shout.

"Victoria, it's me. Nick."

"Hello?" she said again, louder.

"Victoria. Can you hear me?" Nick was shouting.

"Nick? Is that you?"

"Yes, it's me, Victoria. Can you hear me?"

"Hello? I can't hear you."

"Victoria?"

"Nick?"

Nick held the phone out for a moment and sighed deeply. Then he shouted into the mouthpiece as loud as he could, "Can you go someplace quieter?"

"Hold on," she said, "I'm going to go someplace quieter."

"Great," Nick said, softly, knowing she couldn't hear him.

As he listened, the background noises grew fainter. Eventually, she spoke again, this time in a more natural tone.

"Nick, is that you?"

"Hey, honey. Am I interrupting a good party?"

"Fundraiser. You know. Fun really isn't the point, but I

should be in there. Is this important?"

"I just wanted you to know that I took your advice."

"Advice?" she said, after a short pause.

"Yeah. Remember, you wanted me to introduce myself to Keene at the funeral? Fix the relationship, and all that."

"Oh Nick, that's great. But, can we talk about it later?"

"You were right. We hit it off, and he invited me to his house for dinner and to discuss business."

"I knew you had a killer instinct."

"Please don't use that expression."

"Huh?"

"I'm calling from his house right now."

"Good job, Nick, but I really have to go. You can give me all the details when I get home."

"I've got a little problem, though."

Nick could almost hear her tapping her foot with impatience. "What? What is so important that it can't wait until later?"

"Keene's dead, Victoria."

"What?"

"He's dead. Murdered."

"Oh my God! How did that happen?"

"It looks like he was strangled. With my necktie."

"The red one with the little doobies? The one I gave you for your birthday?"

"That's the one."

"Nick, what were you thinking?"

"I wasn't thinking anything!" Nick's voice rose with agitation. "I didn't do it, Victoria. For god's sake, give me a little credit. I know that killing the client is not good for the business relationship."

"But your tie. I mean, really."

"Well, the local cops think it was me, too. They have me under arrest. I think I need an attorney."

"Well, yeah."

"I don't know any attorneys, Victoria."

"I do."

"I know. That's why I called you. You know tons of them through all that political crap you're involved in."

"It's not 'crap,' Nick. It's very important work. We have an agenda. There are important things that need to be accomplished, and Paul is the one with the vision and the credentials to do it."

"I know, I know. Sorry. I guess being arrested for murder has made me a little testy. But can you hook me up with an attorney who can handle this type of thing?"

"Hold on."

Nick listened to muffled talking as Victoria carried on a conversation with someone in the background. After a moment, she came back on. "We'll get someone for you, Nick."

"We? Who's 'we'?"

"Where are you being held?"

"Right now I am at Keene's house on Boca Cheeca Key. The police are still doing their stuff with the crime scene. I don't know where they're going to take me. But who is 'we'?"

"Paul and me. Don't worry, and don't say anything incriminating. Just wait until we get someone out there to represent you. And honey? I want you to know that I believe you didn't do it."

"Well, thanks for the vote of confidence, Victoria."

"You did the right thing calling me. I have to go and set things up. You just sit tight and don't say anything."

"Thanks, honey. Sorry that I . . ." Before he could finish his thought, she had disconnected him.

***

Buddy Grinnell was desperate for a beer. He was a little concerned about his craving and hoped it was less a reflection of his need for alcohol and more his mind's way of coping with the stress of his first murder investigation. He swirled the water around the bottom of the plastic bottle and stared at it with distaste before placing it on the desk without taking a drink.

He looked up at Nick Rohmer. "So you're not willing to make any statement at all?" he asked.

Nick was seated in the little guest chair of the office adjacent to Andrew Keene's, across the desk from Buddy Grinnell. The two large policemen who had been guarding him stood a few paces behind him, blank expressions on their faces.

Nick nodded. "I really don't think I should say anything without an attorney present."

"That's fine. We'll wait for your attorney. In the meantime, take off your clothes."

Nick's eyes went wide and the color instantly drained from his face. "L-L-Look" he said, "I don't think you want to try anything weird. I really do have a lawyer coming."

Buddy Grinnell tried to suppress a grin. "I need to bag your clothes for evidence."

"Oh, right," Nick said, as he started to breathe again. The color came back to his face with a rush, and in a matter of seconds, he went from deathly white to a mortified red. As he started to undo his shirt, one of the officers behind him burst out with a loud laugh.

"Hey, Chief! He thought you wanted to. . . you know? Ha!"

"Shut up, Neely. Go get a couple more evidence bags."

"Okay, Chief," the one named Neely said, and left the room still chuckling.

Buddy watched as Nick untied his shoes. "Just the outer clothing," he said. "Shirt, pants, shoes. You can keep the underwear."

"Thanks."

"And empty your pockets," he added. Then to the other officer he said, "See if you can round up something for Mr. Rohmer to wear. Check with the family, see if they can give you a blanket or some old clothes."

"Roger, Chief."

Nick emptied the contents of his pockets onto the desk, then kicked off his pants and folded them neatly. He handed them to Grinnell, who slipped them into a bag along with the suit coat, shirt, and shoes. "You know I didn't do this," Nick said.

Buddy shook his head. "I don't know anything, except that Andrew Keene was strangled with your tie, and you were discovered kneeling over the body. Maybe you can see why I'm a little suspicious."

"Granted, it doesn't look good when you put it like that, but what reason could I possibly have for killing Mr. Keene? I hardly even knew him."

"I don't know. Maybe he insulted you. Maybe he threatened you. Maybe it was a crime of passion."

"Passion?! This is crazy."

"Murder is crazy." Buddy thought that was a good answer. He wanted to sound like a seasoned murder investigator instead of someone who was on his first case. "You wouldn't believe some of the things I've seen."

"Yeah? Well, if you spend all your time investigating me, I think you're going to let the real murderer get away. You've got a whole house full of suspects."

"Right. Who just happened to wait until you were alone with the victim so they could strangle him with your tie. I think you're the right place to start this investigation. There's no reason to suspect anyone else."

"Hey Buddy." It was Neely returning with the evidence bags. Buddy gave him a cold look. "I mean, Chief."

"Yeah?"

"There's something out here that Ruiz thinks you should see."

"What is it?"

Neely cast a quick glance at Nick before answering. "There's a hole. In the screen."

"And?"

"Well, it's a pretty big hole."

"Your point?"

"Ruiz said it was 'man-sized.' Like maybe someone broke in." He looked at Nick again. "Like maybe someone else?"

"Shit!" said Buddy Grinnell.

"I knew it," said Nick. "There was someone else."

"You!" Buddy said, speaking to Neely. "Stay here and keep an eye on him. And bag the rest of this evidence."

He heaved himself to his feet and spoke to Nick. "Until I say so, you're still a suspect. Don't get too excited over a ripped screen."

"Ruiz said it was cut with a knife," Neely said.

"Cut, ripped, whatever. It was still you in there, and your tie."

"Or maybe someone else," Nick said. "Someone who broke in with murder on their mind. Someone with a reason to kill Andrew Keene."

"It's just a hole."

"But it's a big one," said Nick. "And it's right in the middle of your case."

NINE

If you want success, you have to dress like you're already successful.

From - *Judge This Book by Its Cover. Please.*

It only took Scorch a few minutes to figure out which key worked the front door to Richard Golden's townhouse. He slipped inside and dropped the swag he had lifted from the Keene house onto the floor. He locked the door behind him and turned on the lights.

He was in a marble-tiled entryway lighted by a crystal chandelier hanging overhead. In front of him was the living room and dining room, and to the right, through a small pass-through in the wall, he could see the kitchen.

To his left was a short, dark hallway with stairs barely visible in the reflected light of the chandelier. The far wall of the living room, opposite the front door he had just come through, was made entirely of glass, with a set of sliding glass doors to the outside. The dark night outside was invisible, with the glass reflecting the inside of the room like a wall-to-wall mirror.

Everything was decorated in white, chrome, and glass.

White furniture, white walls, and even white carpeting were complemented by glass tables and brightly colored modern art in heavy chrome frames. He stepped off the tile and his greasy running shoes left dark prints in the rug as he crossed the room. He turned on a lamp in the living room and cringed as the stark brightness of the room assailed him, reflecting from nearly every surface.

The room was hot. Scorch searched for the thermostat, and eventually found it in the hallway. He set the temperature down as low as it would go and smiled as he heard the air conditioner kick on. There were going to be no more hot, sleepless nights for him.

Scorch went up the stairs and found two bedrooms. The bedroom overlooking Biscayne Bay was huge. Just like in the living room below, the far wall was all glass with sliding glass doors opening onto a balcony. With the lights off, it was possible to see the bright Miami skyline floating in the distance. "Shit!" Scorch said, "Nice fucking view." He then turned on the lights and saw nothing but his own reflection coming from every direction.

The inside of the sliding glass doors were mirrored. The ceiling over the king-size bed was mirrored. The walls opposite the bed and behind the bed were mirrored, as were the closet doors that lined most of the remaining walls. It was like a fun-house Scorch had seen once when he was a kid. Everywhere you looked, there you were, visible from one angle or another. You couldn't get away from yourself.

Once he got over Richard Golden's apparent fascination with himself, Scorch noticed the pile of luggage in the corner. There were five big suitcases, packed and ready to go.

"Planning a trip?" Scorch asked. He opened a bag. He was disappointed to find only clothes. He opened another and found more of the same.

Scorch stepped to one of the closets and opened it. It was empty. He went on to the next, and it was nearly so. It held only bare hangers, with a couple of old shirts hanging off to one side. The next closet was filled with a set of drawers, and a quick search revealed that they had been emptied of most of their contents also.

"Looks like Dickie was planning more than a vacation," Scorch said, this time addressing one of his many reflections. "Just a little too late, weren't you, Dickie? Scorch got to you first. Scorch always gets there first." He laughed, and enjoyed the sight of his many reflections laughing too. It really was like a fun-house.

***

Buddy Grinnell was torn. Nick was found on the scene, kneeling over the body, and it was his tie fatally knotted around Andrew Keene's neck. On paper, Nick was an obvious suspect. Yet he had no known motive, and the cut screening seemed to indicate that there was an intruder of some sort on the property who remained unidentified. He didn't feel that he had a case to make against Nick yet and that it would be premature to arrest him.

Walter Hughes felt otherwise and said so. "Don't be so timid, Mr. Grinnell. Nick Rohmer could have had any number of reasons to kill Andrew Keene. Perhaps a fit of uncontrolled anger over the loss of the business. This will become clear over time. We have means and opportunity, with motive to be named later, so to speak. You would be foolish not to arrest him."

They were on the Keene house patio, near the pool, and it was now well after midnight. They talked out of earshot of the Keene family members still milling about, and away from the small room where Nick awaited their decision, under guard in his underwear.

Buddy had called for Walter Hughes because, among his other duties, he was on retainer to the Village of Boca Cheeca Key as legal counsel. Buddy was hoping for an informed opinion, but he was unconvinced.

"If we later find that some unknown intruder committed the murder, would this leave us open to a charge of false arrest?"

"Of course. That is always a possibility with any arrest. But in my opinion, we have good cause." Hughes glanced over at Nick, visible through the open doors. "He could be a very dangerous man. It is your duty to get him off the streets. If you let him go, who knows what else he might do, or where he might flee to, beyond your limited jurisdiction? This may be the only chance you have to arrest him."

Buddy nodded. "Okay, Mr. Hughes. Thanks for your help."

"So what are you going to do?"

"A little of both, I guess."

***

After a long shower, first cold, then hot, Scorch was lying naked on Richard Golden's bed. He admired his reflection in the ceiling as he tried flexing various muscle groups and different poses. He decided a mirrored ceiling was a good idea, but not much fun alone.

He picked up the telephone and dialed. On the fifth ring, the phone was answered by a voice heavy with sleep.

"Yeah?"

"Hey Donna."

"Scorch? What the hell? Do you know what time it is?"

"No. Is it late?"

"Goddamn it, Scorch. It's like one in the morning."

"Yeah? Well, how would you like to spend a little time with me in my new luxury condo on the ocean?" His reflection on the ceiling smiled at him. "The view is fucking unbelievable."

"You have a condo?"

"Shit, yeah. It might be a townhouse. It's got two stories. Don't that make it a townhouse?"

"How did you get a townhouse?"

"'Luxury' townhouse. It says so on the sign out front."

"You can't even afford to pay the electric bill. How'd you get a townhouse?"

"Don't worry about that. I said I'd take care of you, didn't I?"

"Yeah. Then you burned up the trailer."

"Do you got to keep bringing that up?"

"When's this condo scam gonna blow up in your face?"

"This ain't a scam, Donna. A friend of mine died and left me the keys. I can use it as long as I want, with or without you. You want to enjoy this with me, or do you want to hang out at your mother's? I don't give a shit either way."

There was a long pause before Donna answered. "Where is it?"

"You ever hear of Boca Cheeca Key?"

"No."

"It's about the most expensive real estate in Florida. You can't even drive to it. You got to take a boat. Is that cool?"

"You gonna come get me?"

"I'll meet you at the ferry." Scorch gave detailed directions to the mainland terminal. "And bring your black bikini. I want to see if you can give some of these rich old farts a heart attack."

She giggled. "What about you, baby? You think you can stand to have a bunch of old men drooling over me?"

"As long as they don't touch. You leave the touching to Scorch."

She giggled again and hung up.

***

Nick looked up expectantly as Buddy walked back into the room. "Well?" he asked.

Buddy ignored him and addressed his officers. "Neely.

Grab the evidence bags and put them in my cart." He tossed him his keys. "Ernie, I want you to seal up the room where Mr. Keene was killed. Then I want you to post yourself in the hall for the rest of the night, and make sure that no one goes in there. Do we have any more of that crime scene tape?"

Ernesto Ruiz looked sheepish. "We used it all up at that accident the other day."

"Well, figure something out," Buddy said. "Make sure it's clearly marked 'Do Not Enter,' et cetera. Okay?"

"Okay, Chief."

When they were alone, Buddy turned to Nick. "So what am I going to do with you?"

"Let me go home?" Nick asked, hopeful.

Buddy ignored him. "I could arrest you, but it seems a little premature. Then again, I don't want you walking away. You're still a suspect."

Nick watched Buddy wrestle with the problem.

Buddy walked to the open door and looked out. It was so peaceful. He could hear the murmur of conversation drifting over the pale blue water of the swimming pool, and he felt the fresh, cooling breeze coming in off the Atlantic. He took a deep breath and turned back to Nick.

"I may end up regretting this, but you're not under arrest. Yet."

"Thanks."

"But I don't want you leaving town."

"Fair enough," Nick said. "At this point, I just want to go home and go to bed."

Buddy Grinnell shook his head. "I don't think you understand. I don't want you leaving town. This town. Boca Cheeca Key. If you leave Boca Cheeca, I'll have a warrant out for your arrest before you even get to the mainland."

"I've got to stay here? I can't even go back to my apartment in Miami?"

"It's just until the FDLE people get here and finish

questioning you. They can decide to either arrest you or let you go. Probably no more than a day or two at most."

Nick looked down at himself, wearing only socks and boxers. "So this is it for me? You want me to hang around here for a couple of days in my underwear?"

"Didn't anyone bring you anything to wear?"

"Yeah, but I'm more comfortable in my underwear." Nick immediately regretted his sarcasm. "Sorry. No. No one has brought me anything."

"We'll get you some clothes. Hang on." He stepped back out onto the patio, and only Jeannie Keene was still there, waiting quietly at the pool-side table she had occupied all evening. He called her over.

"I have a favor to ask of you, Miss Keene." She just nodded and waited for him to continue. "Would it be possible to dig up some clothes for Mr. Rohmer to wear? We've confiscated his suit for forensic testing, and I'm afraid he's going to be with us for a few days. Maybe something of Nelson's would fit?"

She gave Nick a quick appraisal, making him feel naked in his underwear. "They're about the same size, but Nelson is particular about his stuff. I'll find something."

"Thanks. And make sure it's something you wouldn't mind losing. I don't know when you might get it back."

As Jeannie turned to leave, Buddy said, "Miss Keene?"

She turned back. "Yes?"

"Speaking of Nelson, do you know where he is? No one has seen him since dinner."

Jeannie shook her head. "I haven't seen him either, but if I do, do you want me to tell him to go see you?"

"If you would, please. I have a few questions. We're just trying to establish where everyone was when your father . . . It'll just be a few questions."

She nodded. "I'll tell him," she said.

***

In front of the Keene house, two police vehicles were neatly parked bumper to bumper. They were the standard island electric cart, but painted a warm green and white, with blue bubble lights on top. A third had been parked there earlier, but one of the officers had already left with Dr. Folger and Andrew Keene's body, headed for the walk-in cooler at one of the island's restaurants.

Neely was loaded down with evidence bags. He dumped them in the front seat of the Chief's cart and then started stowing them one at a time in the locking compartment under the back seat. When he was done, he carefully locked up, then left the keys on the front seat, where the Chief couldn't miss them. He then headed back up to the house to see what else he was needed for.

***

Jeannie presented Buddy Grinnell with her find, who in turn passed it to Nick. Nick held up the T-shirt, which was a lurid orange and had a bizarre graphic of a fish on the front. The back read "Phish World Tour" and had a burn hole in it. Next he picked up the shorts. They were black plaid and looked enormous. "Thanks," was all he said.

"Sorry about the pants," Jeannie said. "It was all I could come up with right away. I can probably do a little better tomorrow."

"No. Don't bother," Nick said. "This is great." He stood and stepped into the shorts, and was able to pull them on without even unbuttoning them. They hung off his hips, and the cuffs were well below his knees. He had to hold them up with one hand to keep them from slipping down around his ankles. "A belt might help," was all he said.

Jeannie tried to stifle a laugh. "I guess you and Skip aren't the same size," she said and laughed again, this time without benefit of stifling.

Nick turned around so she could get a 360° view. "I

think this is a good look for me. It's a nice change from wool suits. Now all I need is a skateboard."

Jeannie laughed again. "Sorry, Rohmer. I'll get you something better in the morning. You want to try the shirt?"

"Sure, if you think you can stand it." He pulled the shirt on and it was as oversized as the shorts. "It makes a nice counterpoint to the pants, don't you think?"

"Definitely. You could be setting the trend for accountants everywhere."

"If the fashion show is over," Buddy Grinnell said, "are you ready to go, Mr. Rohmer?"

"Go? Me? Go where?"

"With me."

"I thought you weren't arresting me?"

"I'm not. I'm taking you to my apartment. You've got to stay somewhere while you're here, and this town doesn't have a hotel. You can stay at my place, if you don't mind sleeping on the floor."

"You're not arresting me, you're just going to keep me under your eye twenty-four hours a day."

"It's just a friendly offer. You've got nowhere else to stay, unless you want to bunk up with one of my officers."

"He can stay here," said Jeannie. "God knows we have enough rooms."

Buddy looked from Nick to Jeannie. "I don't think that would be a good idea, Miss Keene. He's under suspicion of murdering your father. I don't think your family would be pleased to be sleeping under the same roof as a suspected murderer."

"Oh, please." She waved a hand dismissively. "Get real. Of all the people in this house, he's probably the only one who didn't have a reason to kill my father."

"The rest of your family may not feel that way."

"Fine. How about if we put him on *Andy's Dream*? No offense to you, Chief, but I'm sure that it'll beat the hell out of sleeping on your floor."

"What's 'Andy's Dream'?" Nick asked.

"It's my father's sailboat. It's fifty-eight feet long, has air conditioning, and it's never used. Plus, it's not 'under the same roof' as my family. That work for you, Chief?"

"It's your choice, Nick."

"Thanks for the offer, Chief, but if it's all the same to you, I'd rather we spend as little time together as possible. The boat sounds pretty nice."

"Fine," Buddy said. "But if I may, Miss Keene, I would like to suggest that you let the other members of the household know where Nick is so no one is surprised."

"Sure. I'll send out formal announcements."

"Sarcasm aside, I think you should let them know."

"Jesus Christ, Chief, you're starting to sound like my mother." Jeannie read the expression on Grinnell's face. "Fine. I'll do it. I'll make sure everyone knows about our dangerous boat guest."

"Thanks," Buddy said. "I'll just make sure everything here is secure before turning in myself. I'll see both of you tomorrow."

TEN

The boardroom, like the bedroom, is no place for false modesty.

From – *The Tao of Success*

Jeannie led Nick back to the small private marina that housed the Keenes' various watercraft. She stepped up to the large white sailboat that Nick had seen earlier when he arrived.

"This is *Andy's Dream*," she said. "It's poorly named, since the only thing that Andy ever dreamed about was money. He never used it himself – too slow, he said – but my mom loved it. She used to take us out on it all the time, before . . . Anyway, here it is."

She stepped on board and extended a hand to help Nick. "She's been closed up for a while, so let's get her open and breathing." Jeannie pulled a key from her pocket and opened the main hatch. A puff of warm air flowed over them, smelling slightly of diesel, fiberglass, and wood. "It'll be fine once we air it out a bit."

She went down a short ladder into the main cabin. Nick followed her and watched as she expertly opened various hatches and flipped some switches on a big electrical panel. As the lights came on, Nick got his first look at the interior.

"Wow," was all he said. The walls and floor were mostly mahogany, like Andrew's office, but with a white ceiling that helped to reflect the light and kept the cabin from feeling like a cave. To his right was a small table and bench surrounded by electronic equipment. Jeannie saw him looking at it.

"That's the nav station," she said, "and this is the galley." She pointed to a U-shaped counter that wrapped from the hull around to the middle of the cabin and that contained a cook-top and sink. "There's a fridge under the counter. I just turned it on, so it won't be cold for a while, but there are some drinks in it if you get thirsty."

She pointed to the front of the boat. "That's the salon, and forward of that, there are two cabins and a head."

"A head?" Nick asked.

"Yeah. That's boat talk for 'bathroom.'" She turned around and brushed past Nick. "And back here is the Captain's stateroom."

She led Nick down a narrow passageway toward the back of the boat. "You can sleep here," she said, as she opened a couple more hatches to let the night breeze in.

The Captain's stateroom consisted of an oversized bed on a raised platform. Two brass reading lights were mounted on the wall and Jeannie switched them on. On either side, the cabin walls were lined with mahogany planking, with a different-colored, lighter wood on the floor. There were drawers built in on either side of the bed, where there might normally be a nightstand in a regular bedroom. One of them had an electric clock on it, blinking "12:00". Opposite the bed, mounted high on the wall was a small flat screen TV. Under that was a stool in a little mirrored alcove with a dressing table.

Jeannie opened a door to her right and turned on another light. "Head," she said, "and over here is the closet." She opened another door, this one louvered, to reveal an empty closet. "I don't suppose you'll have much need for it, but here it is."

Nick moved to the bed and sat on it, lightly bouncing. "I don't know," he said. "Are you sure this is nicer than the Chief's apartment? It doesn't even have cable TV."

She picked up a remote control from the dressing table and tossed it to Nick. "Satellite. One hundred and twenty-two channels."

"Well," Nick said, "I guess it will do for tonight." He laid back and reached as far as he could across the vast mattress. "You know, I think this bed is actually bigger than my apartment."

Jeannie came over to the bed and stood in front of Nick, looking at him. He sat up, a little nervous. "I was just kidding about the boat," he said. "It's great."

He couldn't read the look in her eyes, and when she finally spoke, it was almost a whisper. "Did you see what happened to my dad? Did you hear anything?"

"No."

"You were right there, in the hallway. You didn't hear anything?"

Nick shook his head.

"My brother and his shrew wife are certain it was you." she said.

"I barely knew your father. I wanted his business. I just wanted to talk business, you know?"

"Yeah, I know." She said. "I know. It would be nice if you were the killer, but . . ."

"You think it would be nice if I had killed your father?"

"No, no." Jeannie sat on the bed next to Nick. "I just mean, if you'd done it, we wouldn't all be left wondering. You know. Wondering who. Wondering if maybe . . ."

"Wondering if maybe it was someone in your family?"

Jeannie sat quietly for a moment, staring at the wall. "It's still stuffy in here," she said. "Take a walk with me, while we wait for the boat to air out." She stood up.

Nick glanced at the clock on the bedside table. "Is that clock right? Is it really blinky midnight?"

Jeannie laughed. "Why? Is it past your bedtime?" She took Nick's hand and tried to pull him off the bed. "Come on. We'll walk on the beach. It's cool, and I need to talk." Nick allowed himself to be dragged to his feet. "Besides, you owe me."

"I owe you?"

"Who got you those stylish clothes?"

Nick glanced down at the gigantic pants hanging off his hips. "I'm supposed to owe you for these?"

"If it weren't for me you'd still be walking around in your underwear."

"But I'd have my dignity."

"In those boxers? Don't kid yourself."

Still leading Nick by the hand, Jeannie steered him back on deck. She stepped lightly to the dock, again helping Nick maintain his footing, and they walked north toward the tip of the little island, and around to the ocean side. The breeze coming off the Atlantic was delightful, cooler by ten degrees than the stale air in the sailboat. A half-moon was rising, creating a river of light that ran to the horizon. They walked silently along the water's edge and Nick was glad that he'd come.

"This is nice," Nick said. He glanced up at the stars, slightly dimmed by the light of the rising moon. "I can't remember the last time I did something like this."

"My dad liked it, too. It's the reason he wouldn't air condition the house. He said everyone moves here for the climate, and then seals themselves up twenty-four hours a day in their refrigerated cocoons. If you're going to do that, he'd say, you may as well stay in Minneapolis and hang pretty pictures on the wall."

Nick thought about what it would be like to take a walk at two in the morning in his neighborhood. Somehow he didn't think it would have the same appeal.

The house and marina were now out of sight, blocked

by a thick stand of sea-grape trees. Jeannie sat on the sand, just above the high water mark. Nick sat next to her and looked across the water toward Key Biscayne.

He watched the Cape Florida lighthouse as it pointed a finger of light into the night. Slowly it turned, sweeping over the dark water until it flashed directly at them, and then moved on across the bay.

"It's pretty," he said. "Thanks for bringing me out here."

She turned to face him, but he couldn't read her expression. The moonlight was too weak. Only her eyes were clearly visible, the whites seeming to glow in her tan face.

"You need to help me," she said.

Nick looked at the distant lighthouse again. He should have known that she wanted something. She was too pretty, and the moonlit beach was too pleasant to come without a price. Well, whatever the price was, he wasn't going to pay it. He thought of several possible responses before settling on, "No. I don't."

She ignored him. "You seem like a smart guy."

He shook his head. "Well, I'm not."

"You can help me figure out what happened tonight. I need to understand all the money talk."

"You don't even know me." Nick paused to consider his next words. "I don't know anything about you, or your father, or the rest of your family that I didn't get out of an accounting file. This is a matter for the police."

She scoffed. "Buddy?"

"Or the FDLE. They're coming tomorrow."

She laid a hand on his arm, and he turned to look again into the bright whites of her eyes. "I hated my father," she said. "I probably shouldn't tell you this after what happened tonight, but I've hated him ever since I was old enough to realize he was a bully. He used his physical size to bully those smaller than him. And he used his money to control, buy, or destroy anyone he came in contact with."

She turned her gaze to the water. "Everything was a contest with him. Every interaction was a battle with a winner and a loser, and he was always the winner."

"So why did you stay here?"

"I tried to leave," she said, "but it was just another contest of wills, and I lost."

"I'm sorry you didn't have a happy childhood, or an ideal father, but what does any of that have to do with me?"

She continued as though he hadn't spoken. "I made it a point to be detached from what was important to my father. If he cared for it, I wanted nothing to do with it. If he loved it, I hated it. He loved his goddamned company and his goddamned money more than his family."

She turned back to Nick. "That's where I need your help."

Her hand still rested on his arm, and her touch was soft and warm. Nick found it distracting but tried hard to put it out of his mind. "I missed the transition somewhere, from lousy childhood to needing my help."

"My father was extremely wealthy."

Nick nodded. "Yeah?"

"Not just rich, but obscenely rich. He was also mean and nasty and selfish. But above all, it was his wealth that made him extraordinary."

"Okay. So he was rich, and nobody liked him."

"You heard him at dinner. He was sure that someone was stealing from him. If they were about to be discovered, wouldn't that be a good motive for murder?"

"I suppose," Nick said. "But it may be that he finally pushed someone too far, and they pushed back. Fatally."

"I don't think so. I think he was killed over his money, and you understand money. You were his accountant."

"I worked for his accounting company. I never even met the man before today."

Jeannie took Nick's hand and pressed it with both of hers. "I'll fill you in on who's who and how they're related to each other and to my father, and you just need to make sense of the money part." She squeezed his hand as she got more worked up. "If we can figure out who was stealing from him, we'll know who had a reason to prevent his investigation."

"Just because someone might have been stealing from him doesn't mean they killed your father." Nick pulled his hand free. "Look, I'd love to help you, but I'm not a detective. I'm just an accountant. I add up numbers all day. You need to hire someone who knows what they're doing."

"But," she began, then stopped. She was silent for a moment, and Nick wondered if he had been too abrupt. He heard her take a deep breath and let it out slowly into the night. "Yeah," she finally said. "You're right." She stood up and brushed the sand from the back of her legs. "I'm being stupid. Sorry. There's no reason you should be any more involved than you are."

Nick stood beside her. "I'm sorry, Jeannie. But really, I don't see how I could help you."

"Yeah. You're right," she said. "It must be all the stress. Forget I even said anything."

"Look, if you have any specific questions about the way the company was structured, or anything like that, I'll be happy to try to answer them if I can."

"Okay, Rohmer. I might take you up on that." She started to walk back the way they had come. "Come on. We should head back."

Nick followed without another word. After a few moments, the silence grew awkward, and Nick searched for something nice, but non-committal, to say.

"Thanks again for the walk. It's was nice to get away from the heat."

"Enjoy it while you can, because it'll still be hot when we get back." She stopped in mid-stride, so suddenly that Nick bumped into her. "I've got an idea that'll keep you cool even after you get back."

"What? Is there an all-night Dairy Queen around here?"

"Let's take a swim."

Before Nick could respond, Jeannie had stepped out of her shorts and taken off her shirt. She then proceeded to remove the bikini she wore underneath, which he found both fascinating and odd. Wasn't it intended for swimming?

"Come on," she yelled, running into the light surf. "The water's fine."

Nick stood on the beach like an idiot, in his goofy giant shorts. He watched as Jeannie splashed into the moonlit water. She was so tan that she was hard to see against the dark ocean and sky. Only her pale, white backside was clearly visible, like a white-tailed deer Nick had once seen running into the woods. Nick watched in fascination as it bobbed into the sea, then disappeared as the water rose above her waist.

"You're going to get lonely up there all by yourself," she called.

Nick still hesitated. Statistically, night swimming on an unguarded beach was dangerous. He also thought about Victoria, but rather than raising feelings of guilt, he felt regret for their lack of spontaneity. They were young. They were relatively carefree. Why didn't they ever do anything like this?

"Are you coming in, or are you just going to stand there like an accountant?"

"Be right there," he yelled back and peeled off his shirt.

He automatically folded it neatly and laid it in the sand, then he allowed his giant shorts to slide to the ground. He hesitated when he got to his boxers, but only briefly. After nervously looking both up and down the beach, he kicked them off and ran into the water after Jeannie. Nick felt a pang of guilt, like when he was a little kid and knew he was doing something he shouldn't, but he was enjoying himself anyway.

"Isn't this great?" Jeannie asked when he reached her.

"It's no D.Q., but it's okay." The surf was warm near shore, but it got cooler as they swam out toward deeper water. "Do you do this often?"

"No," she said. "It's no fun by myself." They were treading water now, and she turned toward the moon, her wet face glistening in the pale light. "I love to watch the moonrise, when you can see the river of light stretching to the horizon. When I was little, I thought that if you followed it all the way to the end, it would take you to paradise. It's silly what kids think sometimes, isn't it?"

"I thought paradise was in South America, but it turned out to be Paraguay."

She laughed and splashed water at him. "And I thought you were smart."

She rolled onto her back and floated quietly under the stars for a moment while Nick watched the waves caress the curves of her breasts and hips. "If you want to get really cool," she said, "do this."

In a sudden splash, she was gone, diving below the surface. Nick waited. And waited. Seconds stretched into a minute, and still she didn't reappear. He became anxious, looking around in the dark to see if she had surfaced somewhere distant from him. He called her name into the quiet night, but there was not even an echo to answer him. He was nearing full-blown panic, imagining his next encounter with Chief Grinnell to explain another mysterious Keene death. Before he got to the part where he imagined his confession, Jeannie burst to the surface at his side in an explosion of spray and wet hair and gasping breath.

"It's fantastic," she said, between pants. "The water is so much cooler down deep. You should try it."

Nick's heart was pounding a hundred miles an hour from the adrenaline rush of his fear, and he was feeling almost as out of breath as Jeannie sounded. "Damn! You were down there forever. Are you okay?"

"Fantastic," she said. "My mom used to say I could hold my breath for a week." She dipped her head back into the water so that it swept her hair back from her face. She looked toward the shore. The roof of the Keene house was visible from where they were, and the glow of the landscape lights twinkled like stars through the foliage. "We should head back," she said. "You must be exhausted."

"Well, it has been a long and strange day. I'm kind of looking forward to climbing into bed."

"Me too," she said, and even though Nick knew she meant her own bed, it sent a thrill through him, until he thought of Victoria again.

She swam strongly to shore, with Nick following. As they reached shallow water, Nick tried not to stare at Jeannie, but couldn't help admiring how she looked, wet and winded in the moonlight.

"Hmm, that's odd," she said.

"What?" Nick tried to sound casual despite being acutely aware of his nakedness.

"This is where we left our clothes, right?"

Nick looked past Jeannie at the empty sand. Their footprints were just visible in the moonlight, and it was clearly the spot where they had dropped their things, but the beach was now conspicuously clothes-free.

Nick immediately felt like that little kid again, only this time, he remembered what it was like getting caught doing what he wasn't supposed to. "Shit," was all he said.

As they stood silently looking at the empty beach, Nick heard something like a click-whir sound from somewhere in the bushes. It was a familiar sound, but before he could place it, Jeannie started yelling.

"Nelson! You bring those clothes back right now!"

This did not have the desired effect, and even Nick could recognize the sound of someone running through the underbrush, away from them.

"Damn it, Nelson. You come back here!"

"Is there something I should know?" Nick asked. He thought he sounded very calm and reasonable, under the circumstances.

"I think Nelson stole our clothes," she said. "He does stuff like that. He likes to take things."

"And he took our picture?"

"Yeah. He does that, too. He has this really amazing camera. He can get shots in almost no light at all."

"Great." Nick had thoughts of Victoria receiving a set of prints in the mail.

"But don't worry," Jeannie said. "He almost never does anything with them. It's just something to keep him out of trouble. It usually works better than this."

"So what now?"

"Don't worry. You wait here, and I'll go back to the house and get us both something to wear."

As she turned to leave, Nick had a sudden pang of chivalry. "Do you want me to go?" he asked. "You could wait while I find something."

Jeannie laughed at him. "Sure. Where are you going to find clothes? I can just see you sneaking around the house, naked, trying to score a pair of pants." She laid a hand on his shoulder. "Don't worry, Nick. I'll go. They're my family, and we aren't all that modest, in case you hadn't noticed. Just wait here, and I'll be back in a flash, so to speak."

She turned and ran back toward the house, leaving Nick alone and naked on the beach.

***

Chief Grinnell and Officer Neely stepped out onto the Keene's front drive and hesitated.

"Where's my cart?" Buddy asked.

Neely looked around, and blinked hard. Where there had previously been two police carts, there was now only one. "It was here just a bit ago."

"When you put the evidence bags in it?"

Neely nodded emphatically. "Right. Like you said. And I locked them up."

"And the keys?"

"They're in the cart."

"Which is where?"

Neely answered quietly. "I don't know."

Buddy took a deep breath and counted to ten. After a moment, he calmly said, "When we get back to the security office, you're going to comb every square inch of this island until I have that cart back. With the evidence. Do you understand?"

"Yes, sir."

"Now give me your keys."

"They're in the cart."

Buddy's shoulders tensed, and he could feel the start of a serious headache right at the base of his neck. He was too tired to give a lecture on protecting police property, so he just slumped into the driver's seat of the remaining cart and turned the key. As Neely started to climb in on the passenger side, Buddy stopped him.

"I'll take this one," he said. "You can drive back in mine."

"But yours ain't here, Chief."

"I know," Buddy said, and drove off.

ELEVEN

Sometimes when opportunity knocks, it's best to turn out the lights and pretend that no one is home.

From - *Success on Forty Hours a Week*

When the house had first been conceived by Andrew Keene, his plan was to have as natural a Florida setting as possible - no air conditioning and no artificial separation from the environment. The house was situated to maximize the relatively cool breezes that usually blow in off the Atlantic Ocean, with the windows and large French doors allowing the air to flow into and through the house. The theory was that this, along with the judicious use of ceiling fans, would render the house livable without living in a "climate-controlled cocoon" as Andrew called it.

The plan was mostly successful. For about seven months of the year, the breezes and the temperatures were well within the range of most people's comfort zone. The months of June through October, however, were pretty unbearable. But the temperature wasn't the biggest problem. The biggest problem was the insects.

At the time the house was built, the small islands to the

south, the future sites of Phases I, II and III, were swampy, bug-infested marsh. No amount of breezes or ceiling fans could cope with the invasion of insects that descended on the house every night at sunset.

Faced with a family that refused to live under such conditions, Andrew made the concession of screening the windows on the west side of the house, toward the bay. But rather than screen every door and window on the Atlantic side, he built a gigantic enclosure that sealed the pool, the patio, and both floors of living space behind a thin wall of bug-proof mesh.

It was through a door in this screen enclosure that Jeannie tried to pass unnoticed onto the pool deck and from there to her room. She was not successful.

"You're certainly dressed for the weather."

Jeannie jumped at the sound of Charlotte's voice. She hadn't seen her where she lay sprawled on one of the lounge chairs. "You scared me," she said. "What are you doing out here?"

"I came out here for a dip in the pool and to cool off." She regarded Jeannie's nakedness, then looked down at her own outfit. She was wearing her bikini bottoms and a large, complicated harness-like brassiere that supported her enormous breasts. "I feel a little overdressed."

"I was taking a swim on the beach, and someone took my clothes. I think it was Nelson."

"You shouldn't swim alone at night like that. It's dangerous." When Jeannie said nothing, Charlotte continued, "Or maybe you weren't alone?"

"I've got to go get some clothes," Jeannie said, and she started to move away.

"Oh my God," Charlotte said, "please tell me you weren't with that accountant."

Jeannie blushed under her tan. "We were opening the sailboat, and it was hot, so we took a walk on the beach, and . . . Why shouldn't I be with Nick? He seems nice. And you flirted with him all through dinner."

"I flirted with him to piss off Andrew. What's your angle?"

"I don't have an 'angle.' I just needed someone to talk to."

"Well, don't get too attached. He'll be gone tomorrow unless they pin Andrew's murder on him. In which case, he'll also be gone."

"You don't think he did it, do you?" Jeannie asked.

"No. My money's on Nelson."

"Nelson? Why Nelson?"

Charlotte held up a hand and started counting off on her fingers. "One, he's crazy enough. Two, he's strong enough. Three, he had every reason to hate Andrew, as much or more than the rest of us. And four, no one has seen him since the murder. That looks bad."

"He's always disappearing somewhere," Jeannie said.

"Yeah, but when you disappear after a murder, it doesn't look too good. If you want to help your brother, you should try to find him before Buddy and his rent-a-cops do."

"Thanks," Jeannie said, "but I'm sure that Nelson can take care of himself." She headed off to her room for some clothes, already thinking of places she might be able to find her brother.

***

Nick approached the dock cautiously. The only illumination other than the moon was from the low-voltage landscape lighting, but to Nick, it felt like mid-day. He stood behind a tree for a moment, but neither saw nor heard any movement at all. It had to be past 3:00 am, and he fervently hoped that no one was out prowling the grounds at this hour.

His wait for Jeannie on the beach had been long and lonely and frustrating. The night breeze had quickly chilled his wet body. Within a few minutes of her departure, Nick had gone back into the water, crouching in the shallows. He told himself that it was to stay warm. In reality, though, he just wasn't comfortable standing naked on the beach.

After being touched by "things" in the water, he moved back onto dry land and found a modest perch behind a palm tree. He waited for Jeannie as long as he could, but the mosquitoes, and a growing certainty that she was not going to return, finally drove him back to *Andy's Dream* in his altogether.

He stepped lightly onto the deck of the sailboat and found that the hatches had all been closed. He could also feel a slight vibration in the deck, and heard a muffled hum that sounded to him like an air conditioner.

He slid open the hatch and stepped into the artificially cooled air of the salon. Jeannie must have come back and turned on the air for him, but why had she left him stranded on the beach? Was it some kind of cruel trick? Was she angry that he refused to help her?

Nick was so tired, he didn't even try to figure it out. He was just grateful to be inside and comfortable.

The lights were off, so he felt his way back to the main stateroom, and fumbled his way to the door of the head. It didn't seem to be air conditioned, so he closed the door behind him. He found a light switch and took a few moments to figure out the plumbing. He then took a cold shower, rinsing the salt and sand out of his hair and off his body.

He found a towel and stepped into the deliciously cool air of the captain's stateroom to dry himself. He was ready to collapse.

He threw his towel over the stool by the dressing table and pulled back the bedspread. He slipped gratefully between the sheets, stretching out in the huge bed. And he immediately made contact with another body.

Nick jumped. In a single motion he was out from under the covers, on his feet, and scrambling for the towel in the dark.

Whoever it was had been disturbed enough by Nick's athletics to roll over. A feminine voice, heavy with sleep, asked, "Who is it?"

"It's Nick." Nick's optimistic side chimed in. "Jeannie, is that you?"

There was a rustle of movement from the bed, and then the light was on, revealing a small, rainbow-haired woman with a surprising number of facial piercings. "No," she said, "I'm her mother. Who are you?"

"I'm Nick," he said. "I'm . . . I mean, Jeannie said I could stay here . . ." He glanced down to be certain that he was sufficiently covered by the wet towel he had snatched off the stool. "I'm so sorry to have disturbed you," he said. "There must be some confusion . . . "

She smiled at him, and her eyes ran up and down his length, making him extremely self-conscious. "So, you and Jeannie?" She raised her eyebrow questioningly. "You're a nice change from the 300-pound bikers she usually drags home."

"Oh, we're not together," Nick said. "I only met her tonight. Or yesterday, really."

"Oh? And you thought she would be in your bed? You think highly of yourself."

"She's the only person here that I really know, and that knows where I'm staying, so, I thought . . . maybe?"

"Well, better luck next time. I'm Betty," she said and held out a tiny hand. "Betty Keene – wife number two."

Nick took her extended hand and shook it. "Nick Rohmer," he said. "So sorry for your loss."

"You mean Andrew? That's no big loss. The bastard has had it coming for years. He's the one that got me locked up in a mental hospital."

"I see," was all Nick could think to say.

"Don't worry," she said. "I'm not dangerous, usually." She got out of bed and stood to her full five feet of height. She was wearing a T-shirt that fell below her knees. "It's late," she said. "You must be tired, and I'm guessing by the way you're clutching that towel to your crotch that you don't want to share the bed. I'll take one of the forward cabins."

"You don't have to do that," Nick said. "I can take one of the other cabins."

She waved a hand dismissively. "You take the big bed. I don't need a lot of space." As she passed him, she said, "We'll talk in the morning."

"Thanks," Nick said, and within ten seconds, he was in the bed and asleep.

***

Dressed again in shorts and a tank top, Jeannie first checked all the spare bedrooms in the house, and there were a lot of them. She even looked in her dad's room, though she thought that would be out of bounds even for Nelson.

Next she went through the ground floor rooms and offices. All of them were unlocked, as always, except for Walter Hughes'. She went down the hall in front of her father's office, and nodded to the cop on guard, surprised that he was still awake.

She left the house and walked down to the dock, and when she saw *Andy's Dream*, she suddenly remembered that she had abandoned Nick on the beach. Jeannie swore and ran down to the beach where she had left him, slightly relieved that he wasn't still there waiting for her.

She followed the beach all the way past the house to the little bridge that connected them to the next island, then cut back to the docks again to look in the boats for signs of Nelson. Still nothing. She bypassed the sailboat, not wanting to confront Nick after what she had done to him.

She headed down Keene Boulevard toward the public marina. There were a lot of boats there, and she couldn't search them all, but she didn't think Nelson would go to ground in someone else's boat, anyway. The ferry, however, was another matter.

When the last ferry of the night pulled in, the crew cleaned her up and left everything ready for the next morning. There were no guards, and the big boat was only secured by a plastic chain draped across the gangway.

Jeannie jumped the chain and searched first through the passenger lounge, then she checked all the deck seating, and there was still no sign of her brother. She went to the bow and stood looking over the sleeping maze of condos and townhouses. Only a few lights were on, and those were probably controlled by timers. This time of year, three-fourths of the population of Boca Cheeca was somewhere up north, at their summer homes.

She scanned the quiet streets for inspiration. She was out of ideas. Frustrated, Jeannie sat down in one of the plastic seats on deck to assess her next move. But before she could, exhaustion caught up with her, and she fell asleep.

TWELVE

Without health, there ain't no wealth.

From – *Hip-Hop Up the Corporate Ladder*

The Chicago sun would not rise for another hour, but Gordon McCall was already completing his five-mile run. The doorman of his apartment building watched the security monitor for his return, and could see him heading up Lakeshore Drive. With near-perfect timing honed over a year and a half of mind-numbing routine, he reached the lobby doors just as McCall puffed up to the building. Holding the door wide, he smiled broadly.

"Good morning, Mr. McCall."

As usual, before responding, Gordon McCall worked up a wad of thick, mucilaginous saliva and spit it into the concrete planter next to the door. "Good morning, Jimmy. You missed a good run this morning. You should come with me some day."

Jimmy smiled, as he did every morning, though it was not easy for him. For one thing, his name was Ed, and it clearly said so on his gold-colored, plastic nametag. There had been at least three doormen since one was named Jim.

The other thing that was beginning to wear on him after eighteen months of the same daily exchange was the invitation to go running. Ed felt it was a not-so-subtle dig at his build, which could kindly be called portly. He was built more like a shot-putter than a runner, though he lacked the muscle tone to do either.

"I'd love to, Mr. McCall, but who'd let us in when we got back?" he answered, as usual.

McCall laughed and punched him lightly on his upper arm. "One of these days, Jimmy. Just you and me and the sunrise over the lake."

This concluded their morning ritual, so Ed was surprised when McCall didn't immediately go inside but continued to talk to him.

"I'm going to need a cab to the airport, Jimmy, at 0700. Can you arrange that for me?"

"Going out of town, Mr. McCall?"

"Florida."

"Vacation?"

"Business. Too hot there for a vacation this time of year, and too crowded when the weather's nice. I should only be gone a few days."

"Well, have a safe trip. I hear there's a lot of crime down there."

"It's Florida, Jimmy, not the third world. When I get back, you and me and a quick run along the lake, right?"

"Just like always, sir." And this time, Ed gave a genuine smile. Even just a few days without this inane banter would be like a vacation for him.

***

Nick was running along the beach in his best suit, and the sun was beating down on him. He was hot, sweating under the suffocating layer of wool, but he kept running. He was chasing something, but he wasn't gaining any ground. His wool suit was too heavy, and his leather-soled shoes slipped in the wet sand, but he kept running.

He was chasing Jeannie, who ran naked ahead of him. Her ponytail bounced as she flew over the sand, lightly brushing her back, and the white soles of her feet flashed at Nick with every step she took. She turned and smiled, then waved a hand at him, beckoning him on. She laughed as she ran effortlessly along the water's edge, barely seeming to touch the ground as the distance between them grew.

Nick looked over his shoulder and saw Victoria running after him. She was dressed in a long red bathrobe, her hair wrapped in a towel. She was yelling to or at him, but he couldn't understand what she was saying. He smiled at her, but she didn't smile back. She just ran harder, a grim look on her face.

He looked ahead again, and saw Jeannie, still running and laughing, now farther from him than ever, lightly flying over the sand. Nick watched her as she faded in the distance. Behind him, Victoria was closer, and Nick realized he wasn't sure why he was running. Was he chasing Jeannie or running away from Victoria? He finally stopped. Victoria caught up to him and then ran past him, saying, "You'll never get ahead if you stop running."

Nick called after her. "Ahead of what?"

She was in the distance now and Nick couldn't hear her response.

He awoke with a gasp.

"Would you like some coffee?" Betty Keene stood over him wearing faded cut-offs and a green knit halter top, a steaming cup of coffee in her hand. Nick couldn't help but notice that her navel was pierced. She sat on the edge of the bed. "You seemed to be having a bad dream."

"Was I?" Nick asked. He was wrapped tightly in acres of sheets and drenched with sweat. He tried to remember his dream, but already it was fading like steam on a bathroom mirror.

"Do you have anything to wear, other than that towel?"

"No. Not really."

She stood and handed Nick the cup. "You sip this, and I'll see if I can find you something."

"Thanks," Nick said, as she walked back toward the main salon.

Nick set the cup on the bedside table and untangled himself from the sheets. He fished on the floor for the still-damp towel he had used the previous night. He jumped quickly into the shower again and rinsed away the remains of his dream.

With the towel knotted firmly around his waist, he stepped back into the cabin and found some clothes laid out for him on the bed. He wasn't going to be winning any fashion awards again today. He got dressed, then went to join Betty Keene in the salon.

"Well, don't you look stunning," she said as she took in the effect of her sartorial efforts.

"I know beggars can't be choosers, but is this the best you could come up with?" Nick looked down at the long length of leg showing below his very tiny striped shorts.

"The eighties were an awesome decade," she said. "They set the bar for fashion. And with your legs, I think you pull it off. But don't mess up that tank top, I think Jeannie will want that back."

"I feel like Richard Simmons," he said.

"Here are some flip-flops." She tossed a pair of turquoise colored thongs on the floor at Nick's feet. "Those are Jeannie's, too, but I'm sure she won't mind you using them."

Nick tried to slip his foot into one of them. It was about three sizes too small. "Thanks anyway, but for now I think I'll just go barefoot."

"Ok, but you'll need to find something if you're going to be walking around outside in the mid-day sun."

Nick sat down on the settee, across from Betty. "Thanks for the coffee and the clothes." He took a sip. He needed the caffeine after only about three hours of sleep.

"I don't want to sound ungrateful," he went on, "but is there any food on this boat? I didn't get much to eat last night."

"You must have been at one of Andrew's 'survival of the fittest' dinners. Sorry to say, other than some canned goods, there's really not much on board to eat. I'm sure they'll have some breakfast laid out in the house." She paused a moment. "There's also a snack bar at the ferry terminal and a small coffee and pastry shop that opens for the early commuters. You could try that."

"They took all my belongings into evidence. I haven't got a dime on me."

"Me neither. I guess we're both living off the land."

"Wow," Nick said. "Did we just bond?"

"I think so," she said.

"Great. Since we're friends now, maybe you won't mind me asking why you're living off the land and staying - secretly, I assume? - on this sailboat?"

"That covers a lot of ground and a lot of history. Do you have that kind of time?"

"I think so," Nick said.

"Ok, but first . . ." Betty stepped to the counter and hefted the coffee pot. She refilled both their cups, then sat down and took a big sip. "Where to begin?" she said.

"How about at the funeral yesterday where you were throwing eggs at Mr. Keene?"

"You were there, huh?"

"I knew it!" Nick said. "That was Nelson with you, right?"

"Yeah, but that's more of an ending than a beginning. Let's begin with Andrew's first marriage."

"Fair enough," said Nick. "It's your story."

"Andrew married his childhood sweetheart, right out of high school. Her name was Shirley. She was a sweet girl, not overly bright. Big boned, as we used to say. She's Skip's mother. She and Andrew had Skip about a year after they married, when he was just trying to get on his feet.

When Skip was about five, Andrew's eyes started to wander. He and Shirley split, and she went home to Omaha, gained about 150 pounds, and died young of a massive heart attack. Her mom said she died of a broken heart."

"Did Skip stay with Andrew when they divorced?" Nick asked.

"No. He went home with his mom, but when she died, he moved back in with Andrew. By that time Andrew and I had married, I had already had Nelson, and Jeannie was on the way." She took another long sip of coffee. "We were happy, after a fashion. Andrew was always working, making more and more money, but we were used to him not being around. I raised the kids and he worked. It seemed like a good division of labor."

"That worked for a while, then he got his wandering eye again. He started to follow a local 'exotic performer' from venue to venue. Her stage name was 'Lottie Mellons'. Clever. She was more the Shirley type than little ol' me. I guess he was returning to his roots. Anyway, one day he told me he wanted a divorce. I didn't handle that too well."

Betty paused in her telling of the story, possibly reliving a painful memory. Nick didn't want to be rude, but he couldn't contain his curiosity. "What do you mean, you didn't handle it well?"

"Let's say I lashed out. After twenty-three years of marriage and raising three kids, I felt I deserved better. I started to go to his business meetings - he always had a lot of meetings with zoning boards and environmental groups - and I would heckle him from the crowd. I also may have burned down one of his model homes, but that was never proven. Anyway, apparently he could only take so much of that, and he got a couple of doctors to say I'd had a psychotic break, and they had me involuntarily committed. He got the divorce and married Lottie Mellons . . ."

"You mean Charlotte? She's Lottie Mellons?"

"One and the same. That was about five years ago. I've

been in Colonial Pines most of that time. Whenever I get out, I make it a point to torment Andrew, like you saw yesterday. That always gets me put back in, but it's totally worth it."

"You've never done anything more . . . violent?"

"Subtlety isn't your thing, is it?" Betty smiled at Nick over her coffee cup. "Let me help so you don't have to beat around the bush. No, I didn't kill Andrew, but like most of the rest of the family, I would have liked to."

"I didn't mean to suggest . . ."

Betty reached across the table and patted his hand. "Don't worry about it Nick. It seems everybody on the island's a suspect at this point." She winked at him. "Especially you."

Before Nick could protest his innocence, the boat rocked as someone stepped on deck. Betty held a finger to her lips, warning Nick not to say anything.

"Hello? Mr. Rohmer, are you in there?" It was the voice of Walter Hughes.

Betty nodded to Nick that it was okay to answer and quietly got up and moved to the forward cabin, closing the door behind her.

Nick raised his voice to answer. "Yes, I'm here."

"I hope that you're decent because I'm coming in." With that, the hatch to the main cabin slid open and Walter Hughes descended the three steps to the floor of the salon. He was wearing a pair of neatly pressed pale blue pants and a white guayabera shirt. He had apparently left his shoes on deck as he was now wearing only socks.

Walter looked around the boat with distaste. "I haven't been on this vessel in years," he said. "I was always after Andrew to sell it. It's a non-earning asset, and very expensive to maintain."

He looked at Nick, standing next to the salon table, his coffee in hand. "I see you are now dressed as a pedophile," he said. "It's not an improvement."

"It's all I could find," Nick said.

"I'm not here to discuss fashion. We have unfinished business." Walter looked around the cabin. "Are we alone?" he asked.

"Yeah, of course," Nick said.

"You aren't particularly clever, are you, Mr. Rohmer." He picked up Betty's half-empty cup from the table. "Do you always prepare two cups of coffee for yourself?"

"Well, I . . ." Before Nick could stammer out a poorly formed lie, they both felt the boat move slightly, then heard a splash of something falling, or diving, into the water from the bow.

Walter stepped to the forward cabin, leaving the door open. Nick saw him close a hatch. He returned to the main salon. "So who are you trying to protect, Mr. Rohmer, yourself or your bedmate?"

"I'm not trying to protect anyone . . ."

Walter held up a hand. "Please, I don't care who you choose to sleep with, or where you do it, I am here for one reason only. I need the Keene Construction files that are at your accounting firm."

"Now?" Nick asked.

"Yesterday. That was when you were supposed to turn them over, before your embarrassing efforts to get Andrew to retain your firm. Since that is no longer a possibility, I would like the files turned over to my new firm today." He looked at his watch, an expensive-looking gold and diamond timepiece. "It is now 6:30 am. You have all day to get them delivered to the office of Alberto Herrera, our new CPA. If they are not there by 5:00 pm this afternoon, I will personally see to it that you are held solely responsible for the loss of your company's biggest single client and that you never find another job in your chosen field. Is that clear?"

"That's not as much of a threat as you think, at this point," Nick said. "I'm probably about to be fired."

"That doesn't surprise me," Walter said. "I'd fire you, too."

"This doesn't have anything to do with the pending investigation that Andrew ordered, does it?"

Walter waved a dismissive hand at Nick. "I have no concerns on that count. As you no doubt recall, I made this request before Andrew got it into his head that someone was stealing from him. I don't care about that. But I do need the files moved, and I have another problem that you may be able to help me with."

"You expect me to help you after you threatened to have me fired?"

"Yes. Here's my issue. Richard and I had a partnership that invested money overseas. We did quite well for ourselves, but since Richard's untimely death, I find that our account has been closed and the money is gone. I need someone on the inside at Burnham & Fields to check Richard's personal records to see if we can determine where the funds have been transferred. Sadly, with Richard dead and Alberto at his new firm, you are the only person I know there at this time that might have that kind of access."

"So you want me to break into Burnham & Fields computer system and recover all the personal emails and documents of Mr. Golden that might relate to your missing money?"

"Precisely. I think I can make it worth your effort, too."

Nick was intrigued by the strange turn that this conversation had taken. "How would you do that?"

"If you are able to help me recover my missing funds, I will guarantee you a position with Alberto's new firm, with more prestige, and a significantly higher salary."

"And if I don't help you?" Nick asked.

"We're back to you never working as an accountant again. Your choice."

Nick thought for a moment. "How about cash?" he said.

"Cash?"

"Screw the job with Mr. Herrera. How much would you be willing to pay me for this information?"

"Mr. Rohmer, I'm so pleased to see that you can be bought. This makes things so much easier. I would be willing to pay you $50,000 for the successful recovery of my funds."

Nick whistled softly. "Wow. You must be missing a lot of money."

"It is a sizable sum," Walter said.

"I'll do it for two hundred thousand," Nick said.

Walter smiled. "You may not be as stupid as I first thought. Keep in mind that you will only get paid if my money is recovered, so my interests in this are now your interests as well."

"Am I the only one working on this problem for you?" Nick asked.

Walter flashed him a humorless smile. "This is far too important to me to only have one option in play. There are other actors in this little drama, but you're my inside man, Mr. Rohmer, and I think you have the advantage right now. So, do we have a deal?" Walter held out a cold, thin hand to Nick.

"We have a deal," Nick said, and they shook. "But, I'm not allowed to leave until the police have cleared me."

Walter stood. "Don't take too long about this, Mr. Rohmer. The colder this trail gets, the harder it will be to recover my money. I expect you'll find a way off the island sooner rather than later?"

Nick nodded. "It would help if I knew the name of your joint venture."

"You won't find it in Burnham & Fields official records, but we called it 'Plan B.'"

"Oh? What was Plan A?"

"There wasn't one. It was an inside joke." Walter took a business card from this wallet and handed it to Nick. He pointed to a hand-printed phone number on the back of the card. "I can be reached at this number twenty-four hours a day. Don't hesitate to use it. How can I get in touch with you?"

"The police took my cell phone," he said.

"Well, get another one as soon as you can, then make sure that I have the number," Walter said. "The day is young, Mr. Rohmer, and you have hundreds of thousands of dollars to earn. I suggest you get started."

Walter stood and walked to the ladder leading up to the deck. He turned back to Nick, and said, "Do not disappoint me, Mr. Rohmer. I'm willing to pay you for success, but if you fail or try to betray me, there will be dire consequences for you." With that, he climbed back on deck and slid the hatch closed behind him.

***

Scorch woke himself up with a sneeze. He squinted through half-closed eyes against the light of morning, and the first thing he saw was himself reflected in the mirror over the bed. He had fallen asleep where he lay while talking to Donna. He was still naked and curled into a tight fetal ball against the frigid cold that infused the townhouse.

Scorch tried to stretch but grimaced as chilled muscles cramped and protested. He inched his way gingerly off the bed, and with arms wrapped tightly across his chest, stumbled into the bathroom and a hot shower.

Twenty minutes later, a towel around his waist and Richard Golden's raincoat over his shoulders, Scorch went downstairs and checked the thermostat. It was just as he had left it the night before, turned all the way to the lowest setting. The thermometer read a brisk fifty-eight degrees.

"Damn, that is some fucking cold A/C," he said and moved the dial up to a more reasonable seventy-five.

Scorch cleared his throat, trying to scratch the itch that had been bugging him since he woke up, and decided a hot cup of coffee would do the deed. When his bare feet hit the cold tile in the kitchen, he let out a yelp and hopped to the little mat that lay in front of the sink. The place was an icebox.

He began rummaging for something that resembled a coffee pot, but the kitchen looked like it had been equipped by NASA. Everything had the look of those fancy European catalogs that sold cappuccino latte espresso machines that he could never figure out how to use. He gave up after a moment and stood quietly at the sink as a sneeze began to build. He waited, and at the last instant grabbed a paper towel and filled it with a loud, messy sneeze that he felt to his frozen toes.

"Shit," he said and blew his nose. "That's just fucking great."

He grabbed a fistful of clean paper towels and stuffed them in the pocket of the raincoat. He had a feeling he would need them.

THIRTEEN

Information is money. With the right information, you can buy anything.

From – *Success in the Digital World*

Nelson Keene woke up in the driver's seat of Buddy Grinnell's police-issue electric cart. He was parked in the garage of a partially completed home in Phase III of The Village of Boca Cheeca Key, well out of sight of the road. As the sun came up over the Atlantic, he also rose and stretched and had a look around.

The 3,800 square-foot house-in-progress on the Atlantic side of the island would someday be the part-time home of an extremely wealthy individual who would spend about six weeks a year there. The other forty-six weeks per year, no one would be there to witness a sunrise like the one that Nelson watched, with towering cumulus clouds on the horizon showing pinks and oranges and yellows reflecting in the steely blue-gray sea. Nelson snapped a few pictures.

He went back to the police cart and unlocked all the compartments. He found a portable police radio, a book of tickets, a first aid kit, a portable defibrillator, and a pair of bolt cutters.

When Nelson found the evidence bags, he slowly emptied them one at a time onto the sandy concrete floor of the garage. There was a DNA kit with samples from the crime scene. There was a collection of random blunt objects taken from the desk and shelves that the police thought could have been used to cause Andrew Keene's head wound. He also found Andrew's appointment calendar and his cell phone.

Then Nelson found Nick's clothes and personal belongings.

Nelson quickly stripped to his underwear and put on Nick's shirt and suit. It was a good fit. He then flipped through Nick's wallet before putting it in his back pocket. He also pocketed Nick's business card holder, a cheap ballpoint pen, and his keys.

Nick's socks were not included, so Nelson slipped his bare feet into Nick's wingtips. The shoes were a little big, but it was doable. Nelson slung his camera around his neck and walked up and down the garage testing his new wardrobe.

Nelson returned to the pile of evidence. He looked at Nick's Timex watch but then threw it back in the pile. Next he picked up a pink "While You Were Out" memo slip, with the words, "Gordon McCall, AA flight 1317, 11:19 MIA" handwritten on it. This he studied carefully before putting it in the breast pocket of his shirt.

Nelson picked up his father's cell phone and turned it on. The battery showed half a charge, so he slipped the phone into his pants pocket. Next he picked up Nick's briefcase and hefted it, as though checking the weight. He opened it and found it empty except for a few notes Nick had made for his meeting. He dumped the contents on the ground and snapped it shut. Then, with briefcase in hand, he walked back to the road. He turned north toward the ferry terminal.

***

Buddy Grinnell and Ernesto Ruiz were waiting at the Keene's private docks when the green and yellow Florida Marine Patrol vessel pulled up and delivered the four-person team from the FDLE.

Buddy introduced himself. "I'm Buddy Grinnell, Chief of Police for Boca Cheeca," he said. "Which of you is Alex Sotolongo?"

The lone woman in the group stepped forward and extended a hand to Buddy. "I'm Special Agent Alex Sotolongo." She was tall, only about a half a head shorter than Buddy, well-muscled and about forty. Her eyes were hidden behind dark glasses. She wore an FDLE cap with the bill low over her eyes. She pointed to the three men behind her. "This is my forensics team; Roger Cole, John DuPree, and Red Perlman."

"And this is Ernesto Ruiz," Buddy said, and there was handshaking all around.

"We'd like to get started," Alex said. "Can you take us to the crime scene so the boys can get to work?"

"Follow me," Buddy said and led them up to the Keene house.

As they walked through the main entrance, Philip appeared. "Oh great," he said, "more police. I supposed they'll want to eat, too?"

Buddy introduced him. "Special Agent Sotolongo, this is Philip, the Keene's butler."

"I prefer the term majordomo," Philip said, "not that anyone cares what I prefer."

"Nice to meet you, Philip," Alex said. "We won't be needing any food, but we could use some bottled water if you've got any. It's very warm in here. Is the air conditioning not working?"

"Ha!" Philip said. "You haven't seen anything yet. Wait until the day starts to heat up."

"There's no A/C," said Buddy. "One of the many

quirks of the Keene household." He turned to Philip, "Can you bring the water to Andrew's office?"

"Sure. It's not like I have anything else to do."

As they headed down the hall, Alex asked, "Is he always like that?"

"As far as I know."

When they reached Andrew's office, Buddy was relieved to see that Officer Neely was still on guard, and was actually awake. The door to the office was closed, and there was a ribbon of white paper hanging across it.

Alex stepped up to the door and touched the paper. "Is this calculator tape?" she asked.

"Yes, it is," Neely said.

"Someone has written 'Crime Seen Do Not Enter' on it in pencil. And 'Scene' is misspelled."

"We ran out of the yellow plastic tape," Neely volunteered. "The calculator tape was my idea."

Buddy shook his head. "Calculator tape?" was all he said.

"Is the door locked?" Alex asked.

"Yes, sir," said Neely. "No one has been in or out all night. I've been here the whole time and the key's been safe right here," he said, patting his right front pocket, then his left front pocket. "I mean here." He fished for the key and handed it to Alex.

She unlocked the door and with exaggerated care, tore the calculator tape in half. She opened the door and stepped into Andrew Keene's office, to find it exactly the way it had been the previous night.

Unfortunately, the way it had been last night was with the French doors wide open to the patio. "Were these doors left open all night?" she asked.

Buddy looked to Neely for an answer, hoping for some sort of explanation that would make sense. Sadly, that was not the case.

"Yes," Neely said, "but we put some crime scene tape across those doors too so no one would come in."

Alex could see the calculator tape moving slightly in the weak breeze. "Awesome," she said. She looked around at her contaminated crime scene. "Did you at least bag and tag some of the evidence last night before this room was left open to the world?"

Buddy sighed. "Yeah, we did."

"Well, that's something, anyway," Alex said. "At least we have something to work with. Where is it stored?"

"It's missing," Buddy said. "We think it was stolen."

"Awesome," was all she said.

***

Victoria had not dressed with a sea voyage in mind. She was wearing a bright red skirt and matching jacket over a white blouse. The skirt was a little full, and she spent most of her time on deck with one hand on the railing and the other holding her skirt down so that it didn't blow over her head.

Her shoes were also not a good choice for a boat ride. The red shoes that went with this outfit had what she considered a sensible heel, but it still made walking up the gang plank and balancing on the moving deck difficult.

She had given up on her hair. It had been in a neat bun when she left her apartment that morning, but in the wind of the ferry, and with no free hand to attend to it, it was now a frazzled mess.

For the third time, she asked Paul to go inside to the lounge, so she could get out of the wind and off her feet. He told her to go ahead and that he would stay on deck for now. He was enjoying himself.

In his blue power suit, with his tie safely folded into an inside jacket pocket, he actually looked quite dashing in the brisk breeze. His short, dark hair, slightly graying at the temples, withstood the wind well, and with his jacket buttoned, standing there in his tasseled loafers, he looked like a man at ease with himself and his surroundings.

Victoria admired his panache, even as hers was being blown away by the wind. He just looked so solid and dependable. Even as she continued to fight to maintain her balance and control her skirt, she wouldn't think of going inside without him. Anything less than her full commitment seemed unworthy.

As the ferry turned into the Boca Cheeca channel, it slowed down and the wind dropped with their speed. Victoria tried to smooth herself out. She didn't feel too much worse for the wear, but was pretty sure she would need a mirror to repair her hair.

"What a prosperous-looking town," Paul said as they approached the dock. "This has to be some pricey real estate."

Victoria nodded. "The town wasn't incorporated at the time of the last census, but it's probably number one or two in terms of average household income in the state."

"These are my natural constituents," Paul said. "Why haven't we had any fundraisers out here?"

Victoria looked down at the mostly empty streets and the shuttered townhomes. "The population is very seasonal. There aren't many residents here this time of year."

"I'm sure the ones that are would make it worth our while. Make a note."

"Yes, sir." As they started for the walkway to disembark, she put a hand on Paul's arm. "Thanks for what you're doing for Nick," she said. "I really appreciate it."

Paul patted her hand. "You're welcome, Vic. I'm happy to help." He glanced at his watch. "We will be back in Miami in time for the forum, right?"

"We should have plenty of time," she said. "Hey, is that Nick?" She pointed to a tall, thin young man in a dark business suit waiting to board the ferry. Paul looked where she was pointing, but before he could answer, she realized her mistake.

"No, that's not him," she said, "just a similar build and suit."

"We'll see him soon enough," Paul said, as they reached the dock. "You just leave everything to me."

"I just hope he's okay," she said. "He's not cut out for prison."

***

Nick licked some croissant crumbs from his lips and took another sip of his mimosa. The breakfast buffet laid out in the sunroom of the Keene house was about as different from the previous night's dinner as it could be. There were fresh-baked pastries, eggs, waffles, bacon, some sort of potato hash, three different kinds of juice to go with the coffee, champagne for mimosas, and a Bloody Mary bar. There was probably enough food to feed twenty people.

Nick walked out to the patio and looked for some shade. He found a spot by the pool and sat in one of the lounge chairs carefully balancing his plate and his drink.

Charlotte emerged from the sunroom with her own plate and a Bloody Mary. She sat on the chaise next to Nick. "Enjoying your breakfast?" she asked.

Nick hurriedly chewed and swallowed what was in his mouth. "Very much. Thanks."

"I had Philip lay something out for a crowd. I thought we might have a lot of police tramping about today. It wouldn't pay to have them hungry and cranky."

Nick took a sip of his mimosa. "Is anybody else up?"

"Do you mean Jeannie?" Charlotte gave Nick an exaggerated wink. "I heard you two had some quality alone time last night."

Nick blushed from his neck to his forehead. "We just went for a late swim."

"Is that what you call it?" she said. "Don't worry. What you two do together is no one's business but your own – and mine." She laughed at her own joke. "But no, I haven't seen her yet this morning." She took a dainty fork full of egg. "Skip and Carolyn were here, though. They loaded up a couple of plates and left, thank God. I haven't seen Nelson, and I expect Walter any minute."

"What's the deal with Walter?" Nick asked. "Does he live here?"

"He may as well," she said. "He's here all the time. He has an office and a small room that he stays in when he doesn't feel like going back to Miami, which is most of the time, it seems."

Nick chewed a mouthful of potatoes. "If you don't mind my asking, what does he do for the company?"

"Walter pretty much runs the company. He's CEO and General Counsel and a few other titles. He runs the day-to-day operations, other than the construction crews. Those are run by Skip."

"So what was Andrew's part in all this?"

"Andrew was the soul of the company. He was the one who had the vision and did the deals."

"Did Andrew and Walter get along?"

Charlotte laughed again. "No one got along with Andrew, but they seemed to have figured out how to work together. At one time they were partners in the business, but Andrew bought him out or something. After that, Walter came back as an employee. I think he always resented that a little."

"Really? They were partners?" Nick asked. "Wasn't Richard Golden a partner at one time too? I think Andrew mentioned that at the funeral."

"Was he? I don't know. That was before my time." She reached over and laid a soft hand on Nick's leg. "Aren't you just full of questions?" she said.

"Nick?"

Nick turned around to see Victoria and Paul being escorted by Philip.

"These people are here to see the accountant," Philip said. "I leave them with you. I have to get back to the kitchen since there are apparently more mouths to feed."

Everyone ignored Philip as he left in a huff.

"You look pretty comfortable for someone in police custody," Victoria said, eying Charlotte's hand on Nick's thigh.

Paul ignored Nick entirely and focused his full attention on Charlotte. "I'm Paul Gonzalez-Smith," he said and extended a hand. "And you are . . ?"

Charlotte took his hand lightly in hers and squeezed it softly. "Charlotte Keene," she said. "Andrew Keene's widow."

"I'm so sorry for your loss," he said.

"Yes, it's a real shame what happened," Victoria said. "You have our condolences."

"Thank you," Charlotte said. "It's been very difficult, but we're holding up."

"If there's anything at all that I can do," Paul said, "please don't hesitate to ask. Anything."

"Well, aren't you sweet," Charlotte said. "But you're here to help your friend, right?"

Paul glanced at Nick for the first time. "He doesn't seem to be in any immediate danger, unless someone has called the fashion police."

Paul and Charlotte shared a chuckle over this.

Nick got up from his seat and gave Victoria a kiss on the cheek. "It's good to see you, Victoria. Thanks for coming."

Victoria nodded her head toward Paul and gave Nick a "look". "Thank you, too, Paul, for coming out here for me," Nick added. "I know it's a busy time for you."

"Anything for Victoria's fiancé," he said taking Nick's seat next to Charlotte. "I'm here to help," he said, taking Charlotte's hand in his again, "in any way that I can."

FOURTEEN

If you're on time once, people will expect it every day.
Watch those expectations.

From – *Aim Low, Hit High*

Scorch was late meeting Donna at the ferry. He found her standing there on the dock by herself, dressed for a day at the beach. She was wearing a long shirt over her bathing suit, a big floppy hat, and dark sunglasses. In her hand, she had an enormous beach bag.

"Hey baby," he said and tried to kiss her.

Donna hit him, hard, across the face with her free hand. "Why can't you be on time for once, Scorch? Why do you make me wait here like a fool while everybody else goes about their business?"

Scorch rubbed his cheek. "I'm not that late," he said, with a little more whine in his voice than he intended.

"Fifteen minutes," she said. "Fifteen minutes that I had to stand here wondering if you screwed me again."

"Hey, have I ever let you down?" he asked.

She just looked at him.

"Well, this is different. You're gonna love the condo."

He took her hand and walked with her through the faux-cobbled streets of the town. The sunshine and humid heat cleared any thoughts of a cold from Scorch's head. By the time they reached Richard Golden's condo, he felt like a million bucks.

"Here it is, baby," he said as he unlocked the door and let her pass.

"What's all this shit?" she asked. She used her foot to indicate the debris that was blocking the entrance hall.

"What, this?" Scorch picked up a golden shovel and turned it over in his hands. "It's just some valuable shit I found last night." He picked up a golden hammer mounted to a wooden frame and handed it to her. "Do you think this is solid gold? It's real heavy."

"No one makes a hammer out of gold, Scorch. It's probably just paint."

"Really?" He scrutinized it more closely and scraped it with a fingernail. "It doesn't feel like paint."

"Where'd you get all this, and why is it in front of the door? You can't even get in here."

"Sorry, baby," he said. "I was keeping it here until I got around to selling it." He picked up the golden shovel and a gold-covered bulldozer and shoved them in a closet with the mounted hammer. "Forget about this stuff," he said. "Check out the apartment."

Donna stepped into the living room. "Wow," she said. "This is beautiful. It's even better than you said." She walked to the sliding glass doors and looked at the view. In the daylight, the Miami skyline stood out above the bay, with a line of dark cumulous clouds behind it making a dramatic backdrop.

Donna unlocked the sliding glass door and tugged on it. It was made of hurricane-proof glass, and was four feet wide and eight feet tall and weighed over 250 pounds. It didn't budge.

"I'll get that for you, baby," Scorch said. He grabbed the door handle, put his weight into it, and it started to roll. It picked up speed and threw him off balance, sliding open hard and banging into the opposite wall, bouncing back slightly. "Shit!" he said. "That's what I call a door!"

She stepped onto the patio that overlooked the bay. It was surrounded by a low wall and brightly flowered shrubs for privacy. Beyond the flowers, she could see the turquoise blue waters of the bay. She took a deep breath. "It even smells expensive. It's like a resort. How long can we stay here?"

Scorch tried to stifle a sneeze. He wiped his nose on his forearm. "As long as you want, baby. No one's living here right now, except us."

"I'm going to call my mom," she said, "then you're going to take me to the pool and show me off to those old men." She ran inside with a giggle.

Scorch smiled. "Before you call your mom, let me show you the bedroom."

***

Nick was once again sitting across the desk from Buddy Grinnell in the small room that adjoined Andrew Keene's office. This time, however, Buddy was joined by Alex Sotolongo, and on Nick's side of the desk were Victoria, to his right, and Paul Gonzalez-Smith next to her. Victoria was holding Nick's hand to show her support.

The desk was littered with half-empty water bottles and plates bearing remains from the buffet breakfast. The ceiling fan was turning at full speed. Everyone was wearing too much clothing for the heat, except Nick in his shorts and tank top. He realized he looked ridiculous, but at least he was somewhat comfortable.

Alex had a file open in front of her and had to hold the papers down against the wind from the ceiling fan. "Tell me what you saw when you came into the room," she said.

Paul held out his hand toward Nick. "Don't answer that," he said.

"Why not?" Alex and Nick asked simultaneously.

"It could be incriminating," Paul said.

Nick ignored Paul's advice. "I didn't see anything when I came in the room, at least not at first. Just my jacket on the sofa and my briefcase on the floor. It wasn't until I moved further into the room that I saw the body."

"Ok, good," Paul said. "That's not incriminating."

"Did you see any blood?" Alex asked.

"My client reserves the right to not answer that question," Paul said.

"Mr. Smith," Alex said.

"That's Gonzalez-Smith."

"Mr. Gonzalez-Smith, is there a reason that you think your client shouldn't answer that?"

"I don't know what he's going to say. The first thing they teach you in law school is if you don't already know the answer, object to the question."

"It's okay, Paul," Nick said. "Yes, there was a little blood under Mr. Keene's head. Not a lot."

"Did you notice any footprints in the blood?" Alex asked.

Paul looked at Nick and shook his head, indicating he shouldn't answer.

Alex turned toward Paul. "Mr. Smith . . ."

"That's Gonzalez-Smith," he said.

"Señor Gonzalez-Smith," she said, "¿Cómo es que usted encuentra algo que objetar a todas las preguntas?"

"I'm sorry," Paul said. "I didn't quite get that."

"Do you speak Spanish, Señor Gonzalez-Smith?

"I'm not fluent," he said, "but I am doing Rosetta Stone."

"If you're going to insist that people tack 'Gonzalez' onto your name," Alex said, "you might try learning something about the language and culture that you're attempting to embrace. It would come off as more sincere."

"Thank you. That's a very good tip. Vic, write that down."

Nick turned to Victoria. "You let him call you Vic?"

She released his hand and wiped her sweaty palm on her skirt. "Of course," she said. "It's not like 'Vic' rhymes with Paul."

She took out a notepad and Nick watched as she wrote "embrace Hispanic culture/learn Spanish."

"You can't be serious," Nick said.

"Don't be small-minded," Victoria said. "It's not becoming."

"Ok, hold it," Alex said, holding up both hands. "This isn't couples therapy. And you," she said, pointing at Paul, "if you continue to object to every question I ask, we're going to be here a very long time. Do you want to go home to your air-conditioned house at some point? I know I do."

"As a matter of fact," Paul said, "I have some very important meetings to attend later today."

"And I need to get to work," Nick said, which got a curious glance from Victoria.

"Great," Alex said. "So, we're all in agreement. We want to get this over with quickly, right?"

Everyone around the desk nodded their agreement.

"Ok, then. Mr. Rohmer, did you see any footprints in the blood under Andrew Keene's head?"

"No, I don't think so. I was pretty fixated on my tie that was knotted around Mr. Keene's throat, though."

"What kind of shoes were you wearing?" Alex asked.

"Why do you ask that? You have them. Chief Grinnell took them along with everything else I was wearing."

Alex glanced at Buddy, but he refused to make eye contact. "For the record," she said, "what kind of shoes were you wearing?"

"Black wingtips."

"Do they have a crepe sole?" Alex asked.

"No," Nick said, "just leather. Why?"

"How well did you know the victim?" Alex asked.

"I had just met him that day at a funeral. He was a

major client of my company, but I don't normally deal with the important clients . . ."

"Don't sell yourself short, Nick," Victoria said, "your clients are very important in their own way."

"I guess," Nick said, "just not in a money or career way."

"If you weren't involved with this client, why were you here for dinner?" Alex asked.

"It's kind of a long story," Nick said. He tried to summarize the events of the past three days, starting with the news of Richard Golden's death and culminating with him finding the body of Andrew Keene.

Alex turned to Buddy Grinnell and asked, "Does this other death, this," she looked at her notes, "Richard Golden, have anything to do with Andrew Keene's murder?"

Buddy shook his head. "That was an accident. He took a tumble out of his cart and broke his neck. It's not unheard of."

"And that happened here on the island?" she asked.

"Yes." Buddy didn't offer any further explanation.

"You've had a rough week in this exclusive little burg," she said.

"Tell me about it," Buddy said and took a sip of water.

Through the open doors, Nick saw Jeannie walking quickly across the patio on the far side of the pool. "Excuse me a moment," he said, and he stood up abruptly and stepped outside, leaving four bewildered sets of eyes to follow him as he crossed the patio to intercept her.

"Who's that?" Alex asked.

"Andrew Keene's daughter, Jeannie," Buddie said. "She's on the list." He pointed to one of the papers that Alex was holding in place on the table.

They all watched as Nick stopped Jeannie. Both Nick and Jeannie appeared a little formal initially. Then, Jeannie put her hand to her head, like she had forgotten something, and Nick waved his hand to indicate that it didn't matter. She nodded, then turned to go, but he grabbed her arm. She tried to pull away, but as Nick spoke, she stopped resisting, then seemed to be interested in what he was saying, then reached up and wrapped her arms around him, giving him a hug. He returned the hug, then remembered that he was being watched and looked nervously back at the room where he had left the two police officers, Paul, and his fiancée.

Nick pried himself loose from Jeannie. She looked at her watch and the two of them nodded, then Jeannie went back in the house, and Nick returned to his interrogation.

"Care to explain that?" Alex asked. It was clear from Victoria's expression that she found this the most interesting question so far.

Nick paused a moment, and after a glance at Victoria, said, "She asked me for help with an accounting issue, and I just agreed. That's all."

"It didn't look like an accounting issue to me," Victoria said.

"What is your relationship with Miss Keene?" Alex asked.

"I don't have one. She's just a potential client."

"Did you ever meet her before yesterday?"

"No."

Alex changed tack. "Do you know of any reason that someone would want to kill Mr. Keene?"

Nick shook his head. "I barely even knew the account, let alone the people involved. My only interaction with Mr. Keene was at the funeral . . ."

"Where he was threatened and attacked by his ex-wife and son," Alex said.

"Threatened?"

Alex read from her notes. "I quote: 'It's you that should be in that box.'"

Nick nodded. "She did say that, but 'threatened and attacked' seems a little strong. Harassed would be a better word for it."

"At the dinner you attended, did they appear to be a happy family?" Alex asked.

Both Nick and Buddy laughed at that. Alex gave Buddy a stern look and he went back to playing with his water bottle.

"Why do you find that question amusing, Mr. Rohmer?"

"Well, they weren't exactly the Waltons."

Alex raised an eyebrow. "Who are the Waltons?"

Nick shook his head. "Sorry. What I mean is, they seemed to have a lot of tension in the family. Mr. Keene claimed that someone was stealing from him and that put the group on edge. Everyone was angry at everyone else. It wasn't a relaxed atmosphere. If you need background on the family relationships, I'm not the guy to talk to." As Alex noted the file, he asked, "Can I go now?"

Without looking up, Alex answered. "We're done for now, but don't leave the island."

***

Walter Hughes was sitting at his desk tapping his pen when there was a knock on his office door.

"Come in."

Philip came into the office and stood uneasily in front of Walter. "You needed to talk to me, sir?"

"Philip, don't be so nervous. I just wanted to commend you on this morning's breakfast buffet. You did a very creditable job on such short notice."

Philip smiled. "Why thank you for noticing, sir. Most of the people on this island wouldn't know a good meal if it bit them back, and as for the police, well –"

"I'm sure," Walter said. "And now with Andrew gone, I'm certain the evening meals will be of equal quality. It will be nice to see your talents finally put to good use."

"Thank you, sir," he said. After a pause, he asked, "Is that all? Did you need anything?"

"No, that's all. I just wanted to pay you a long overdue compliment. Well done."

"Thank you." Philip turned to leave. As he laid his hand on the door knob, Walter spoke again.

"By the way, Philip, who are the two strangers here this morning – the man in the suit and the woman in the red dress? They don't appear to be police."

Philip turned so he could gossip more efficiently. "They're here with the accountant. She's his fiancée, and the man is some kind of lawyer from Miami. The lawyer can't seem to leave Mrs. Keene alone for a minute. It's disgusting."

"And you're sure about the girl being Mr. Rohmer's fiancée?"

"Well, that's the way she was introduced. Her name's Victoria . . . something Polish. And the lawyer's running for some kind of office. The way he's all over Mrs. Keene, though . . ."

Walter's telephone rang. "Thank you, Philip," Walter said. "You can go."

"Oh. Well, okay then," Philip said turning on his heel. He closed the door behind him and Walter picked up the phone on the third ring.

"This is Officer Ruiz, sir, Boca Cheeca Police."

"And?"

"Well, sir, I have a light on the board at Richard Golden's."

"A light?" Walter asked.

"The board lights up when someone enters the property without punching in the security code. Normally we call the homeowner, but with Mr. Golden dead . . ."

"I see." Walter contemplated the situation for a moment. "When did the light go on?"

"About fifteen minutes ago. The strange thing is, though, that it appears that it also lit up last night around midnight, but there was no one here to see it, what with everyone up at the Keene house."

"What is your customary protocol in this kind of situation?" Walter asked.

"We'd usually send someone out to check on the property, but we're spread pretty thin still. Everyone's either up at the Keene house, or they're out searching the island for . . . um . . . evidence."

"Don't worry about it," said Walter. "You did the right thing calling me, but rest easy. Richard's ex-wife is at the townhouse. She told me she was coming to arrange for the disposition of some of his possessions. No need to worry."

"Very good, sir," Officer Ruiz said, sounding relieved. "I just wanted to make sure that someone was aware. I'll mark the log."

"Thank you for your service, officer. You have a good day."

Walter thought a moment, then opened his desk drawer. From a large ring of keys, he pulled one off that was marked "Golden".

From another drawer, he pulled a large plastic case and snapped it open to reveal a Beretta nine millimeter semi-automatic handgun. Walter picked it up gingerly and weighed it in his hands. He slid out the magazine to check the load, then slid it back in, double checked the safety, and placed the gun into his briefcase.

FIFTEEN

Get a driver as soon as you can afford one. You can turn your commute into productive time, plus it looks cool.

From – *Maximize Your Life*

After his interview, Nick went back out onto the pool deck where most of the Keene family was milling around, waiting their turn with Alex and Buddy. Nick got a glass of juice from the buffet and looked for a place to sit. He spotted Skip, for once without Carolyn at his side.

Nick walked over to where Skip was sitting, and pulled up a seat next to him. "Mind if I sit here?" he asked.

"As if that would stop you."

Nick sat. "I guess you're waiting for your interview?"

Skip ignored him.

"It wasn't too bad. The lady cop seems to know what she's doing."

"She can't be that good if she still hasn't arrested you."

"I know it must have been quite a shock for you to find me over the body like that, but you can't really believe that I did this."

Skip gave a snort in response.

"Look. I know you were part of the decision to get rid of my firm, but no hard feelings. Business is business. It's just too bad about the timing. It really looks bad for you."

"What do you mean?"

"Well, your accountant of thirty years dies, and the first thing you do is decide to get a new accounting firm - before he's even buried. Then, when your dad says he's going to do a full audit of the books, he gets murdered. It looks like there's something that someone's desperate to hide."

"We have nothing to hide. You don't know what you're talking about."

"I know I'm a little green," Nick said, "but I'm not stupid. As general manager, you run the construction crews. You arrange purchases of materials. A lot of money passes through your hands. There are a lot of opportunities for someone to skim a little here, or take a kickback there. Anything like that's going to come to light in a thorough audit." Nick looked at Skip's face. "But of course, I'm sure there's nothing like that."

"No, of course not. What does it matter now, anyway? There isn't going to be an audit."

Nick laughed. "Of course there will. It may not be done by my company, but with your father dead, Keene Construction is going to have to go through probate. An audit will be required. There's no getting out of that now."

"You don't know what you're talking about," Skip said.

"Maybe. Like I said, I'm a little green. But hey, now you'll probably own the company, or a big part of it. You'll be the man. It has to gall you that your wife is a VP and you're not. And Charlotte president? Come on."

Skip turned and looked at Nick for the first time. "Are you seriously suggesting that I killed my dad for a promotion?"

"No," Nick said. "But if they're looking for motive, you've got to be a pretty interesting target. All this," he indicated the house and pool with a sweep of his arm, "to be inherited. And there's proximity. Other than me, you were the closest to the body."

"I was looking for my dad to discuss work issues. I'm not the one that was found over the body."

"You were seeing your dad by yourself? Seems to me, you and Carolyn always come as a pair. Where was she when you came downstairs?"

"She's in bed by 9:30 every night. Early to bed, et cetera."

"Sounds like a ball of fun."

"You're wasting your time if you think I had anything to do with what happened. There are a couple of very unhappy people in this family who had no love for dad. You should be harassing them."

"Oh? Like who?"

"Betty for one," Skip said. "And Jeannie for another. Why don't you go bother her? She's hated dad ever since he told her she wasn't going to college. He made her stay to take care of Nelson. I don't think they've said a civil word since, and that was five years ago. And what about Nelson? No one's seen him since the murder." Skip got to his feet and looked down at Nick. "You're barking up the wrong tree with me."

With that, he walked back into the house.

***

Nelson retrieved the family's black Mercedes, still covered in egg, from the private parking area at Dinner Key Marina. He fought his way up I-95 in heavy traffic, then took the 836 west and crawled the rest of the way to Miami International Airport. He left the car in short-term parking and crossed the elevated walkway into Terminal D.

He bought a spicy empanada and a cup of coffee. The empanada was gone in two bites. He kept the white paper bag that it came in, and with Nick's pen, he wrote "McCall" on the back of the bag. He then went to stand at the end of the concourse to await the arrival of McCall's flight.

There was a steady, unending, stream of people filing past Nelson. In a sea of motion, he was the only living thing that didn't move. After about fifteen minutes he became restless, and started to take pictures of the passersby. With the camera in one hand and his makeshift sign in the other, he picked out random individuals that caught his eye and stalked them with his lens. When one target moved out of sight, he selected another.

He was focused on a large family struggling with five small children and all the attendant luggage, when a man in a suit stopped in front of him, blocking his shot.

He looked up into an impatient face.

"You Rohmer?" Gordon McCall asked.

Nelson tried to hand him one of Nick's business cards.

"Tip: you don't have to give your boss your business card," McCall said. "Let's get moving. Which way to the car?

Nelson pointed to the exit.

McCall held up his leather overnight bag. "I've got my luggage," he said, "so let's go. You lead."

McCall followed Nelson back over the pedestrian walkway to the car, while delivering a monolog about airline inefficiency, cramped leg room, and poor food. When they reached the Mercedes, he said, "If this is your car, Golden was paying you too much." He looked at the gunk baked onto the roof and hood. "Here's another tip: if you know you'll be picking someone up at the airport, it wouldn't hurt to have the car washed. This vehicle is a mess."

Nelson unlocked the car and held the back door open for McCall.

"You're not a goddamned chauffeur," he said, and he got in the front passenger seat. Nelson closed the back door, put McCall's bag in the trunk, and then slid into the driver's seat.

McCall gave him his orders. "Take me straight to the office. Apparently, that situation can't wait another minute. I can check into the hotel later."

Nelson nodded and put the car in gear. Before they had cleared the parking garage, McCall was on his phone making a series of calls that engaged his full attention.

Nelson exited the airport. With no particular destination in mind, he pointed the car west on the 836. When he reached the interchange, he merged onto the Florida Turnpike and headed north toward Jacksonville.

***

Jeannie came and sat next to Nick, in the seat vacated by Skip. "That didn't look like it was a very friendly conversation."

"I was just probing to see if he was nervous about the audit."

"Was he?"

"Hard to tell. He always seems indignant so I can't tell if I got under his skin with that or not. He told me you did it."

"Me?" Jeannie said. "Did he say why?"

"He said you hated your dad because he didn't let you go to college."

She let out a short laugh. "That's one of the reasons. Let's say it was an area of disagreement. I wanted to study nursing. He said that was stupid."

"You a nurse?"

"I'm very nurturing," she said. "Can't you tell?"

Nick looked around the patio area. "Have you seen Walter? I had an interesting conversation with him earlier."

"Yeah? What did that old creep have to say?"

"I'll tell you later. First, I want to talk to her." He tried to point discreetly at Carolyn, who had just come out of the house. "What can you tell me about her?"

"Well, she and Skip have been married for about

fifteen years. I can barely remember a time she wasn't part of the family. And she's kind of a grouch. She's always unhappy about something."

"She isn't fond of me," Nick said.

"As far as I can tell, she's not fond of anyone."

"Is she an early riser?"

"That's an odd question."

"Skip said she was in bed by 9:30. That seems awfully early, but if she gets up with the dawn . . ."

"I doubt he knows when she goes to bed. They have separate rooms. We used to tease Skip about it, but he got kind of sensitive on the subject. He's got one of those CPAP machines –"

"A what machine?"

"CPAP, for sleep apnea. She says it keeps her up. That's her story anyway."

"She seems perpetually angry," Nick said.

"Lately, she's been pissed at Skip. She thinks he should stand up for himself and demand more responsibility in the company. She wants to be the wife of the Big Man. I heard them fighting about it the other night and she said if he didn't do something about it, she would. So, maybe she did."

"You think I should go talk to her?"

"I dare you," she said.

***

Walter Hughes stood in Richard Golden's townhouse, gun in hand, and looked around. It was apparent that someone had been here – there were muddy shoeprints on the white carpeting, and the kitchen had apparently been ransacked, though Walter couldn't tell if anything was missing.

Walter inspected the second floor to find a rumpled bed and wet towels thrown on the floor. He did a quick inspection of the packed suitcases and decided that the packing job was too neat for whoever was here now. They must have been packed by Golden in preparation for a quick departure.

Whoever it was, they hadn't forced their way in, so they must have a key.

Walter returned to the first floor and called the maintenance department with instructions to change the locks and leave at least two copies of the new keys in his office at the Keene's house. He then called the police department and asked for Officer Ruiz.

"Officer Ruiz, this is Walter Hughes."

"Yes, Mr. Hughes. What can I do for you?"

"Mrs. Golden is finished in Richard's townhouse and has left instructions for the locks to be changed. The new keys will be in my possession. Please reset the security code for the alarm to 3-5-1-9."

He could hear Ruiz scrambling for a pad and pen. "Yes, sir," Ruiz said. "3-5-1-9. Got it."

"If any more 'lights' come up on your board for this property, please notify me at once. Can you do that?"

"Yes, sir. I'll have maintenance call me when they're done with the locks and reset the code at that time."

"Thank you," Walter said. "Please be sure that anyone that is on duty knows to call me. Can you do that?"

"Already done, sir. You'll be notified if any unauthorized parties enter the property."

Walter smiled. "It's comforting to know that the Boca Cheeca Police are on the job," he said and hung up the phone. He then set about methodically searching the townhouse from top to bottom.

***

Nick approached Carolyn warily, like he was stalking a dangerous animal. She was about forty and wore her dark hair short. She was wearing a T-shirt tucked into a pair of shorts. With her tennis shoes, she reminded Nick of his high school's softball coach. All she was missing was the whistle.

He stopped next to her and asked, "Got a minute?"

"Not for you," she said. "You shouldn't even be here." She walked away, but Nick followed.

"I was just talking to Skip," he said. "He seems a little nervous about the audit. Should he be?"

"Oh, please," she said. "You have some nerve talking to me about Skip when you're the one they should be investigating."

"He did seem to be pretty excited about increasing his involvement in the company, though. You must be pleased."

Carolyn turned and gave him a scathing look.

"I mean, I heard that you weren't too happy with Skip's position in the company. You didn't think that his father properly valued him." Nick said.

"I don't know who told you that," Carolyn said. She squinted while scanning the patio looking for the culprit. "It sounds like something Jeannie would say. She should talk. She's still driving boats after all these years."

"So Skip being only GM and Charlotte being President didn't bother you?"

She turned and fixed her stare on Nick. "Skip's father very much valued his contributions to the business."

"He just didn't value them enough for a promotion, is that it?"

"That would have come in due time."

"When?" Nick asked. "When his father was dead?"

Carolyn took in a sharp breath. "If you're suggesting that my husband had anything to do with Dad Keene's death . . ."

"I didn't mean to suggest anything. It just that, objectively, it looks like you and Skip had a lot to gain by Andrew's death," Nick said.

"You know who had a lot to gain? The Harlot. She's got plenty of motive."

"The Harlot?"

"Charlotte. She was totally on the outs with Dad Keene, and I heard that he had talked to his attorney about a divorce. And they had a prenup, so she'd get nothing. It was going to be back to exotic dancing for her."

"Wow," Nick said. "When you open up, you really open up."

Carolyn gave him a cold look with her dark eyes, turned on her heels, and left.

***

Nelson and McCall were halfway to Fort Lauderdale when Nelson's cell phone rang. McCall looked up from his own conversation, annoyed when Nelson dug the phone from his pocket and answered.

"Yeah?" was all he said.

"Nelson, that you?"

"Uh-huh."

"Where you been, boy? You had my truck all day yesterday and no sales. Today you don't show up. Everything okay?"

"No."

"Well where the hell have you been?" the voice asked.

"Funeral."

The caller calmed a little with that news. "Sorry to hear that. Who died?"

"Dad."

"That sucks. My dad died a few years back. It's tough. Sorry I yelled at you, but I need someone to pick up one of my trucks. Damn driver quit on me and just left it in Flamingo. Can you imagine that? I need someone to go pick it up for me and drive it back up here. It's worth a hundred bucks to me to get it back here today. Can you do it?"

"Yeah."

"Any chance you can get there by noon?"

Nelson looked at the time on the dashboard. "One," he said.

"One's okay. Great! It's supposed to be parked near the visitor center. The keys are in the freezer. You got all that?"

"Yeah."

"Great. Sorry again about your dad, man, and thanks for your help."

Nelson hung up and took the next exit, and then circled around to get back on the turnpike headed south.

McCall hung up on his own phone and noticed for the first time that they were not yet in Miami.

"Where the hell are we?" he asked.

"Miramar," Nelson said.

"Are we headed to Miami? Shouldn't we be there by now?"

Nelson didn't answer but just kept driving south toward the Everglades.

SIXTEEN

Set your goal and go for it. Don't have a fallback. Don't have a contingency plan. A contingency plan is just a plan to fail.

From – *Succeed or Die Trying*

Nick walked over to Charlotte, where she was seated with Paul Gonzalez-Smith. She looked up at him and smiled. "I saw you talking to Carolyn," she said. "You're braver than you look."

"I can see how she would be a perfect fit for human resources. The employees must love having to deal with her," Nick said.

Charlotte laughed. "No one in their right mind would go to her. She has a very pleasant assistant who deals with people. Carolyn is more of a behind the scenes person."

Nick looked around the patio. "I don't see Victoria anywhere. I thought she'd be here with you."

"To keep an eye on Paul?" Charlotte said.

"I don't need a minder," Paul said. "Mrs. Keene and I are just having a friendly conversation. Vic's gone in search of a bathroom, or something."

"Do you mind if I join you?" Nick asked.

Charlotte waved her arm as though indicating that whatever was hers was his. "Please, pull up a chair. I'm sure that Paul doesn't mind sharing me."

Paul cleared his throat. "Actually, we were just talking about my campaign –"

"Oh, Paul," Charlotte said. "That can wait a moment. Can't you see that Nick wants to ask me some questions? You do, don't you?"

Nick dragged a chair close and sat facing Charlotte, his back to Paul. "I'm just a little curious. In talking to the others, some have suggested that perhaps you and Andrew were having problems."

Paul came to her defense. "I don't see how that is any of your business," he said.

"It's okay, Paul. I don't mind. The police are going to ask me the same things." She turned her attention back to Nick. "We had the occasional lovers' spat, but generally, I think we were very happy. Andrew took care of me like a husband is supposed to. And for a man his age, he was surprisingly virile."

"There was a big age difference between you, though. You're even younger than Skip."

Charlotte smiled. "I'm actually only a few years older than Jeannie, but that was never a problem. In some ways, our age difference was the basis for our relationship."

"Someone said that Andrew had been in touch with his divorce lawyer."

"Hearsay!" Paul shouted.

"This isn't a trial, Paul. You can relax," Charlotte said. "I imagine that Carolyn is the source of that rumor." Her smile never wavered.

"You two had a prenuptial agreement, isn't that right?"

"You don't have to answer that," Paul said.

Charlotte ignored him. "Of course. He was a very wealthy man, so it only made sense that he would protect his assets."

"If he was considering divorce . . ."

"He wasn't."

". . . that would have left you with nothing but your own personal assets," Nick said, fighting, but failing, to keep his eyes from flicking to Charlotte's chest.

Years of training allowed Charlotte to ignore Nick's eyes on her. "You're just fishing," she said. "If you're really in need of a motive to kill Andrew, you should take a look at Walter Hughes. There's a man with a chip on his shoulder."

"What kind of chip?" Nick asked.

"Walter's gay," she said. "He's from a time when that was the kind of thing you just kept hidden. He still thinks that no one knows. Andrew held that over his head for years. Andrew would torment the man with threats of exposing his secret. The only time that I ever saw Walter really lose his temper was during an argument where Andrew threatened to expose Walter's 'proclivities,' as he called them. Andrew won the argument, but if looks could kill, Andrew would have been dead right then."

At that moment, Alex and Buddy emerged from the office where they had been conducting interviews.

"Can I have your attention, please?" Alex said. "I really appreciate everyone's help and patience so far, but we're going to need about an hour break from the witness interviews. Anyone that we have not spoken to yet, can you please be available here again in about an hour? Thanks."

Like they had heard a signal from a starter's gun, the family dispersed in all directions simultaneously. Only Charlotte remained calmly seated where she was.

"It looks like your pool of suspects has evaporated," she said.

"They're not my suspects," Nick said. "I was just trying to get a feel for the family dynamic."

"Of course. Well, I hope you figure out who did it. I know our relationship was not conventional, but I really did care for Andrew. I would hate for his killer to go unpunished."

***

After Scorch introduced Donna to Richard Golden's mirrored bedroom, he took her, as promised, to the pool. Donna was disappointed that there were no rich old men for her to strut in front of. The pool area was mostly populated by older women, and judging by their expressions and hushed whispering, they were more interested in Scorch's tattoos than they were in her.

Donna was lying in the shade with a magazine, her hat and glasses still in place, and she was slathered in sunscreen. Scorch, on the other hand, was convinced that the sun was going to cure his budding cold. He was avoiding the shade. He had removed his shirt, exposing his heavily tattooed but pale torso to the sun, while still maintaining his dignity by wearing his jeans.

"You want some sunscreen?" Donna asked him. "You've been in the sun a long time."

"I'm good," Scorch said. "I can feel the sun working."

Donna put her magazine down and looked over at the group of white-haired women gossiping on the other side of the pool. "I'm bored," she said.

So was Scorch, but he hadn't wanted to admit it. "You're the one wanted to hang out by the pool," he said. "You got something else you want to do?"

"Let's go get something to eat."

"There's a place near the ferry. You got any money?"

"Oh, Scorch, you're such a gentleman." She slipped on her cover-up and grabbed her bag. "Come on," she said. "I'll buy."

Scorch pulled on his shirt, wincing as it hit his skin. They walked to the café near the ferry and ordered two sandwiches and some beers. "Let's find a seat in the shade," Scorch said.

As they ate, Donna reached across the table and pressed a finger to Scorch's forehead.

"Ow," he said.

She removed her finger and watched the spot she had been pressing turn from white to pink. "You're burned," she said. "I told you to use sunscreen."

"I'm fine," he said and sneezed into his food. "Shit. I still got this cold, though."

"Come on," she said. She stood up. "Let's go back to the condo. I think I know a way to make you feel better."

Scorch downed the rest of his beer and they walked back to Richard Golden's townhouse. Scorch dug the key out of his pocket and slipped it into the lock. It wouldn't turn. He pulled it out and shoved it back in the keyhole hard, and still it wouldn't turn.

"What the fuck!" he said.

"You got the right key?" Donna asked.

"Yeah, I got the right fucking key."

Donna hit him in the arm. "Don't shout at me!"

"Hey, I'm trying to work the lock here. Don't hit me." Scorch furiously jiggled the key, then kicked the door. "I think they changed the lock," he said.

"Another great plan. Way to go, Scorch. You said you had permission to use this place."

"I did – I do . . . Sort of."

Donna hitched her bag onto her shoulder. "I'm out of here," she said. "I'm going back to my mom's."

"Wait," Scorch said. "Wait right here. I'll go around back and come in through the sliding glass doors. I'll open the front door for you in a minute."

"Now you're gonna break in? Great."

"It's not breaking in if the back door is still open, right? Give me one minute."

He jumped down the steps and ran to the corner of the building. There were four units, and Golden's was on the end. He started toward the back but found his way blocked by an eight-foot high stucco wall. There were thick shrubs planted at the base of the wall, so it was hard for Scorch to get close enough to jump up and climb over. He stepped slowly into the bushes like he was wading into heavy surf. He slowly inched closer to the wall. As branches scratched and pulled at him, he became acutely aware of his sunburn.

When he was close enough, he jumped up and scrambled over, only to find more bushes on the other side. He dropped as carefully as he could, but still suffered a couple of stabs, cuts, and scrapes from the branches.

Once through that barrier, it was easy to find Golden's walled patio, but this was also surrounded by dense shrubs.

When the consultants were designing security systems for the condos and townhomes in Boca Cheeca, one of the strategies they suggested was planting thorny bushes around the first-floor patios and windows as a deterrent to intruders. This was such a low-cost way to keep people out that Keene construction never installed many of the recommended video cameras, but went all out with the Crown of Thorns plant. It grows easily in the Florida climate and requires minimal maintenance. The one-inch thorns and the poisonous sap were an inconvenience to the groundskeepers, but they had learned that they could deal with it with heavy leather gloves and thick protective clothing.

Scorch had neither of these, and he plunged directly into the dense thicket that surrounded the patio wall. As the thorns tore at his clothes and his sunburned skin, he let out a yell that could be heard as far as the ferry terminal.

Scorch was not one to be deterred by a lack of equipment, preparation, or knowledge, and he plunged on through the menacing thicket of thorns. He eventually reached the base of the patio wall, and climbed up and over, dropping, bloody and torn, to the flagstones.

He paused for a moment to catch his breath and assess the damage. Blood was seeping through his shredded shirt in more than a dozen places, but he had been able to keep his head and arms above the worst of it, and they were relatively undamaged.

He got back on his feet and plucked a few thorns from his jeans. He then stepped up to the sliding glass door that he had used earlier, hoping that it was still unlocked.

He grabbed the outside handle and tugged, but it didn't budge. He tried again, harder, but still nothing. Scorch then grabbed the handle with both hands, and bracing his feet against the door jamb, pulled with all his strength. The door gradually started to move, then with increasing speed, flew open and slammed against the opposite door jamb. Scorch released his grip, and with his feet not set firmly on the ground, he fell hard onto the patio.

"Son of a bitch!" he said, then laughed. "I knew you'd be open, you stupid fucking door. I knew it!"

He stood and brushed himself off, then ran his hands through his hair. "I'm coming, Donna!" he shouted, and he crossed the room to the front door. He whipped it open, a look of triumph on his face, only to have it fade when he saw that no one was there. Donna had not waited for him.

"Fuck you, Donna!" he shouted to the world. "Fuck you," he said again more quietly and slammed the door.

***

Buddy Grinnell and Alex Sotolongo stood in the garage of an unfinished mansion in Phase III, looking despondently at the jumbled pile of what was once evidence. Buddy's men had found the abandoned police cart and its contents, and after sending word to Buddy, had duly marked the area off with more calculator tape.

Alex squatted and moved a few items around with a pen. "Do you have a complete list of everything you bagged last night?" she asked.

Buddy nodded.

"Let's do an inventory and see what's missing, then

let's get all this dusted for prints and see if we can't at least find out who did this."

She stood and scanned the unfinished concrete and sand that was the floor. "There're some shoe prints here that look like a match to the print at the murder scene. Can you get a cast of these?" she asked Buddy.

"No," he said. "We don't have anything to do that."

"No problem," she said. "I'll get Roger and John down here with their evidence kits. Can you get one of your guys to fetch them?"

"Sure," Buddy said and made a call on his radio.

She looked again at the scene. Even in the shade of the garage, just standing was causing her to break into a sweat. She took off her cap and wiped her forehead with her hand, then wiped her wet hand on her pants. "Any theories, Chief?"

Buddy sighed. "Based on the size and type of shoe prints, my guess would be that it was Nelson. He's the only Keene we haven't been able to establish a timeline for, other than his mother. She's on the loose somewhere, and this is definitely the kind of thing she'd do, but she's a tiny woman. These prints couldn't be hers."

"Hey, Chief?"

Buddy turned to face Neely, who was holding a clipboard, trying to look alert and efficient.

"We checked the list. Ain't nothing missing except the clothes and briefcase we took off the kid, and Mr. Keene's cell phone."

"You're sure that's all?" Buddy asked, taking the clipboard and scanning it. "Or do I need to have Ernie double check?"

"I think that's everything," Neely said, "but there's stuff here that ain't on the list."

"Like what?" Alex asked.

"There's a pair of shorts, a T-shirt and a pair of flip-flops." Neely pointed them out to Buddy and Alex.

"That looks like Nelson's stuff," Buddy said.

"And I'll bet those sandals match the prints at our crime scene," Alex said. "Looks like we need to put an APB out on your boy Nelson."

Buddy gave a slow nod. "Yeah, I guess we do," he said. "You should probably have the dock master at Dinner Key Marina check on the Keene family's cars, too. They have a number of them. If one is missing, it should be added to the APB – Nelson's probably driving it."

"What should I give for a description?" Alex asked.

"About six feet tall, 170 pounds, light brown hair." Buddy looked at the clipboard with the missing evidence marked. "And it appears that he's dressed in a dark wool suit and black wingtip shoes."

***

Nick and Victoria were sitting side-by-side on a chaise lounge on the patio. They were close, but not touching, Nick looking down at his bare feet, and Victoria looking out at the ocean. Paul was on the other side of the pool still speaking with Charlotte Keene.

"So," Nick said. "This isn't really working, is it?"

Victoria shook her head. "No. It doesn't seem like it."

"What happened?" Nick asked. "We used to be so great together. We were like a team – you and me against the world."

"That's the problem, Nick. You see the world – you see reality – as something to be fought against. It's not. You need to grow up and be part of the world. I feel like you're still trying to find a better way, and there isn't one. This is it. This is life. You need to embrace it and do the best you can with it."

"You sound like one of those self-help books you gave me."

"Did you even read them?" she asked.

Nick laughed. "I sure did. They're fun. They're mostly full of really obvious ideas wrapped in catchy phrases, along with some platitudes, and psychobabble, and the occasional very bad suggestion. I read every one."

"I'm sure you didn't have the right attitude about it. You've got to want to improve."

"I'm sorry I'm not good enough for you, Victoria. I'm sorry that I wasn't out there trying to make the world a better place through candidate forums and fundraisers."

Victoria looked across the pool at Paul. He was still chatting with Charlotte, their heads close together as though sharing secrets. As she watched, he hopped up and ran to get her another Bloody Mary. "He sure looks the part, doesn't he? Even in this heat and in a suit, he pulls it off."

"He's kind of an idiot," Nick said.

"Your jealousy is not becoming, Nick. He's not an idiot, he's just . . . He's just . . . Okay, he may not be the smartest man in the room . . ."

"Even when he's alone."

". . . but he has good instincts. If I can help get him elected, I think he'll do good things." She trailed off as she realized Paul wasn't the issue. She looked back at Nick. "What about you, Nick, what are you going to do?"

"Well, first off, I'm probably going to get fired. My attempt to salvage the relationship with Keene Construction appears to have gone spectacularly wrong."

Victoria chuckled. "Yeah. It's hard to see how it could have possibly gone worse."

"The day is still young. I may surprise you."

They sat for a moment in silence, then Victoria slipped the ring off the third finger of her left hand and gave it to Nick. "Sorry," she said. "I think this was a mistake."

Nick took the ring and held it in his fist. "Yeah, me too," he said.

"So that's it?"

Nick nodded. "I guess so."

They stood and gave each other an awkward hug.

"Thanks for coming to my rescue, Victoria. I guess I

didn't really need legal help, but then again, Paul isn't really much of a lawyer."

"That's why he's in politics," she said. "I better get over there and prevent a scandal with the widow Keene. You take care of yourself, okay Nick?"

"Thanks," he said. "You too."

Nick watched Victoria as she crossed the pool deck and sat down beside Paul, playing chaperone. It looked like she was going to have her hands full.

SEVENTEEN

It's okay to follow the beat of your own drummer. Just make sure your drummer has rhythm first.

From – *Your Mother was Right: You'll Never Amount to Anything*

Scorch emerged from the shower feeling better. He used the towel gingerly on his sunburn, but it still came away bloody due to the open wounds from his encounter with the Crown of Thorns bush. He put his dirty jeans back on, but couldn't face the prospect of a shirt on his burned shoulders.

When he went downstairs to rummage for some beer, he discovered he had left the sliding glass door to the patio open and the temperature of the room had climbed into the eighties. He pulled on the door, and again found it stuck.

"Not again, you stupid, fucking door," he said, and prepared to do battle.

He grabbed the inside handle with his right hand, and the outside handle with his left, and again placed his right foot against the door jamb for leverage. With one big heave and a kick the door gave and shot back across the opening, dragging him with it. It slammed shut as he was letting go, and it caught the last three fingers of his left hand, crushing them between the door and the metal frame.

Scorch howled. And he kept on howling. Inarticulate at the best of times, he couldn't even form the basic curses that made up the foundation of his vocabulary. All he could do was scream like the wounded animal that he was.

After a moment, his brain began to function again, and he tried to free his trapped hand. With his right hand and foot, he flailed and kicked at the door handle, trying to get it to open. He eventually was able to get hold of the handle in his good hand, and with an adrenalin-enhanced push, slide the door enough to pull his crushed fingers free.

When Scorch saw the damage he'd done to his hand, he turned white under his sunburn and almost passed out. The three fingers that had been trapped were bent back at a ninety-degree angle right across the middle joint, and they were bleeding where the frame of the door had scraped the skin away. The fingers were crushed nearly flat.

Scorch ran whimpering to the kitchen and got some ice in a towel and applied it to his hand. He couldn't bear to look at his fingers at their unnatural angle, so he closed his eyes and just pressed his hand to the cold towel.

After a few minutes, he peeked, and then he started cursing the door, his luck, Richard Golden, Donna, and the door again.

His cursing was interrupted by knocking.

"Donna!" he yelled. "I knew you'd be back." He wrapped his hand in the towel and went to the front hall.

He swung the door open. "Shit," he said. "Now what?"

"May I come in?"

Scorch stepped aside to allow the man with the gun into the townhouse.

***

Nick slipped into the room and closed the door behind him. The shutters were closed against the heat of the mid-day sun, and he couldn't see a thing in the gloom after the brightly sunlit corridor. "Jeannie!" he whispered loudly. "Are you here?"

He heard a toilet flush, then running water, and then Jeannie stepped out of the small bathroom that adjoined her bedroom. "Nick," she said, "you found me."

"It wasn't easy," he said. "This house is huge."

"Yeah, we have a little more space than we probably need. That was my dad's style." She waved him in. "Have a seat."

"Where?"

"Oh, wait," she said. In the dim light, Nick watched her walk across the room. She opened a set of shutters, letting light in through a pair of French doors.

As the room became visible, Nick looked around for a place to sit. Nothing obvious came to view. The room was painted a cool, pale blue, with a white tile floor. It was half filled by an unmade king-sized bed that was buried under layers of clothes. There was also a small sofa and an armchair that faced a wall-mounted TV. The sofa was occupied by a scuba tank, a laptop computer, and an open pizza box that still held half a pizza. It didn't look fresh. The chair was filled by a large cardboard box containing what looked like textbooks. On the floor between the sofa and the TV was a game console and two controllers, with at least a dozen games strewn about.

"Sorry," she said. "The place is a little messy." She closed the pizza box and threw it into a corner. "Here you go."

Nick stepped gingerly through the debris field and sat on the sofa, careful not to knock the air tank onto the computer.

"I don't let any of the staff into my room. It's the only

place that's my own," she said and swept a pile of clothes off the bed and onto the floor. She sat cross-legged on the bed. "So, you said you had an interesting conversation with Walter? What's up with him?"

"There's something very strange there," Nick said. "What can you tell me about him?"

"He's a dick," she said. "And he thinks he's better than everyone else. Why? What's Walter got to do with anything?"

"He's real anxious to change accounting firms."

"That's it?" she said. "You've got a whole theory about Walter because he wants a different accounting firm? I've got news for you, Nick – no one cares that much about their accountants."

"He came to see me this morning on the boat and was making weird threats to get me fired if I didn't get his records moved. Then he told me he wanted me to get my hands on Richard Golden's personal records. I told him I'd do it for $200,000, and he agreed."

Jeannie whistled. "I take it back," she said. "Apparently Walter cares a great deal about his accounting." She thought about it a moment. "That sounds strange. Why would he want that stuff so badly?"

"I don't know, but he started agitating for the papers the minute Richard Golden died. Now he says Richard moved some of his money and he wants it back. That's what he's willing to pay me for. He says he and Richard had a business venture together. You ever hear anything about that?"

"That's news to me, but like I said, I didn't have anything to do with the business. I basically just handled the boats for my dad."

Nick's short shorts were riding up on his thighs as he sat on the soft sofa. He tugged at them discreetly while Jeannie was looking down at her fingers spread on the bed sheet.

"I also spent some quality time with your family this

morning," Nick said, "while they were waiting to be interviewed by the police. It seems like everybody would have benefitted from your dad's death. Plus I think they were really unnerved by the threat of the audit."

"That doesn't surprise me."

"I'd like to go through the company files and see who's got something to hide. If I can review the records at my office, maybe I can figure out what they were up to. That could tell us who had a real motive to murder your dad."

"That's going to be hard, with you stuck on the island."

"That's why I need your help," Nick said.

Before Jeannie could respond, the shutters were thrown open revealing a balcony beyond the French doors. Betty Keene stepped into the room.

"Mom!" Jeannie said.

"Hi, baby," Betty said, then picked her way through the litter on the floor to give her daughter a hug. "Your room is a pigsty." She looked over at Nick. "This is no way to entertain a gentleman caller."

Jeannie released her mom and said, "I've told you I don't want you climbing up here to sneak into my room. It's dangerous."

"It's only one floor up," she said. "Don't be such a baby."

Jeannie pointed to Nick. "This is Nick Rohmer. He was here for dinner last night when dad was killed, so the police haven't let him leave yet."

"We've met," Betty said. "We briefly shared a bed last night."

Nick waved. "Hi again," he said.

"Oh my God!" Jeannie said. "The boat! I forgot you were out and I let Nick use the boat. I hope he didn't scare you."

"I think I scared him," Betty said, "but we're buddies now. Who do you think dressed him this morning?"

Jeannie looked at Nick's clothes for the first time and said to her mother, "You're cruel."

"I guess it runs in the family," Betty said. She looked around for a place to sit, and decided on the bed. Jeannie sat next to her.

Betty played with the many rings on her fingers as she spoke. "I've been eavesdropping on the Keystone Cops," she said. "They aren't too hard to overhear with those squawking radios of theirs."

"What's the latest?" Jeannie asked.

"They just put out an APB on Nelson."

"What's an APB?" Jeannie asked.

"A notice to all local police to be on the look-out for Nelson, and arrest him if they spot him," Betty said.

"Why?" Jeannie asked. "He didn't do anything."

"They think they found his shoe print at the crime scene, and he stole all the evidence that Buddy had collected last night. It looks bad."

"He wouldn't do that to Dad. He couldn't."

Betty placed her hand over her daughter's. "I know that, and you know that, but all the police see is a crazy son who was apparently interfering with the investigation by tampering with the evidence. And they can't find him. It looks like he left the island."

"Just because they can't find him doesn't mean he's not here," Jeannie said. "They can't find you either."

"I know," Betty said. "They aren't the sharpest. That's why I want you to check all of Nelson's usual haunts and see if you can find him first."

Jeannie's shoulders slumped. "I spent half the night looking for him. I couldn't find him anywhere either."

Betty sighed. "Well, that's not good."

"Is there anything that I can do?" Nick asked.

Both Keene women shook their head. "Nelson's our issue," Betty said, "but thanks for asking."

"Nick thinks he can figure out who killed dad," Jeannie said.

"Maybe," Nick said. "I think we should follow the money."

"What money?" Betty asked.

Jeannie explained about the audit and Nick's thought that someone might have been desperate to stop it.

"I doubt any of that bunch has the balls for a physical confrontation, at least not with someone like Andrew," Betty said.

"But someone did."

"Maybe they hired someone," Jeanne said.

"Maybe." Betty drew the word out like she was thinking of something else. "Why don't you follow the money, Nick? Jeannie and I'll see what we can do to help Nelson."

"He can't do anything without his files," Jeannie said. "He's got to get to his office. I've already done what I can to find Nelson and come up blank. Why don't you stick around and keep an eye on the police investigation? I'm going to help Nick get to the mainland."

Betty nodded her assent. "Ok," she said. "But now that they're looking for Nelson, they're watching the ferry and the marina."

"Maybe I can sneak out with one of the skiffs," Jeannie said.

"I don't think you'd get too far. Take my jet-ski. It's beached under the bridge. Buddy's men haven't found it yet. You should be able to get to it without too much trouble."

"You have a jet-ski?"

"It's borrowed," Betty said.

"Borrowed like I shouldn't get caught on it or I'll be arrested?"

Betty nodded. "Yeah, that kind of borrowed, so be careful. I don't want the police putting out an APB on both my children."

Jeannie wrapped her arms around her mother. "Ok," she said. "You be careful, too."

Betty pointed at Nick. "And you take care of my daughter, okay?"

Nick nodded. "Yes ma'am," he said. "But it's more likely that she'll be taking care of me."

***

As Nelson passed through the gates of Everglades National Park, Gordon McCall was on his phone with the police.

"That's right. I'm being kidnapped," he said. "Yes, I think I'm near Florida City. I just saw a sign." Pause. "In Florida." Pause. "Well, that was the number saved on my phone for emergencies." Pause. "I can do that? If I dial 9-1-1, they'll know where I am?" Pause. "Hello? Hello?"

McCall looked at his phone. There were no bars.

He looked out the windows at the seemingly endless vista of scrub and sawgrass. He turned to Nelson. "You know, Rohmer, you're not only going to be fired for this, but I'm going to press charges. Is that what you want?"

As usual, Nelson didn't respond. McCall thought again about overpowering him, but he had visions of the car running off the road into a swamp and not being found for weeks. He decided to stick to his plan of waiting for the car to stop before making his move.

After forty-five minutes of monotony, during which they didn't see another car, McCall eventually spotted what passed for civilization in the Everglades – a small marina and a visitor center.

Nelson pulled the car up to the visitor center, next to a blue and white ice cream truck. He parked and got out, pocketing the keys.

McCall followed him out of the car and was assaulted by the heat and humidity. He could already feel the sweat forming under his arms. "I'm guessing this isn't a very popular spot in August," he said, not expecting a reply.

Nelson climbed in the back of the truck and after a few moments emerged with two ice cream sandwiches, one of which he handed to McCall.

"Thanks," McCall said. He tore into it, realizing for the first time that he was hungry. It was just about the best thing he ever tasted, and it was gone in three bites. "That really hit the spot," he said. "You got any more?"

Nelson jumped back in the truck and came out with another ice cream sandwich. He handed it to McCall, and pointed to the passenger seat of the truck.

"You want me in there?" McCall asked. "Are you crazy? I'm not going anywhere with you." He stood his ground and started eating the second ice cream sandwich.

Nelson shrugged his shoulders and climbed into the driver seat. When he started the truck, McCall realized he was about to be left stranded somewhere in the Everglades with no phone and no means of transportation. "Fine!" he said. "I'm coming." He climbed into the passenger seat.

As Nelson put the truck in gear, McCall said, "Hey, you forgot my suitcase."

Nelson shifted into park and hopped down to open the trunk of the Mercedes. Once he was alone, McCall jumped into the driver's seat and slammed the truck into reverse. He backed up fifty feet until he hit a curb, then he threw the truck into drive and did his best to peel out of the parking lot. He laughed in triumph as he headed back toward the park entrance.

Nelson watched him go. "Damn," he said and snapped a picture of the receding truck.

After forty-five minutes of driving through swamp, McCall's phone beeped as he came within range of a cell tower. He opened the GPS on his phone and pulled up directions to the Burnham & Fields office in Miami. The program indicated forty minutes. It wouldn't be a minute too soon for him.

EIGHTEEN

It may be lonely at the top, but on your way up, you're going to need friends.

From – *Crowdsourcing your Success*

Nick and Jeannie found Betty's jet-ski right where she had left it, under the bridge that connected the middle and northern islands of Boca Cheeca. It was tucked up tight under the little bridge and well out of sight from above.

They pushed it back into the water, and Jeannie climbed on. She patted the seat behind her. "Come on, Nick. Climb aboard."

Nick looked at the machine with concern. "Do you know how to drive one of these?" he asked.

"If it floats, I can pilot it. Come on. We need to get out of here before we're spotted."

Nick climbed on and scooched close to Jeannie as she started the motor. It was quieter than he expected.

She turned to him and said, "I'm going to head east, toward the Atlantic. We'll shoot south on the outside and cut back into the bay south of Elliott Key. They're less likely to be looking for anyone going in that direction."

"Isn't that the wrong way?" Nick asked.

"Yeah. That's why they won't be looking."

"Shouldn't we have life vests or something?" he asked.

"Yep," she said. "Hold on."

Nick wrapped his arms around Jeannie's middle and she opened the throttle slightly. The jet-ski puttered east in the little channel that divided the two islands. When she was in open water, she gave it a little more gas and turned south along the eastern shore of Boca Cheeca. When they were opposite the southernmost isle, Jeannie opened it up and they flew. They were doing at least sixty miles per hour, throwing a tall rooster tail up behind them, and bouncing over the light chop. Nick was terrified at first, and clung tightly to Jeannie, but he soon began to enjoy the ride.

They ran down the seven-mile coast of Elliott Key, and then Jeannie cut their speed and turned into a small channel just to its south. She motored west back into Biscayne Bay, then turned south again along the west side of Key Largo.

She slowed as they approached land, and then piloted them into a small channel. "Where are we?" Nick asked.

"Steamboat Creek."

"We're a long way from Miami."

"Don't worry," Jeannie said. "I have a plan."

They continued up Steamboat Creek to where it intersected Card Sound Road. Jeannie turned up a side canal that paralleled the road for about three hundred yards until they came to what looked like a derelict shack that was in imminent danger of falling into the water. She maneuvered between a few small boats and, giving the jet-ski a final burst of speed, she drove up onto the beach next to the shack.

"Here we are," she said.

"Where?"

"Keelows. It's a kind of biker and boater bar. Locals, mostly."

Nick looked the place over. From where they were standing, it looked abandoned. The wooden structure didn't have a spot of paint on it and was weathered a uniform pale gray. The roof was mostly raw tar paper, with a tattered blue tarp hung over one end that was apparently held in place with loose concrete blocks and an old tire. The remains of a deck jutted over the canal, but most of the floor was missing and one side was sagging almost to the water.

Jeannie followed his gaze. "They don't use the deck anymore."

"Really?"

She laughed. "Come on. It looks better on the inside."

She led him up the bank of the canal and around to the front, which faced onto a gravel access road. There were eight large motorcycles lined up in front, along with one pickup truck. A hand-painted sign hung above the door reading, "Keelows – always open."

Nick followed Jeannie through the front door. The bar was so dark that Nick was practically blind after the bright light of the afternoon. He wished his sense of smell had been equally dulled as he was assailed by a nauseating mixture of odors. The smell was equal parts stale beer, urine, and mold, with a strong undercurrent of vomit.

Jeannie stood a moment letting her eyes adjust, then stepped up to the bar. "Hey, Pat," she said.

Pat flashed a big smile that was missing a front tooth. "Hey Jeannie!" he said. "Long time."

"Been working. Can you set us up with a couple of beers?" she said, indicating that Nick was with her.

Pat looked suspiciously at Nick. "Sure," he said.

"What do you have on draft?" Nick asked.

Pat gave him a long, cold, look. "Beer," he said.

Nick gave a nervous laugh. "Ha. That will be great. Thanks."

As Pat drew their beers, Jeannie asked, "Is Biggie Johnson or Little Willie around?"

Pat slid a beer to Jeannie. "Biggie's in the back. Haven't seen Little Willie in weeks." He spat into Nick's beer, then slid it across the bar to him. "He might be out of town."

Nick looked at his beer, with the large gob of spit floating on top of the foam.

"Everything okay?" Pat asked.

Before Nick could answer, Jeannie slapped a ten dollar bill on the counter. "Everything's peachy, right Nick?"

Nick just nodded.

"Thanks, Pat," Jeannie said, then to Nick. "Grab your beer."

They stepped away from the bar and started threading their way through a mix of mismatched chairs and tables, some clearly broken beyond repair or use. Not for the first time, Nick wished he had his shoes. He had to peel his feet off the sticky floor after every step. "Why'd he spit in my beer?" Nick asked.

"I don't think he liked you," Jeannie said. "Let me do the talking from now on, okay? You just stand there and look good."

"Okay," Nick said. "But is this guy's name really Biggie Johnson?"

They had reached a door at the back of the bar, and Jeannie stopped and turned to Nick. "Yeah, that's the name he goes by. Little Willie, too."

"It seems that someone is trying to compensate for something," Nick said.

Jeannie held up her hand, signaling Nick not to talk. "These guys are a little touchy. I don't want you to speak. Don't ask any questions. Don't even breathe audibly unless I say to. Just stand there and drink your beer."

"Umm," Nick said.

"Just pretend to drink it then. Here we go," and with that, Jeannie opened the door to the back room.

The 'back room' was everything that the front of the bar wasn't. It was well-lit and clean, and instead of smelling like a neglected gas station bathroom, it smelled pleasantly of freshly fried food. Nick's feet didn't stick to the floor and there was a jukebox playing sixties rock in one corner. The bar itself occupied the entire wall to their right and was manned either by Pat's twin or by Pat himself, who had somehow gotten there before them.

The booths and tables were in good repair and were fairly crowded, with about half of them occupied by what appeared to be a motorcycle gang. They were wearing jeans and boots, and leather jackets or vests. They all had the same design on their backs - a pirate skull overlaid on a ship's wheel, with the words "Nautical Wheelers" across the top, and "Florida Keys" across the bottom.

Jeannie headed directly to a booth in the corner. "Hey, Biggie," she said.

Biggie looked up at Jeannie, and a broad smile broke through his scraggly beard. He stood, and she almost disappeared as he enfolded her into a hug.

Biggie Johnson was aptly named. At over six and a half feet, he was close to four hundred pounds, most of it muscle. He was dressed like the others in biker attire, with boots, jeans, and a leather vest over a T-shirt with the words "Bad Dude" across the front. His long hair was salt and pepper and mostly held back by a red bandana. He appeared to be somewhere between forty-five and sixty years old.

"Jean-bean," he said. "Where have you been?"

"You know me, Biggie. Always something going on."

"You still live in that big-ass house? You want me to come by and scare your old man again?"

Jeannie shook her head. "Thanks. Not right now, but I do need your help." She grabbed Nick's arm and pulled him closer. "We need to get to Miami, and I can't use any of my family's cars."

Biggie looked at Nick. "This a friend of yours, Jean-bean?"

She nodded.

"He must be a very brave man to come in here dressed

like that." Biggie called across the room to a skinny man drinking at the bar by himself. "Peck! Get over here."

Peck set his beer down and walked unsteadily over to where Nick and Jeannie stood in front of Biggie. He was about thirty and was dressed in dirty jeans and a dirty sweatshirt over a heavily tattooed chest.

"Give Jean the keys to your bike," Biggie told him.

"I'm fine," Peck said. "I can drive."

"You ain't fine, and that's not why you're giving them your keys. They need your ride."

Peck looked at both Jeannie and Nick. "I don't know them," he said. "Nobody rides my bike but me."

"Unless I say so," Biggie said. "I'll make sure you get home okay, and they'll make sure you get your bike back. Jean's loaded."

Peck looked Biggie up and down a moment, then handed his keys to Jeannie. "Okay," he said. "It's the red Switchback out front."

"Thanks." Jeannie turned to Biggie. "There's a jet-ski out back if you want it. It's not actually mine, but . . ."

"Okay," Biggie said. "I know someone who could use the parts. You gonna stay a minute and chat?"

"Sorry, Biggie. I've got to go. But I'll be back with the bike, or I'll let you know where to find it." She tried to give him a hug, but her arms didn't even go halfway around his massive girth. "I owe you," she said.

"Yeah, you do," Biggie said. "If you're in trouble or need anything else, you just call Biggie, okay?"

Jeannie nodded. "You bet. Thanks again."

As they turned to leave, Peck asked, "You guys gonna drink those beers?"

"Nope," she said. She grabbed Nick's beer and handed both to Peck. "Enjoy, and thanks for the loan of your bike. I'll take good care of it."

Nick and Jeannie hustled out the front and found Peck's red Harley. Jeannie climbed on, and Nick got in his usual spot behind her.

"Shouldn't we have helmets?" he asked.

"Yep," Jeannie said, then she started the motor and headed off down the gravel track toward Card Sound Road.

***

Alex and Buddy stood over the chilled body of Andrew Keene. He was in a black body bag on the floor of the walk-in cooler of the marina café. Dr. Folger was with them.

"We'll be doing a full autopsy at our facility," Alex said. "But I heard you had a good look at the body in situ. What do you think killed him – the tie or the blow to the head?"

Dr. Folger unzipped the bag to expose Andrew Keene's head. The tie was still knotted around his throat. "The blow to the head is what caused the bleeding, but I don't think it killed him. There was only a small break in the skin. The skull didn't appear to be fractured. I would say he was hit by something with a corner or sharp edge, hard enough to stun him, but not kill him."

He reached down and opened one of Andrew's eyelids. The whites were blood red. "The subconjunctival hemorrhaging indicates strangulation. The petechiae around the eyes and cheeks," he said, pointing at what looked like a red rash on Andrew's face, "is also consistent with strangulation. I'm pretty sure the necktie killed him."

He zipped the bag closed.

"Would it take a lot of strength to strangle him like that?" Alex asked.

"Not really," he said. "Not if he wasn't resisting."

Alex shook his hand. "Thank you, doctor, for your help. Would you like a copy of the autopsy when we have it, just to compare notes?"

"No, thanks," he said. "I suspect I'm right, and if I'm not, well, I'd just as soon not know that."

They stepped from the cooler back into the café's

kitchen. "We'll call you if we have any other questions," Alex said.

After the doctor left, Alex and Buddy walked out to the marina as the marine patrol boat arrived to take the FDLE team, with their recovered evidence and the body, back to the mainland.

"What else do you need from me?" Buddy asked.

"It would be nice if you could find Betty Keene," Alex said. "Also, keep an eye on the marinas so you know who's coming and going. And make sure you get those security cameras up and running again. You don't want any more dead millionaires popping up unexplained."

"What are your next moves?" he asked.

"We'll be doing some grunt work for now – checking backgrounds, phone records, that kind of thing. I'll let you know if we have any breaks."

"And what about Nelson?"

"He'll turn up," she said. "When he does, we'll have a little talk and see if we can't get inside his head."

***

Nick and Jeannie reached Brickell Avenue at about 4:00. Jeannie found a spot for the motorcycle, and they walked the half block to the offices of Burnham & Fields. As they waited for the elevator, Nick explained his plan.

"There's a good chance I'm going to be fired the moment I walk in, so I'll need you to keep them busy while I try to access the records."

"What about the files? We need the files, don't we?"

"There are no files," Nick said. "I tried to review them before I met with your dad, but Richard had shredded them all. The whole thing's very fishy."

The elevator dinged its arrival. They stepped in and Nick pressed the button for the eighteenth floor. "I think I know how to get the information we need, but I need a few minutes on the computer."

As they stepped off the elevator, the first thing that Nick saw was Lydia's moon face.

"Nick!" she said. "Where have you been? The office has been so worried about you." She looked at what he was wearing, and asked in her loudest stage whisper, "Why are you dressed like a male prostitute?"

"Lydia, this is my friend Jeannie," he said, pulling Jeannie forward to Lydia's workstation. "She's going to tell you about the worst twenty-four hours of my life, but first I have to get a few things from my desk." He started toward his cubicle, then turned to ask, "Have I been fired yet?"

"No, Nick, I don't think so," Lydia said. "Who could fire you? No one else is here."

"What about McCall?" he asked.

"You were supposed to pick him up at the airport. Did you go to the airport?"

"You mean he isn't here yet? Great. Jeannie, I'll be back in ten minutes."

Nick power-walked down the hall, bypassing his cubicle, then ran up the stairs to the executive offices. With McCall not yet there, it was the perfect chance to get at Richard Golden's computer.

Joanna's desk was still empty, so Nick dug Richard's key from her desk drawer and unlocked the office. He stepped to Richard's desk and started his computer. While he waited for it to boot, he started looking through the desk for anything that he might have missed the day before. There were no paper records of any kind, but in a bottom drawer, he found something that he could use. It was Richard Golden's backup hard drive.

Nick signed into Richard's PC. Fortunately for Nick, Richard seemed to use the same password for everything. It was always "Passw0rd1". Richard thought the zero instead of "o" was genius.

Nick hooked the drive up and started backing up all of Richard's emails, correspondence and any other documents that he could find. There was a lot of material, but the drive was fast.

While the files were being transferred, he logged in and accessed Dorothy, the company's database of scanned documents. He had administrator privileges, and quickly set up a new account for remote access under the username "GMcCall", then signed out. As soon as the file transfer was complete, he shut down the computer. He stuffed the portable hard drive into an interoffice envelope and headed back down to the lobby.

As he reached Lydia's desk, the elevator dinged, and two police officers, escorting an agitated man in a business suit, stepped off. As they approached Lydia, Nick and Jeannie stepped back out of the way.

The first officer spoke. "This man claims to work here, ma'am. Do you know him?"

"I'm Gordon McCall," the man said. "We spoke on the phone."

"Mr. McCall," Lydia said, "it's so very nice to finally meet you. Everyone here has been so worried about you. Welcome to Miami."

"Ma'am," the officer said, "are you able to identify this man as working here?"

"We've never actually met," she said, "Mr. McCall was flying in today from Chicago. Is he under arrest?"

"See?" McCall said. "May I go now?

"No. We still have the matter of the stolen ice cream truck. The bomb squad is on the way now to check it out."

"The bomb squad?" McCall asked. "Seriously?"

"The way you were circling the block was very suspicious, as was the way you abandoned the vehicle directly in front of the building," the officer said.

"I was looking for a parking space!" McCall yelled. "And I only took the ice cream truck so that I could escape."

The officer looked at his notepad, "Escape from your kidnapper? Mr. Nick Rohmer?"

"Yes. When are you going to arrest him? He's the one that's responsible for all this mess."

"Once the bomb squad gives us the all-clear, we can examine the truck. In the meantime, you'll have to come with us regarding the stolen vehicle."

Nick eased Jeannie into the elevator and pressed the button for the lobby.

"If you're looking for Nick," Lydia said, trying to look around the three men blocking her view, "he's right there." She pointed to the closing doors of the elevator.

The three men turned as the doors were beginning to close and Nick stared straight into the eyes of Gordon McCall.

"That's not Nick Rohmer," McCall said. "I've never seen that man before –"

The closed elevator doors blocked the rest of McCall's statement. "When we get to the lobby," Nick said, "we probably shouldn't hang around."

"Back to Boca Cheeca," Jeannie said.

As the elevator reached the first floor, Jeannie's phone rang.

"Hello? . . . Yes it is. . . Un-huh, do you know where he is? . . . Okay. Don't let him leave. We'll be there in twenty minutes."

"What was that about?" Nick asked.

"That was Nelson's boss. He needs us to come pick up Nelson."

"Nelson has a job?"

"Yeah. Come on. We have to get him before the police do," she said, then turned and started running back to where they had parked the motorcycle.

NINETEEN

What you don't know CAN hurt you.

From – *The Big Book of Business Platitudes*

Scorch sat in Richard Golden's kitchen, taping forks to his broken fingers. He had tried knives first, thinking they would be more bad-ass, but it hadn't worked as well as he had hoped. With a separate knife on each finger, it was hard to control what he cut or stabbed every time he moved his hand. Also, the handles were too long and got all crowded in his palm, causing his fingers to splay out in odd directions.

The forks were a little more manageable. The handles were thinner and shorter, and so better fit in his hand. With the forks extending from the ends of his fingers, he convinced himself that he was like Wolverine from X-Men.

That was, until the first time he snagged one of the forks on the back of a chair. Then he caught an edge of a doorway with one and almost passed out from the pain. They seemed to get caught on everything. He needed to come up with something better.

Scorch found a pot pie in the freezer and heated it up in the microwave. As he ate, he slowly peeled the tape from his mangled fingers and threw the forks into the sink.

Everything that had gone wrong – his cold, his sunburn, his scratched and torn body, and now the crushed fingers of his left hand – everything was the fault of Mr. Smith, or whatever his name was. And now he was stuck here when he could be with Donna for a little sympathy and first aid.

Scorch should have been more surprised when the man pushed his way into the condo with the gun, but he wasn't. With the day he'd been having, a crazy guy with an automatic seemed about right.

"You must be Mr. Scorch," the man had said. "Please sit down and don't make any sudden moves."

Scorch recognized the voice. This was the guy who had hired him to rough up Richard Golden. He went to the living room and sat in one of the white leather chairs. "I know who you are," he said.

"I sincerely doubt that," the man said, "but if you need a name, you can call me Mr. Smith." He pointed at Scorch's left hand with the gun. "What's under the towel?"

"I hurt myself," Scorch said.

"Let's see."

When Scorch unveiled his crushed fingers, Mr. Smith turned pale. "Oh my," he said. "You can cover them up again."

Scorch put his fingers back in the icy dish towel, then let out a powerful sneeze. He wiped his nose on his forearm. "Why're you waving that gun at me?" he asked. "What do you want?"

"I may have need of your services."

"You didn't pay me for the last time. Why should I do anything for you?" Scorch asked.

"If you can help me with my present circumstances, I will pay you for the bungled job you did on Richard Golden, plus a hefty bonus."

"Not interested," Scorch said. "I'm injured."

"So you are," said Mr. Smith. "But you need to be interested. First, because I'm holding a gun on an intruder so I can shoot you anytime I decide to. Second, because I happen to know there are a number of souvenirs from the Keene household in the hall closet. I assume you stole them and that they have your fingerprints on them. I could easily tie you to the murder of Andrew Keene. I just need to make a phone call."

"The murder of who?"

"Whom."

"Whatever," said Scorch. "I'll just tell them that you hired me to kill Richard Golden."

Mr. Smith laughed. "That would be an interesting allegation to prove, don't you think?"

"Fine," said Scorch. "What do you need? It better not require two hands."

"I may need you to do a little babysitting. I'm going to bring someone here, and I need you to keep them safe, but not let them leave or use the telephone. Do you think you can do that in your present condition?"

"Can I tie them up?" Scorch asked.

"Yes, but I don't want anyone injured or molested. If you need to use bonds for control, that's fine. Are you okay with this assignment, or should I notify the Boca Cheeca police about your activities here?"

"I'll need more money. Kidnapping's serious," Scorch said.

"So is murder, and you're already on the hook for that." He threw a cell phone to Scorch, who snatched it out of midair with his good hand. "That is what they call on television a 'burner phone.' Keep it close. If I need you, I'll call."

He turned to go, but paused at the front door. "See if you can splint those fingers with something. You may have need of both hands."

Once he was alone again, Scorch started to experiment

with the kitchen utensils. First he had to straighten his fingers, and the pain almost made him pass out. Once they were all pointing in the same general direction, he found some tape and grabbed a knife.

After he had exhausted the possibilities the kitchen had to offer, he turned his attention to the utility room, without success. Next, he tried the hall closet. In addition to his gold-plated souvenirs of the other night, there was a set of golf clubs and a vacuum cleaner. He toyed with the clubs for a few minutes, but they were too thin. The vacuum attachments seemed to offer some potential material, but he didn't want to go around with vacuum parts on his hand.

He looked at the golden hammer mounted to the wooden frame. The plaque read, "To Andrew Keene, in appreciation of his support. Florida Carpenters Local 332." He stood on the frame, and with his right hand, yanked the hammer off. He hefted it and liked the feel. He gently placed his left hand on it and tentatively molded his fractured fingers around the handle.

"Oh yeah," he said. "This'll work."

***

South Florida Ice Cream and Frozen Novelties Company had their international headquarters in Florida City, in southern Miami-Dade County. It consisted of rented freezer space, a two-room office, and a parking area that held their five ice cream trucks. They had a few regulars who leased a truck by the week and ran a fixed route, and some of the trucks were only rented out for special events.

Nelson had a weekly lease, and more often than not, he just drove the truck around South Florida at random, stopping and selling ice cream when the idea occurred to him. His route was paid for by Jeannie as a way to keep Nelson engaged and out of trouble, and he seemed to like the freedom.

When Jeannie and Nick pulled up on their borrowed motorcycle, they found Nelson sitting on the ground in the parking lot, leaning against the front wheel of the Mercedes. He had his camera out and was taking pictures of something in the sky that only he could see.

Jeannie parked the bike and came over to her brother. "Hey, Nelson," she said. "What're you doing?"

Other than taking a quick photo of Jeannie, he ignored her and went back to taking pictures of nothing.

Jeannie turned to Nick. "You stay here and keep an eye on him, okay? I'm going to go talk to Danny."

Nick nodded and watched as Jeannie went into the office. He observed Nelson for a few moments, then asked, "What are you taking pictures of, Nelson?"

Nelson fiddled with the camera and handed it to Nick. On the screen, at extreme zoom, a hawk was visible, wings outstretched, soaring on the wind. Nick looked up, and could see nothing more than a speck high overhead.

He handed the camera back to Nelson. "That's one hell of a zoom, and you have a sharp eye," he said.

Nelson nodded and resumed taking pictures.

"You know, that's my suit you're wearing. I don't think you're doing it any favors by sitting in the gravel."

Nelson stood and brushed off the pants.

"Any chance you'd be willing to swap clothes so I can get my suit back?" he asked.

Without a word, Nelson set down his camera and started to undress. When he was down to his underwear, he handed the bundle of clothes to Nick. "Thanks," Nick said. "You can have this wonderful outfit." He set his suit on the ground and stepped out of his short shorts and tank top and gave them to Nelson before redressing in his own clothes. He draped the suit coat over his shoulder, since it was still over ninety degrees.

"Where're my shoes?" he asked, looking at Nelson's bare feet.

Nelson just shrugged.

"How about my briefcase?"

Nelson jerked his thumb over his shoulder, indicating the briefcase was in the car.

Jeannie returned from the office. As she crossed the steaming parking lot, she said, "Well look who's all suited up again. I like the 'no tie, no shoes' look. Very office casual."

"Thanks" Nick said.

"You ready to go?" she asked and opened the car door.

"What about the motorcycle?" Nick asked.

"The three of us can't all ride on a motorcycle, can we?" She climbed into the driver's seat and started the motor. "Well, come on," she said. "Who wants to ride shotgun?"

Nick opened the back door but hesitated to get in. Nelson was still taking pictures, this time of Nick and Jeannie.

"Nelson, are you coming?" Jeannie asked.

Nelson just shook his head.

Jeannie's voice became firm like she was talking to a child. "Nelson, come on. We have to go home."

"No," he said.

Jeannie cut the engine and climbed out of the car, planting herself in front of Nelson. "Nelson, we have to go home. You can't stay here," she said.

He just shook his head.

"What's the matter?" Jeannie asked him, her voice more gentle.

"Dad."

"Dad's dead, Nelson. He can't hurt you anymore."

Nelson shook his head again and started to cry.

"What is it?" Jeannie asked. She laid a hand on his shoulder. "What's the matter?"

"I," he said, sobbing. "I . . . I . . ."

"You what?"

"Killed . . ."

"No you didn't, Nelson," Jeannie said, her voice firm.

"I . . ." he said, still sobbing. "Pushed . . ."

"You pushed him?"

Nelson nodded.

"You pushed him and he hit his head, right?"

Nelson nodded again.

"That's not what killed him, Nelson. Do you hear what I'm saying? He hit his head and was knocked out, but that isn't what killed him. Someone came in while he was unconscious and put Nick's tie around his neck and . . . You didn't kill him."

"Pushed," Nelson said. "Shoved. He tripped. Hard."

Jeannie put her arms around Nelson and held him tightly. "It wasn't you," she said. "You and dad just had a fight, like always. Someone else killed him, Nelson. It wasn't you."

Now both Nelson and Jeannie were crying in each other's arms. Nick didn't know if he should watch or look away, so he ended up kind of glancing, then looking away, then peeking again. Eventually, the tears subsided and Jeannie released her brother.

"Come on, Nelson," she said. "It's time to go home." She wiped her tears, and then wiped her brother's. "It's okay. Everything's okay now."

She walked back to the driver's side door and signaled to her brother. "It's time to go."

Nelson got in the passenger seat, and Jeannie started the car. With a short spray of gravel, they were off, headed back to Boca Cheeca Key.

***

Victoria sat in the lengthening shadows of the Keene house, with a disconsolate eye on Paul Gonzalez-Smith. He had not left the side of Charlotte Keene for more than ten minutes since their arrival that morning. He and the widow were still engaged in a tete-a-tete, and Victoria had had about all she could take. She should have left when

Paul had told her to cancel that night's forum. He suddenly had "pressing matters" that would prevent him from attending.

She checked her watch and decided that she was leaving on the next ferry with or without Paul. She walked over to where the pair were urgently whispering to each other and cleared her throat.

Paul looked up. "Yes, Vic?"

"I've got to leave. I have commitments in the city that I have to keep," she said.

"Okay," he said. "Thanks for waiting for me, but I'll catch a later boat."

"It was so nice to meet you," Charlotte said and extended a hand.

Victoria took her hand out of habit. "We have a couple of appointments for tomorrow morning," she said to Paul. "Should I assume that you'll be there?"

"Of course, Vic. If anything changes, I'll call you."

"Fine," she said. "See you tomorrow."

She gathered her things and stepped from the patio into the Keene house, not sure at that point which way to turn to find the front door.

An older gentleman whom she had seen a few times moving about on the patio saw her hesitation and came up to her. "Are you Victoria?" he asked.

"Yes, I am. And you are?"

"I'm Walter Hughes," he said and extended a hand. "I work for Keene Construction. Nick is working on a special project for me."

"Nick is working for you?"

"Yes," Walter said. "He seems like a real go-getter. I think that we've come to a mutually satisfactory understanding about this accounting business. You're very lucky to have found such a conscientious young man."

"Thank you," Victoria said. "Conscientious?"

"Extremely," Walter said. "I wish that we had been working directly with him before. He's such a breath of fresh air after stuffy old Richard Golden."

"Wow," Victoria said. "I guess he really stepped up. I always knew that he had it in him."

Walter offered Victoria his arm, and she took it. "If you like," he said, "I can show you back to the ferry. However, Nick and I are due to meet shortly to conclude our business. I thought we might have a celebratory dinner. It would make the evening infinitely more interesting if you could join us."

"Oh, I don't know," she said. "I should really get back to Miami. I have a full slate of appointments for tomorrow."

"Don't be silly. We'll have you back home tonight. How often do you get to celebrate something like this with your fiancé?"

Victoria realized that Walter was not aware of their split, and she decided this was not the time to get into that. Besides, after the way that Paul had treated her all day, it might be nice to have a little attention paid to her.

"All right," she said, "but I really need to get back to Miami tonight."

"You have my word," Walter said, as he took her arm and guided her out of the Keene house.

TWENTY

If no one is following you, you're not a leader. You're just weird.

From – *Worker Bees Never Get to Enjoy the Honey*

Jeannie pulled the black car into the parking lot at Dinner Key Marina. After she killed the engine, she turned around to face Nick.

"I don't think they'll be watching for us on this side. If we take one of the Keene boats, we probably won't have a problem until we get to Boca Cheeca. That side will be trickier."

"We can't afford to have this hard drive confiscated," Nick said. "We have to find a way to get ashore without being seen."

"I know. Here's my plan – I'll go around the back way, like we did this afternoon, and drop you and Nelson at the beach where we went swimming. Then I'll come around the island and pull into the marina by my little ol' self. What do you think?"

"You're the boat expert," Nick said. "If you think it'll work . . ."

"What about you, Nelson?" she asked. "You okay with that?"

He just shrugged.

"Okay. Grab your stuff and let's go."

They made their way along the maze of docks, passing boats of every description. In every direction Nick looked, there was a forest of sailboat masts and rigging. They eventually reached a dock blocked by a locked gate marked "Private". Jeannie worked the lock, and they were through, among the many vessels in the Keene Construction fleet. There were tugs and barges, speedboats, cabin cruisers, fishing boats, skiffs and jet boats of every size. All were painted some variation of green and yellow.

"You guys own all these?" Nick asked. "Why?"

"When you run a construction company from an island," Jeannie said, "you tend to collect boats. Come on. Here's our ride." Jeannie stopped in front of an open deck boat with a single outboard and a console in the middle. "Hop in."

"This is it?" Nick asked as Nelson jumped on board. "It seems kind of small."

"That's so we can get up onto the beach to drop you off. Anything bigger, you'll have to swim to shore."

"I don't mind swimming," Nick said.

"I doubt that hard drive would survive."

"Oh, yeah." Nick reluctantly and carefully climbed onto the boat and looked for a place to sit.

"At least it's bigger than a jet-ski," Jeannie said.

Jeannie and Nelson cast off with the easy rhythm of long practice, and they quickly made their way out to the channel. She opened up the throttle, and the boat rode up out of the water and bounced lightly from swell to swell. It wasn't as fast or as exciting as their ride earlier in the day, but it was a lot drier.

The heavy clouds that had been hanging in the west over the Everglades had dissipated and the bright afternoon sun lit the sky and water an almost uniform blue along the eastern horizon. A flock of pelicans in a lopsided V formation soared north, across their path. Nick watched as one of them plunged into the sea, its bill thrust forward and wings folded back. It came up with something in its pouch, and tilting its head back, swallowed it down.

"Hey, Nelson, can I borrow your camera?" Nick asked. He made a gesture like he was snapping a picture. Nelson passed it over, and Nick spent several minutes taking shots of the pelicans, the blue sky, and the distant outline of Boca Cheeca Key.

Nick felt relaxed for the first time in days. He was enjoying the motion of the boat on the water and the wind in his hair as they cut across the bay to the southeast.

As they neared the middle of the bay, Jeannie's phone rang. She pulled it from her pocket. "Unknown caller," she said to Nick.

"Better answer it."

Jeannie throttled the engine back, and as the boat settled into the water, she picked up the call.

"Is this Jeannie?"

"Yes," she said. "Who's this?"

"This is Walter Hughes. I'm looking for Nick Rohmer and I thought there was a good chance that he might be with you."

She looked at Nick and mouthed "Hughes".

Nick held out his hand for the phone. "Yes, Mr. Hughes?"

"Aw, Mr. Rohmer. Do you know what time it is?"

Nick glanced at the phone's screen. "It's a little after six."

"Good. You're aware of that much at least. And what were you supposed to have done by the end of the business day? Do you remember?"

"Of course. About that . . ."

"I sense an excuse forming," Walter said.

"Not at all. I have what is probably both good and bad news," Nick said.

"A dichotomy. I can hardly wait."

"There are no files to transfer. Richard shredded them all."

"I assume that's the good news?"

"Well, yeah. The bad news is there are no files to transfer."

"I'm going to give you the benefit of the doubt here and assume that you are telling me the truth. It sounds very much like something that Richard would do. Covering his tracks before he leaves town." Walter paused. "What about my other project?" he asked.

"I'm working on it," Nick said.

"You have nothing to report on that front?"

"Not yet."

"Well, I have some good news and some bad news for you, Mr. Rohmer. Would you like the good news or the bad news first? Don't answer," he said. "Here's the bad news. I'm rescinding my offer to pay you a finder's fee if you locate my missing funds."

"Okay," Nick said, "So I guess I'm off the case?"

"Not at all," Walter said. "I still need you 'on the case,' as you put it."

Nick hesitated a moment before asking, "Why would I do that? Why would I still be helping you?"

"Aha!" Walter said. "Now we get to the good news. I have your fiancée here with me. Say hello, Victoria."

"Nick," Victoria shouted. "Call the police! I'm –"

"Shut her up!" Walter yelled to someone on his end of the call. Then he said to Nick, "There's your incentive, Nicholas. If you don't find my money, I will make very bad things happen to your lovely bride-to-be."

All of the color drained from Nick's face and the hand that held the phone started to tremble. He stood up in the boat and looked toward Boca Cheeca in the distance. "If you so much as touch her, I swear to God . . ."

"What? You'll do what? You can't do a thing. You're impotent. If you call the police, I'll kill her. If you try to find her, I'll kill her. If you don't find my money by this time tomorrow, I'll kill her. In fact, if I don't get progress reports from you every three hours, I will start to cut parts of her off and save them for you in little baggies."

Nick heard Hughes take a deep breath. "So, there's your incentive, Nicholas. Call me in three hours with an update."

With that, the call was disconnected.

***

Walter Hughes put his phone down and turned to Scorch and Victoria. "You don't think that was over the top, do you?"

Victoria, tied to a chair and with a dishtowel jammed in her mouth, was unable to answer. Scorch shook his head. "You've got to make 'em sweat if they're gonna do what you tell them."

"Thank you for your constructive feedback, Mr. Scorch. I'm sure that it is well intended." Walter did a quick survey of the townhouse. "Please make sure that you keep all the shades drawn, and don't let her near any doors or windows. And please keep your phone out of her reach."

He walked to the kitchen and looked in the refrigerator. "Do you need any food or supplies?"

"How long we gonna be here with her?" Scorch asked, nodding in the direction of Victoria.

"Shouldn't be more than twenty-four hours," Walter said, "but you never know. I'll bring a few things when I come back. In the meantime, just please keep her under control."

"Who do you think you're talking to?" Scorch said.

"You," Walter said. "I'll be back in a few hours. Call me if there are any problems."

Walter left through the front door, locking it behind him.

Scorch turned to Victoria. "You like that rag in your mouth?"

She shook her head.

"If I take that out, you promise not to scream?"

She nodded.

"If you're lying, you're gonna be really sorry. See this hand here?" He raised his hand, wrapped and taped to the golden hammer. "You make so much as a whimper, and Thor here will smash you upside the head."

Victoria flinched at his touch as he pulled the towel from her mouth and dropped it at her feet. "That's gotta feel better, right?" he said. "I know I hate it when they stuff shit like that in my mouth. Makes me gag."

"Thank you," Victoria said, her voice almost a whisper.

***

Jeannie nudged the beach with the bow of the boat, and both Nick and Nelson jumped off. With little more than their feet wet, they moved up the sand while Jeannie put the motor in reverse and backed off into deeper water.

"I'll meet you in my room," Jeannie said. "Get started on those files, and keep Nelson out of sight."

Nick gave Jeannie a thumbs up, as she powered away to the south. He turned to Nelson. "What's the best way to get into your house unseen?"

Nelson pointed down the beach, toward the screen-enclosed patio.

"Okay," Nick said, then he stopped. "Hey, where's your camera?"

Nelson put his hand to his chest, then looked at their small boat as it receded to the south.

"Don't worry," Nick said. "Jeannie'll take good care of it. Let's go." He started to walk along the shore, just above the tideline. After about ten yards, he turned to ask Nelson a question, only to find that he was now alone on the beach. He turned and ran back, retracing his path in the sand until he got to the point where Nelson's footprints had diverged from his, turning off the beach into the undergrowth.

"Nelson!" Nick said, in a whispered shout. "Nelson!" Nick tried to track Nelson's footprints, but they quickly became untraceable in the brush. "Son-of-a-bitch!" he said.

After standing indecisively on the beach for a few moments, Nick turned and headed again toward the Keene house's beach access. He stepped through the screen door, and found the patio mostly empty, except for the figures of Paul Gonzalez-Smith and Charlotte Keene cozied up to a portable bar that had been set up near the house.

Nick stepped up to Paul and gave him a shove that almost pushed him off his stool.

"Hey!" Paul said. "What was that for?"

"Where the hell is Victoria?"

"I don't know," Paul said. "She left here about two hours ago. She's probably home by now."

"Really? Did you walk her to the ferry? Do you know if she got home okay, or were you too busy schmoozing with Lottie Mellons here to care?"

"Victoria knows how to take care of –. Lottie Mellons?"

"Didn't you know?" Nick said. "That was her stage name before she married Andrew Keene."

Paul turned to Charlotte. "Really?" he said. "Of the Pittsburgh Mellons?"

Charlotte patted his arm like she was comforting a child. "No. A different branch of the family," she said. She turned to Nick. "I assure you there's no reason for concern. This is a very safe community."

"Well it wasn't very safe for your husband," Nick said. He turned to Paul. "And you're an asshole."

Paul and Charlotte watched Nick as he walked away in his bare feet and suit, his briefcase in hand.

"What do you suppose that was about?" Charlotte asked.

Paul shrugged. "You got me," he said. "I've never really understood what Victoria sees in him."

***

Officer Ernie Ruiz was on duty at the front desk of the Boca Cheeca security office, reading a recent Sports Illustrated that someone had left, when he heard the door open and sensed someone standing in front of him. Without glancing up from his magazine, he held up one finger. "Be with you in just a moment," he said and went on reading.

After the promised moment, he looked up and gave his visitor his full attention. "Holy shit!" he said and hit the button that locked the front door. "Good evening, Nelson. We've been looking everywhere for you. Please have a seat."

Nelson sat and waited while Ernie called Buddy Grinnell on the radio.

"Yeah, what is it?" Buddy asked.

"You'll never guess who just walked into the station, Chief."

"I don't want to play games, Ernie. I'm trying to eat dinner. Who is it?"

"Nelson Keene's here, sir. He's in the waiting area and I have it locked down."

"No shit! Don't let him leave. I'll call Alex and let her know they can cancel the APB. I'll be there in ten minutes."

Ernie turned his attention to Nelson. "Can I get you anything, Nelson?"

Nelson nodded and made the universal gesture for "I need a pen and pad to write on."

Ernie came around the counter and handed the writing supplies to Nelson, then watched as he wrote a long paragraph. After a few minutes, Nelson handed it back. Ernie read it. "Wow," he said. "This is serious stuff. You want me to call your attorney or someone?"

Nelson just shook his head.

"I need to you sign this," Ernie said and handed it back. Nelson signed it and held out his hands, as though to be cuffed.

"No need for that right now. Let's wait for the Chief."

Ernie got back on his radio. "Chief?"

"What is it, Ernie?"

"Nelson just wrote out and signed a confession to the murder of his father. I think we just solved our first murder case."

"And hopefully our last," Buddy said. "Hang in there a few more minutes. I'm on my way."

There was a knock on the door to the security office as Buddy disconnected. Ernie looked out through the glass and saw the rainbow-haired form of Betty Keene.

She banged on the door again. "Let me in!" she shouted. "I'm here to confess to the murder of Andrew Keene."

TWENTY-ONE

You can rest when you're dead.

From – *CEO or Else*

When Jeannie got to her room, she found Nick cursing and gripping the laptop so hard, she thought he was about to snap it in two.

"Easy, boy. You're going to blow a gasket," she said.

Nick released the computer, but was so frustrated, he couldn't speak.

"I take it everything didn't go as planned," she said. "Is there something wrong with my laptop?"

"No!" Nick tried to compose himself. "Sorry, Jeannie. No. Your laptop's fine. It's me. I'm an idiot."

"Take a deep breath and tell me what's going on."

"It's the hard drive. It's encrypted and I can't open a goddamn thing."

"Why? You were able to use it at the office, right?"

"Yeah. Apparently it's only usable when connected to Richard's computer, or if I have the password. We don't have that computer and for once, Richard used a different password that I can't guess. We're screwed, and now

Walter's going to kill Victoria because of me."

"This isn't your fault," Jeannie said. "We'll figure this out and get her back." She came and knelt next to Nick and put an arm around him. He was on the floor in front of the sofa, where he had cleared a workspace. "You can do this, Nick. I know you can."

"Victoria never believed I was good enough," he said, "and I'm proving her right."

Jeannie removed her arm and slapped Nick on the back of the head.

"Hey," Nick said. "That hurt."

"Pull it together, Nick. That attitude isn't going to do you or her any good." Jeannie climbed onto the bed and sat with her legs crossed. "Where's Nelson? I have his camera."

"Oh. That's another screw-up that's my fault. Two minutes after you dropped us on the beach, he disappeared into the bushes and I lost him. I have no idea where he's gone."

"Damn him," Jeannie said. "That's not your fault either. He's impossible. I never know what's going on in his head. I hope he hasn't done something stupid."

"I'm sorry. I just turned my back for a moment . . ."

"I lose him all the time," Jeannie said. She walked over to her balcony and looked down at the pool and patio for a moment, then came back in and stood over Nick. "I just hope he stays out of sight. He's good at that."

She watched Nick as he typed on the laptop. "What are you doing? Can you do anything without the password?"

He nodded. "I set up a backdoor account into the company's computer so that I can access scanned files and financial statements. It's not going to tell us how Richard moved his personal funds around, though. That's what we need to know."

"What will it tell you?"

"I might be able to see what kind of financial irregularities are going on with the company. It might give us something we can use against Walter."

"Is there anything I can do to help?"

"I think if we're going to figure this whole thing out, we're going to have to go back to Burnham & Fields and log back into Richard's computer."

"Yikes," Jeannie said. "That may not be so easy a second time." She paused a moment. "Why don't you do what you can right now with what you've got? Figure out what Walter's up to. I'll go get us something to eat and see if I can find my mom to let her know Nelson's back on the island. We need to rest and regroup. What do you think?"

"Sounds like we're wasting time. We've got to find Victoria and get her out of that crazy man's hands."

"The only way to do that is to figure him out, so get to work."

"One other thing," Nick said. "I found these cell phones in the briefcase. Do you know whose they are? One looks like it might be Nelson's."

Jeannie picked up the phone with a case that looked like an old Hasselblad camera. "This is Nelson's." She picked up the other one and turned it over in her hand. "I think this is my dad's," she said. "It must have been in the pile of stuff that Nelson stole from the police."

"Can I see it?" She passed the phone to Nick and he turned it on. "Do you know the PIN?"

"1 - 2 - 3 - 4. My dad wasn't into complex passwords."

Nick entered the PIN and pressed a few icons. Suddenly, Andrew Keene's voice was saying: "Note: Why are we changing accounting firms? Consider scheduling a full audit? Discuss with Walt."

"What the hell is that?" Jeannie asked.

"Your dad used the phone's voice memo function for reminders. This is a note he made when I met him after Richard's funeral." Nick pressed the screen a few times and Andrew's voice spoke again: "Note: Invite Nick Rohmer to dinner to discuss decision of the 'Audit Committee.'"

"I think he used this a lot," Nick said. He went to the next message: "Note to Phil: One guest for dinner. Let's put on a show."

Nick pressed the screen again: "Note: Schedule full audit with Burnham & Fields. What were Walt and Richard up to?"

"So he really was going to request a full audit. You know what that means?"

Jeannie shook her head.

"That means we'll have a motive if we can show Walter was stealing from the company." He queued up the next message: "Note: Schedule an appointment with Doctor Garrison to commit Nelson."

"And that sounds like a motive for Nelson," Jeannie said.

"That's the last note," Nick said. He played it again. "It doesn't mean that Nelson knew, or that he did anything."

"Can I see the phone?" Nick handed it to her, and with a few touches on the screen, she deleted the last message. "He didn't do it," she said in answer to Nick's look. "We have all the motive we need for Walter. Why else would he be holding Victoria? Let's concentrate on getting him put away, and getting Victoria back."

Nick took the phone back and turned it off without saying anything.

"You mad?" Jeannie asked.

"No," Nick said. "You're right. That'd just be a distraction. Nelson isn't our problem right now." Nick looked at the time on the computer screen. "I've got to call Walter in about ninety minutes with a status report. Let me see if I can find something to tell him."

"Okay. I'll be back." She put her hand on Nick's shoulder. "You can do it, Nick."

"I guess we're going to find out," he said.

***

Buddy Grinnell sat across from Betty Keene with her signed confession in his hand. He read it through for the third time, then set it down. He considered her five-foot frame and guessed her weight at no more than one hundred pounds.

"So you overpowered Andrew? Exactly how did you do that? Your confession isn't clear on that point."

"I'm stronger than I look," she said. "I snuck up behind him and hit him over the head with one of those brass bookends. Once he was down, I just strangled him."

"And how did you strangle him?" Buddy asked.

"It's all right there, Buddy. I used the accountant's tie that was sitting there."

"What color was the tie?"

Betty hesitated. "It was hard to see in that light. Blueish red?"

"And the stripes?" Buddy asked.

"I don't know. They were dark."

"There weren't any stripes. It has small dots on it."

"Stripes, dots, what difference does it make? I did it. I killed him."

"Betty, why're you doing this? You and I both know you didn't kill Andrew."

"That's not true. I did it, just like I said there," she said, pointing at her confession.

"I have a written confession from Nelson, too. You know that, right?"

"Everyone knows that Nelson's crazy," Betty said. "You can't believe anything he tells you."

Buddy smiled. "This from the lady that was committed to the looney bin."

"We don't call it that anymore," she said. "We prefer the term 'nut house.'"

"If you're trying to protect Nelson, you don't need to. I'm reasonably sure that he didn't do it either."

"There you go," she said. "We both agree that he didn't do it." She idly twisted one of her eyebrow studs. "So, tell me why you think it wasn't Nelson."

"We got the autopsy report this afternoon. Andrew was strangled, much as you describe it in your statement here, with the necktie. Funny thing is, Nelson makes no mention of the tie in his confession. He says they had a shoving match, Andrew tripped and hit his head. He thinks that was what killed him. It wasn't."

"So you're not going to arrest Nelson?" Betty asked.

"The FDLE will take him in and question him. They may hold him for a while, but I don't think they can make a case, even with this confession. Nelson was gone before Andrew was killed." Buddy held up Betty's confession. "You're not helping him with this. You want to help your son, get him some good legal counsel and maybe some psychiatric treatment. The boy's got issues."

"I need to be with him," Betty said. "If they lock him up alone, I don't know what kind of damage it might do to him. Can I stay with him once the FDLE takes him in?"

"It's not summer camp. You two can't share a cell. But if you tear this up, I think I can arrange that you'll be kept close for the whole time he's in custody. I think I can get them to agree to that much."

"Let me see that confession again," Betty said.

Buddy handed it over and Betty tore it up. "Thanks, Buddy," she said.

"Get him some help, okay? Now that Andrew's gone, maybe your family can start to heal."

She smiled. "Look at the tough guy getting all touchy-feely. Next you'll have us all holding hands and singing Kumbaya."

"I would never do that unless there were s'mores involved." Buddy got up and offered a hand to Betty. "Come on," he said. "Why don't you wait with Nelson? The FDLE won't be here for a while yet."

***

Gordon McCall sat alone in an interview room at the Miami-Dade Police Department. He had been there about ten minutes when a tall dark-haired man in an expensive suit was ushered in to meet him.

The man held out a hand. "I'm Jimmy Delgado. Your office in Chicago retained me to represent you."

McCall took the offered hand and shook it with a force born of relief and gratitude. "Thank God," he said. "I'm Gordon McCall."

"So, Mr. McCall –"

"Gordon."

"So, Gordon, how are you enjoying your visit to Miami?"

Gordon looked around at the gray institutional and windowless walls, the well-worn metal table and chairs, and the stained ceiling of the interview room. "I can't say much about the accommodations," he said.

Delgado gave McCall one of his business cards. "I hear you've had a strange day," he said. "I suspect a few details either got lost or mangled in the retelling. So how about you tell me how it is you left Chicago this morning a respected business professional and ended up in Miami this afternoon as a car thief."

"You're going to want to sit down for this," McCall said. "And take notes. It gets a little weird."

McCall recounted the whole story: being picked up at the airport, getting abducted to the dark heart of the Everglades, making his daring escape in the ice cream truck, and eventually being arrested just feet from the office that had been his goal.

"You've had a full day," Delgado said.

"It's been memorable."

"I can get you released on bond. Tomorrow, I'll talk to the owner of the ice cream vending business that owns the truck and get his side of this to see if we can't figure out what happened. With no harm to the vehicle, my guess is we can get this dropped."

"That would be great. How soon can I get out of here?"

Delgado looked at his watch. "There's some paper-work, and you'll have to come up with the bail money. I'd say about an hour. So hang in there."

McCall stood and took Delgado's hand in both of his and started shaking it vigorously again. "Thank you, Jimmy. You're the only person that's been willing to help me. I really appreciate it."

"I hope you appreciate it just as much after you receive my bill."

TWENTY-TWO

Before you stick it to the man, make sure the man isn't you.

From – *The Cubicle Insurgency*

Jeannie returned to her room with a large bag of potato chips and a wrapped sandwich on a plate.

"Sorry I was gone so long," she said. "I finally found Nelson and my mom."

Nick was still working on the computer and scribbling notes on a pad of paper. "Oh?" he said.

Jeannie tried reading over his shoulder, but it was all hieroglyphics to her. "Yeah. Nelson turned himself in and then my mom turned herself in to protect him. It's a mess."

"Yeah?" Nick said.

She kicked him lightly with her bare foot. "Did you hear what I just told you? My mom and brother turned themselves in to the police. They're competing to see who can take the rap for my dad."

"Sorry," Nick said, looking up at her for the first time. "I wasn't listening. So they've been arrested?"

"Yeah, I guess. The cops are going to hold onto them."

"You don't seem too upset about it."

"No one believes they did it, so I guess it could be a good thing," Jeannie said. "At least now I know where they are and they're out of harm's way."

"Is that food?" Nick said.

Jeannie sat down next to Nick and set the plate between them. "Yep. I tracked down someone in the kitchen. It's a BLT. It's all I could scrounge up."

"I'm starved," Nick said. He grabbed half of the sandwich and swallowed it in two bites. "You gonna eat the other half?" he asked.

"I already ate mine," she said. "It's all yours."

"You rock. Thanks."

She looked at his scribbled notes again. "What're you working on there? Looks complicated."

"There's a lot of funny business going on with the company books," Nick said around a mouthful of half-chewed sandwich. "Everybody seems to have a hand in the pot. You familiar with the term 'financial malfeasance?'"

Jeannie shrugged. "Sort of, I think."

"That's when someone intentionally messes with the company finances for personal gain. In other words, they steal from the company. In the case of Keene Construction, it looks like it was fun for the whole family. You got anything to drink?"

"Sorry, no. You can get some water from the sink. Tell me what you figured out."

Nick got up and stepped to the bathroom. He came back with a plastic cup of water. "Ok," he said. "There are several things that would get flagged in an audit, some of them pretty serious, but the really big one is the scam that Richard and Walter were running."

"Okay, so what were they doing?"

"It's kind of complicated and technical."

"You want me to ask you to explain it, don't you?" Jeannie said.

Nick nodded. "Yeah. I really want to lay it out for you."

"Can you just summarize it? I don't have much tolerance for accounting."

"I'll try." Nick grabbed his pen and pad and sat on the bed. "Sit here," he said. "I have to draw some of this, and my legs are sore from sitting on the floor."

She sat next to him and he turned to a clean sheet of paper.

"Keene Construction makes most of their money buying raw land, improving it, then selling it off in small pieces for a lot more than they paid for it. They also make money from building the houses and condos and such, but the big money is in the land."

"Okay," Jeannie said.

"Let's take this island as an example." Nick drew a rough circle on the page and labeled it 'island'. "The company buys this island and it's 1,000 acres." Nick wrote "1,000 acres" in the corner of the page.

"Now they've got to 'improve' the land, meaning get it ready for building. They knock down all the trees, fill in the swampy areas, grade it out all nice and smooth. Then they have to put in roads and water lines and sewers." Nick drew random lines around the perimeter of the 'island' and crisscrossed the middle. "These are the roads and utility rights-of-way. They use up land. So of the original 1,000 acres, maybe fifty acres are now roads and can't be sold." He scribbled "- 50" in the corner.

"This is an upscale development, right? So there have to be some green spaces and parks and stuff like that." Nick started to draw irregular blotches on the 'island' and filled them in. "These are the parks. There are also some facilities that take up space, like a water treatment plant, and the police department. Maybe a library." Nick sketched some stick buildings on his drawing. "In Boca Cheeca, they had to build the marina and all the surrounding structures, and that takes up more land that can't be sold." He wrote "-200" in the corner.

"Okay," Jeannie said.

"So, of the original 1,000 acres, we now have only about 750 left for building." Nick started to draw lines perpendicular to his 'roads'. "Now the remaining land gets divided into lots to be sold, like this. Up until now, the company owned all this as one big lump. Now they have to get the land platted so they can sell off the individual lots. The land is surveyed and maps are submitted to the county showing where the lots are, and the county clerk records who owns the lots, so when they're sold, the county has a record, and everybody knows who owns what and you don't have any land disputes. The lots get sold off for many thousands, or in the case of Boca Cheeca, millions of dollars and that all goes back to Keene Construction. Profit made."

"Okay," Jeannie said. "So where's the problem?"

"If you did this to a perfectly square and flat piece of land, with regular roads and parks and stuff, it would always come out the same. You'd start with X number of acres of raw land, use Y number of acres for infrastructure, and sell exactly X minus Y acres as lots. But the real world is messier. Land is irregular, roads curve, municipal buildings and utilities have to fit the terrain. It's not always the same."

"And?" Jeannie said.

"And, I think Richard and Walter were taking advantage of your father's 'big picture' approach and fudging the math on the improvements so that more land was being sold than Keene Construction recorded."

"Huh?"

"Using this example," Nick said, indicating the now unrecognizable drawing of his hypothetical island, "they may have used only 200 acres for improvements, but showed on the books that 250 were used. So the company only expects to sell 750 acres and Richard and Walter sell the other 50 acres for themselves."

"How? The land's still here. They can't steal it."

"Ah, but they did," Nick said. "When Walter sent the plat map to the county, he showed that most of the lots were owned by 'Keene Construction, Inc.' We'll call that company 'Keene Inc.' Keene Inc. sold the lots to the new property owners and that money went on the company books. But, for some of the lots, he showed the owner as 'Keene Construction, Ltd.' When those lots got sold, the money went to Keene Ltd."

"Who's Keene Ltd?"

"Aha! That was my question. I thought it might be a foreign subsidiary of Keene Inc., but it isn't. It doesn't show up in any of the company financials. Turns out, it's a Bahamian shell company. I found the records online."

"Okay. So let me see if I understand this," Jeannie said. "Walter put some of the lots under the name of a fictitious company that he and Richard controlled, and when the lots were sold, the money went to their fake Bahamian company instead of my dad?"

"Yeah. And since Richard was doing the accounting and auditing, he could fudge the books to cover their tracks. If they've been doing this for a while, and I think they have been, then they may have stolen many millions of dollars from your father."

"How many?"

"It's just a guess, but from what I've seen here," Nick indicated the computer, "it could be anywhere from twenty to thirty million dollars over the past eight years or so."

"Holy shit! No wonder Walter was so anxious to get the accounting records moved."

"Without Richard to conceal what they were doing, someone would've noticed this," Nick said. "They'd have been nailed sooner or later. This has to be the money that Walter's looking for."

Nick looked at the time on his computer screen. "I've got to check in with Walter. What should I tell him?"

"Tell him you're making progress. Tell him you need more time. I wouldn't tell him you figured out his scam, though. I don't see how that would help."

"Ok," Nick said. "I just need a minute." He got off the bed and paced the cluttered floor for a moment, trying to collect his thoughts. He stepped out on the balcony and took a few deep breaths, then came back in.

"Ok," he said. "I think I'm ready. Can I have your phone?" She passed the phone over and Nick dialed the last number that Walter called from.

After three rings, Nick heard the now-hated voice of Walter Hughes.

"So you can be punctual," Walter said. "What a relief for Victoria. She'll get a three-hour reprieve. What can you tell me?"

"I'm making progress," Nick said, "but it's slow."

"Need I remind you that time is not on your side?"

"I know. We got some files and emails, but they're encrypted. It's taking a while to get access to them."

"It's not like Richard to use encryption. I didn't think he was that technically sophisticated."

"Yeah, well it surprised me, too. We're going to be at this most of the night. You still want me to call you in three hours?"

"If you don't, I'm afraid that Victoria will pay the price. Talk to you soon," Walter said and disconnected.

Nick held the phone so tightly his fingers turned white. He fought the urge to throw it across the room. "I swear to God," he said. "I'm going to kill that man."

"Not until we get Victoria back," Jeannie said. "What's our next move?"

"I've got to get into these files. I found some programs online that're supposed to be able to break the encryption. Let me give that a try."

"Go for it," Jeannie said. "I'll be right here if you need me."

***

Walter went to the second floor where Scorch was holding Victoria. The blinds were drawn, and Victoria was seated in a kitchen chair, her hands and feet bound by wide leather straps, chained together. Her cheeks were smudged with tear-streaked makeup. Victoria's eyes were closed, but she wasn't asleep.

Scorch, on the other hand, was sprawled on the bed, snoring. Walter stepped over to the bed and nudged Scorch with the barrel of his gun. "Wake up. You're supposed to be watching our guest."

"She ain't goin' nowhere," he said and rolled over. "Leave me alone."

"Your work ethic astounds me," Walter said, and he poked him harder with the gun. "If you won't do your job, then I don't need you. Think about that."

"Fine," Scorch said and sneezed. He wiped his nose on the bedspread and sat up. "She can't go anywhere. She's handcuffed."

"Those aren't handcuffs. They're bondage cuffs and they're made for sexual games, not security."

"Really?" Scorch said. "I wondered what they were doing in the nightstand." He got up from the bed and scrutinized them more closely. "Huh. You sure?"

"Yes," Walter said. "I've read about them. Tie her up in something more secure. I'm going downstairs to see if I can find something edible, then I'm going to sleep while you stand watch. Later, I'll let you sleep while I guard Miss Victoria. Does that sound fair to you, Mr. Scorch?"

"Sure, I guess."

"I'm so glad that we see eye to eye on this. I'll relieve you in about three hours," Walter said, and left the room, closing the door behind him.

"Prick," Scorch said to the closed door. He looked at Victoria, her eyes still closed. "I know you ain't sleeping. You're not fooling me."

Victoria did not open her eyes, and Scorch shifted his focus to his left hand. He brought the bandaged fingers, still taped to the hammer, to his nose. "Shit," he said. "This stinks." He started peeling the tape.

It took him almost twenty minutes to separate his hand from the hammer, and with each layer of tape removed, the smell grew stronger. When he finally got down to his bare skin, the stench was nauseating.

Victoria opened her eyes to see what Scorch was doing to cause such a foul odor. When she saw his hand, she flinched. The skin on and around the damaged fingers had turned a dark red, almost purple, color. She watched as Scorch popped a black blister that had formed on the back of his hand, and was almost immediately overcome by the smell it released.

"What the hell," Scorch said. He went into the bathroom and Victoria could hear him in the sink. He came back a few minutes later with a towel wrapped around his left hand. In his right, he had a bottle.

"I think it's infected," he said to Victoria. "You think this'll help?" He showed her the bottle of rubbing alcohol that he was holding.

"I think you need a doctor," she said. "I've never seen anything like that before."

"Doctors don't know shit. They take my money and give me pills that don't do nothing. Fuck that. I'm gonna wash it with this."

He took the bottle of rubbing alcohol and went back in the bathroom. He came back ten minutes later with a package of sterile gauze and some white medical tape. "Look what Dick had in his bathroom," he said.

Victoria watched as he sat on the edge of the bed and proceeded to wrap his hand with the gauze. He started with his fingers, which were now almost black, and worked all the way up to his wrist. The back of his hand was discolored, and when he pressed it, Victoria could hear a crackling sound.

When the hand was wrapped and taped, Scorch carefully molded it to the handle of the hammer again, then proceeded to tape the hammer to his hand. "Here comes Thor," he said.

When he was finished, he carefully inspected his handiwork. "That's better," he said. He brought the back of his hand to his nose and sniffed it again. "Much better."

***

"Nick, wake up."

Nick shot to a sitting position. He was completely disoriented for a moment before he realized he was in Jeannie's room and that he'd fallen asleep while he should have been working to save Victoria.

"What time is it?" he asked.

"It's almost time for another phone call."

Nick rubbed his eyes and checked the computer to see if the hacker program that he'd downloaded had been able to unencrypt Richard Golden's files. It hadn't. What it appeared to have done was totally destroy Jeannie's laptop. It was unresponsive and no amount of rebooting was going to help.

"I think I fried your computer," Nick said. "Sorry."

"No problem. I know you were just trying anything you could think of." She was sitting on the bed fiddling with Nelson's camera. "Take a look at this," she said and passed the camera to Nick. "I can't make out what this is. There are a lot of shots like this."

Nick took the camera and stared at the screen. He turned it ninety degrees first one way, then the other. He worked the zoom and then brought it closer to his face. "Oh my God," he said.

"What? What is that?"

"You don't want to know," he said.

"Why? What is it?"

"Dirty pictures. Taken in very low light. Here, look."

Jeannie took the camera and went through the same contortions as Nick. "Oh my God!" she said. "There are literally hundreds of these on here."

"So much for Nelson's hobby keeping him out of trouble."

"At least it was keeping him busy," she said.

"As fascinating at that is, it doesn't help us right now."

"Okay," she said and turned the camera off and set it down. "Right now, it's time to call Hughes." She handed her phone to Nick.

Nick held the phone and took a deep breath before hitting the dial button.

"Anything new to report?" Walter asked.

"No."

"This is getting repetitive."

"I have to go back to Richard's office and access his computer," Nick said. "It's going to take time."

"Haven't they fired you yet? I would have. Oh, wait – I did."

"I don't think so," Nick said, "but even if they have, I know how to get in and get the information I need, but I have to do it before the office opens. I'm headed there now."

"With the help of Miss Keene? I'm concerned about your loyalty to your betrothed. You seem to have grown very close to Miss Keene over the last few days. Should Victoria be concerned?"

"She's just helping me."

"And why is she doing that, Nick? What's in it for her? Have you asked yourself that question?"

Nick glanced at Jeannie, then turned his attention again to the phone call. "She wants to know who killed her father. She thinks his death is tied to this business of yours. Pretty coincidental that Andrew gets killed the night he decides he needs a full audit of the company books, don't you think?"

"He didn't order an audit."

"He was about to."

"And how would you know . . . Oh yes, that stupid memo app that Andrew insisted on using. So you have his phone?"

"Yes."

"I'll want that, too. If that falls into the hands of the police, it will not go well for Victoria."

"Sure, you can have it, and I'll find your missing money, and you'll give me back Victoria. After that, you'll be through."

"After that, it won't matter," Walter said. "You're becoming a concern for me, Nicholas. Here's what I'm going to do. I'm going to assign you a chaperone for the duration of our collaboration."

"What do you mean, a chaperone?"

"One tasked with ensuring proper behavior," Walter said. "I need to make sure you're looking for my money and not collaborating with the police or trying to figure some stupid heroic means of saving Victoria. He'll meet you at the Keenes' private docks in thirty minutes. You'll recognize him by the hammer taped to his left hand."

"What?" Nick said, but there was no answer. Walter had disconnected the call.

TWENTY-TREE

No one succeeds in business unless they're ruthless. Nice guys really do finish last.

From – *Promote This!*

Nick and Jeannie stood on the dock waiting for the man with the hammer. There was a half-moon rising that was ducking in and out of the clouds, and the wind had picked up, blowing steadily out of the east. Nick could hear the sound of waves breaking on the Atlantic beach. In the bay, toward Miami, he could see flecks of white as the wind stirred the water into a light chop.

He held a pillow case with the items he thought they might need – a hammer, two screwdrivers, a pair of pliers, and a pry bar, all taken from the tool box on *Andy's Dream*.

Jeannie had finally agreed to allow Nick to borrow some of Nelson's clothes, so he was dressed in a pair of cargo shorts and a golf shirt that more or less fit him. She was in dark jeans and a dark top, like she was prepared for a commando mission behind enemy lines.

Nick asked, "Which boat are we going to take?"

Jeannie pointed to the boat they had arrived in six

hours earlier. "The small one," she said. "It gives us more options."

"Is that big enough? It looks like it's getting rough out there."

"We'll be fine in the bay," she said. "I'm going to get the boat ready. You wait here for our guest."

A few moments later, Scorch arrived. "You Nick?" he asked.

Nick nodded.

"Where's the girl?"

Nick pointed to Jeannie where she was prepping the boat. "Over there," he said. "What do we call you?"

"I'm Scorch," he said. He held up his left hand to show Nick the golden hammer. "And this is Thor."

"You named your hammer Thor?"

"Yeah," Scorch said, "just like in the comic books."

"Actually, it's the man who's named Thor. That's not the name of his hammer."

"Really? What's the hammer called?"

"Mjölnir."

"What the fuck! I ain't calling it that. I don't even know what you said. This is Thor." He shook his hammer hand at Nick. "That's what I call it and that's what you're gonna call it. Now get in the fucking boat." He gave Nick a shove with Thor.

Nick jumped into the boat, and Scorch, with only one good hand, followed more slowly, taking care to keep his footing.

"This is Jeannie," Nick said. "Jeannie, this is Scorch. His left hand is called Thor."

"Not the hand, the hammer," Scorch said. He brandished it in front of Jeannie's face. "Thor and I are here to keep an eye on you two, make sure you don't do something stupid."

"Like tape a hammer to our hand?" Jeannie said.

Scorch drew his hand back to swing at Jeannie, but Nick stepped between them and grabbed his arm. "Easy, there," he said. "We need her to drive the boat. If you hurt her, we're done, so everybody just settle down."

He turned to Jeannie. "We ready to go?"

"Yeah. You sit over there," she said to Scorch. "Nick, you release the stern line."

Nick stepped to the back of the boat and tried to remember what he had seen Nelson do earlier. He pulled on the line that ran to the dock, moving the boat close enough that he could reach over and untie it from the dock cleat. He shoved the boat away again and let the rope fall into the water.

"Bring that line in, Nick," Jeannie said. "Otherwise, it'll foul the prop. That would be bad."

Nick hauled in the wet rope and let it lay in a pool on the deck.

Jeannie put the motor in gear, and they headed out of the slip, into the dark waters of Biscayne Bay.

Scorch shouted over the sound of the engine. "Where we headed?"

"Brickell Key," Jeannie said. "I'm going to look for a place I can tie up near Nick's office."

Scorch shook his head. "No. We'll go where I tell you. I'm in charge. We're going back to the marina where that ferry docks. If we have to go somewhere from there, I drive."

"You're the boss," she said, and she altered their course and adjusted their speed for maximum discomfort so that they were pounding the chop. She watched out of the corner of her eye as Scorch grimaced with each slap of the hull on the water.

Ten minutes out they hit their first squall. The wind built suddenly and a moment later they were overtaken by heavy rain. Jeannie held their course. After a quick two minute drenching, the wind dropped again and the rain stopped. They continued toward Dinner Key, now sodden and cold in the early morning wind.

***

Gordon McCall was released from jail well after midnight. The paperwork had taken longer than Jimmy Delgado had guessed, but at least he was out and free. Jimmy hadn't been able to wait for him, and at $400 per hour, McCall didn't want him to. He arranged for a taxi, and at about 12:45, finally made it to his hotel.

Unfortunately, when McCall had failed to check in, the hotel released his room and was now fully booked. Rather than fight with them, he got his cab back and gave the driver the address of the offices of Burnham & Fields. He was too wound up to sleep, and he had a temporary employee pass and the alarm codes that Lydia had given him before the police took him away. He might as well use them.

The office was blissfully serene. Not even the Muzak was on. He walked the cubicles and savored the quiet order of the place, absorbing the power of GAAP accounting that suffused the atmosphere.

He found his way to Richard Golden's office, only to find the door locked. He looked at the information that Lydia had given him and called her number.

Even groggy with sleep, she was anxious to know what prison was like and if he was still going to fire Nick Rohmer and why he was in the office at one in the morning. McCall deflected what he could, answered what he couldn't avoid and eventually got the information that he was looking for about the key to Golden's office.

Once in Golden's inner sanctum, he did a quick reconnaissance walk of the perimeter, then settled on the guest sofa for a short, but well-deserved rest.

***

Except for the sound of the wind whistling through the rigging of a hundred sailboats, the marina was quiet.

Jeannie tied up their little boat, then turned to Scorch.

"We need to get from here to downtown Miami. What's your play?"

"We'll take one of your cars," he said.

"That'd be great if I was planning to drive and brought keys. I wasn't, so I didn't. You have a backup plan?"

Scorch took a moment to catch up. "You mean you came all the way over here and didn't bring car keys?"

Jeannie nodded. "Didn't need them the way we planned it. Now what?"

"You got a car here, right?" he asked Nick.

"Yeah, but the police took my keys. We were going to dock near the office and –"

"Never mind," Scorch said. "We'll take my car."

They worked their way through the marina to the parking area and found Scorch's Impala parked under a tree. The windows were partially down. "I try to keep it in the shade," he said. "The A/C don't work."

"I like the way the trunk lid and the driver's door are contrasting colors," Jeannie said. "And the rust gives it an urban chic look."

"Shut up and get in," Scorch said.

Jeannie opened the back door and climbed in. "Jesus Christ," she said. "What died in here?"

Scorch was grappling with the driver's door handle, which was broken and apparently difficult to open with one hand.

"You need help with that?" Nick asked.

"No! Just get in the fucking car."

Nick got in the passenger seat and waited. Scorch was able to open the door and sit down, then struggled to close the door with his hammer, finally using the claw to snag the door handle.

"That was easy," Jeannie said.

"If you ain't giving directions, don't talk," Scorch said. He looked at Nick. "You. Tell me which way to go."

Nick directed him out of the lot and north on US 1. At

that time of the night, it was an easy drive, and they were soon in front of the parking garage where Nick parked for work, just off Brickell.

Once in and parked, Nick led them to the elevators and up to the eighteenth floor. The elevators were separated from the reception area by a set of closed and locked glass doors.

Nick pulled his employee badge out of his pocket. "Let's hope they haven't fired me yet," he said, then swiped it in front of the reader. It gave an encouraging chirp and they could hear the sound of the electric lock releasing. "Easy-peasy," Nick said and pushed the door open.

The next obstacle was the alarm, which began beeping insistently once they were past the doors. Nick stepped up to the alarm pad and entered the six-digit number, and the beeping stopped.

"I guess we didn't need all this stuff," Nick said and held up the pillowcase of tools. "We still have to go up one floor. Stairs are this way."

He led them through the quiet office and up the stairs to the executive suites. They stepped around a corner and Nick saw that the door to Golden's office was open. He held up his hand to signal everyone to stop while he crept up to the door to peek in.

At first, he didn't see anyone. The desk was empty, as was the conference table. Nick swept the room with his eyes and spotted McCall, sprawled on the sofa, apparently asleep.

He returned to Scorch and Jeannie and signaled them to follow him away from the open office. When they were at a safe distance, he told them what he had found.

"We need to get him out of the office," Nick said, "or this was all a waste."

Scorch said, "Thor and I can take care of him." He made a swinging motion with his hammer hand.

"That could kill him," Nick said.

"How about we pull the fire alarm?" Jeannie said. "He'll evacuate and we'll have the run of the office until he gets back."

"The fire department will come and we'll have to evacuate too, or hide, and once they're gone, McCall will be back." Nick thought a moment. "I have an idea. Let's go back downstairs."

Nick led them back to Lydia's reception desk, reset the alarm, and relocked the glass doors. "Here's the plan . . ."

Moments later, Jeannie was on her phone calling 9-1-1. "I'd like to report a suspicious looking man in the Burnham & Fields building. . . He has a bag over his shoulder and he looks like he's trying to break in . . . About fifty, five foot eleven, wearing a dark suit. He looks crazy, or drunk, or drugged, or something . . . He's waiting for the elevator. I think he spotted me! I have to go!"

Nick counted to thirty, then said to Scorch, "It's Thor time."

Scorch stood and, with one powerful swing of his golden hammer, smashed the glass entrance door. At the same moment, the alarm started to beep urgently.

"Time to hide," Nick said, and they followed him to the employee lounge, where they all squeezed into a storage closet. Nick left the door ajar just enough so that they could hear what was to follow.

***

Gordon McCall was so profoundly asleep that the light didn't even wake him up, at first. It was just there, hovering above him, moving slightly from side to side, like a bright sun seen from a gently swaying hammock.

Then a rough hand shook him awake and he opened his eyes to the flashlight being directed into his face.

"Hey," he said and tried to block the light with his forearm.

"On your feet, sir," said a voice behind the light.

"What's going on?" McCall asked. He sat up, irritated now by the light. "What is this?"

The office lights came on and McCall saw two uniformed police officers, one with his gun drawn and pointed at the floor in front of him, the other holding a flashlight in one hand and a heavy-looking pillow case in the other.

"Please stand and place your hands behind your back, palms outward," the officer said.

"What is this –"

"Sir! Please do as you are directed."

McCall slowly stood and turned to face away from the police officer, his hands behind his back as directed. The cuffs were applied, and Gordon McCall was under arrest for the second time in twelve hours.

***

Nick Rohmer stepped off the elevator as the police were leading McCall past the broken glass of the reception area.

"Hold it right there, sir," one of the officers said.

Nick stopped. "Is everything okay, officer? I got a call from the security company that the alarm had gone off." He looked at the broken glass and then at Gordon McCall. "Is this the guy?"

McCall tried to approach Nick but was restrained. "You," he said. "You were here the last time I got arrested. You were in the elevator."

Nick gave the officers a neutral look. "He's right. I was here earlier and saw this man being arrested. I think it was for car theft, right?"

This time, McCall tried to lunge at Nick. He was yanked back by the officer holding his arm.

"I'll need to see some ID, sir," the officer said to Nick.

After showing his work ID and demonstrating that he knew how to reset the alarm, the officers let him pass. "I'll stick around until the glass company can get here," he told them, and he took a seat at Lydia's desk. It was from that vantage point that he watched the elevator doors slowly close, and he had a long last look into the enraged eyes of Gordon McCall.

TWENTY-FOUR

There's no substitute for the combination of brains and good luck, but hard work is a close second.

From – *Success for the Average Joe (or Joanne)*

After the offices were cleared, Nick got down to work on Golden's computer. Jeannie found the hidden bar and made herself at home. Scorch napped on the sofa.

Nick checked in with Walter on schedule and had been working at the computer for over two hours, making notes, printing emails and documents, and making the occasional grunting noise.

Jeannie came over to stand behind him as he worked, clinking the ice in her glass. "Have you noticed an odd smell in here?"

Nick nodded. "Yeah. Smells like old roadkill."

"I think it's our friend over there," Jeannie said, indicating the sleeping Scorch. "He's got a stench coming off him like rotting meat."

"I don't think his hygiene is up to contemporary standards," Nick said.

She tried reading his notes, but they were indecipherable to her. "You making any progress?"

"Yeah," Nick said. "See if this makes sense to you." Nick picked up his pad. "Remember how the scam worked with Walter and Richard fraudulently transferring land to their shell company?"

Jeannie nodded. "Yeah. The one they set up in the Bahamas."

"Okay. I have copies of bank statements from a Bahamian bank for that shell company. Money would flow into it as the lots were sold, then the funds were transferred to a bank in Switzerland."

"That can't be good," Jeannie said. "The Swiss won't help us, will they?"

"That's been their tradition. They built their reputation on secrecy. That's why the rich and powerful, and criminals, have always favored Swiss banks. But," Nick held up a finger to show he was making an important point, "a few years ago, the Swiss government signed a treaty requiring them to share banking information with the rest of the civilized world. Crooks can no longer find a safe haven there. Apparently, Richard was concerned about it, because it appears that all the money, about $37 million, was transferred to a bank in the Cayman Islands."

"And?" Jeannie asked.

"That's it," Nick said. "That's as far as I can trace it. There aren't any bank statements in Richard's computer from the Cayman Islands bank. The trail ends there."

"So what do we do now?"

"I don't know." Nick looked at his notes. "The money was transferred to a company called 'NWBC Cayman Ltd.' I've been trying to find some info on it, but they don't come up in an internet search, and other than the wire transfers, the name isn't anywhere in Richard's records."

"What did you say the company was called?"

"NWBC Cayman, Ltd."

Jeannie slowly set her drink on Golden's desk and

turned to look out the window at the still dark bay. "Oh my God," she said.

"What? Does that name mean something to you?"

"It might," Jeannie said and turned back to Nick. "I have to make a call." She pulled out her phone and dialed.

***

"Hello. Keelows."

"Hello, Pat. It's Jeannie. Is Biggie around?"

"Don't know. Let me check." Jeannie heard a clunk as the phone was set down. After a moment, Pat was back. "Hold on."

Biggie Johnson's voice boomed over the phone. "Hey Jean-bean, what's up?"

"Hey, Biggie. Did you get the bike back okay?"

"Yep. It was just where you said. Is that why you're calling at 4:00 am?"

"No," Jeannie said. "I've got something I have to ask you."

"Shoot."

"You ever hear of a company called NWBC Cayman Limited?"

The line was silent except for the sound of Biggie's breathing.

"Biggie?" Jeannie said.

"You don't want to ask me about that," Biggie said, his usual booming voice now several decibels quieter. "And, you don't want people to know that you're asking about it, either. I can do a lot of things for you, Jean, but if you piss off these people, you're on your own."

"Okay, Biggie. Thanks. I didn't mean to stir up trouble."

"Sounds like you might be sticking your nose in someplace you shouldn't. You be careful, okay?"

"Thanks. I will."

***

"Okay," Nick said. "What the hell does your biker friend have to do with all this?"

"Do you remember Keelows?" Jeannie asked.

"It's not a place I'll soon forget," Nick said.

"Remember I told you it was sort of a biker and boater bar? That was a little understated."

"Meaning . . . ?"

"It's the hangout of a bike club in the Keys. Being the Keys, they do things a little different, so it's kind of a biker slash boater club. Most of the guys have a Harley and some sort of boat. They call themselves the 'Nautical Wheelers.' You may have seen it on the back of some of their jackets."

"Yeah," Nick said. "I remember."

"Nautical Wheelers Bike Club," Jeannie said.

"So? I'm still not seeing the connection."

"Nautical Wheelers Bike Club. NWBC."

Nick paused a moment to try to assimilate this new information, but he wasn't quite able to make it fit the other pieces of the puzzle. "I don't get it," he finally said. "Why would Richard Golden be wiring millions of dollars to an offshore account controlled by a motorcycle club?"

Jeannie let out a long breath. "Most of their members are good people. They're just working stiffs looking to have some fun on the weekends. They have families and jobs and some are professionals, but there's an element, a hard core, so to speak, who use the club for some outside income."

"Meaning criminal activity? Like drugs? Prostitutes?"

"I have no idea," Jeannie said. "But whatever it is, it's cash business."

"So, are you saying that Richard was using his offshore funds to launder money for a biker gang?"

"They really hate to be called that," Jeannie said. "They prefer the term 'Bike Club.'"

"Okay, so he was laundering their money?"

"It makes sense," Jeannie said. "Every couple of weeks they were sending large bundles of cash from Keelows to Boca Cheeca."

"And you know this how?"

"I was the one delivering it," Jeannie said.

***

"Hey!"

Nick and Jeannie looked at Scorch, who was awake again on the couch.

"You two plotting?" Scorch stood slowly, wobbled a little, then sat heavily back on the sofa.

"You okay?" Nick asked.

"Fuck you," Scorch said, and stood again, this time maintaining his footing. He sniffed the air, then brought his damaged hand up to his nose. "Christ, this is ripe. Time to change the bandages."

He walked over to Richard Golden's private bathroom but stopped before he went inside. "You got any tape I can use on this?" he said, indicating his arm. "I got to rewrap it."

"Check the secretary's desk out there." Nick pointed to Joanna's desk. "I'm sure she must have some packing tape or something like that. And there's also a first-aid kit somewhere."

"Go get it," Scorch said. "I got to start unwrapping this."

Nick was back in a few moments with a roll of packing tape, a portable first-aid kit, and a pair of scissors. He brought them into the bathroom for Scorch and recoiled at the sight and the smell.

"What the hell is wrong with your arm?"

"Nothin'. Leave the stuff and go."

When Nick was gone, Scorch slammed the door and surveyed the damage to his arm.

The good news was that his hand no longer hurt. In fact, he couldn't feel anything below his wrist. Less encouraging were the black blisters and purple discoloration that had spread to his forearm. He popped the blisters and almost threw up from the smell.

He opened a dozen small packets of antibiotic ointment and spread it from his fingers to his elbow. Then he used the whole roll of gauze to wrap his arm. Once that was in place, he brought it to his nose for an exploratory sniff. It still wasn't good.

Scorch looked around the bathroom for something to kill the smell. He found a half bottle of Richard Golden's cologne and thoroughly doused the bandages.

Last, he grabbed the hammer, molded his dead hand around it, and taped it in place with the packing tape.

Scorch gave it a few half-hearted swings. He had to admit, he felt like shit. He looked at himself in the mirror, but he couldn't tell if he was red in the face from his sunburn or his fever. He put his hand to his forehead. It felt hot to him, so he rummaged again in the first aid kit, and swallowed a handful of aspirin with water from the sink.

He looked at his reflection again and told himself, "Pull it together, asshole. There's enough fuckin' money in this deal to set you up for life."

"Not if you don't collect it."

Scorch whipped around to see who said that. There was no one there. He looked in the mirror again, and said to his reflection, "Now you're hearing things."

"It's about time you heard some sense," the voice said.

Scorch turned again, and there was Donna, standing behind him in the little bathroom, still in her beach togs and floppy hat.

"You ain't here," Scorch said.

"You said you'd take care of me, Scorch. You promised. How can you take care of me if you don't get what's due to you?"

"I'm gonna get my money. I just have to be patient."

"He ripped you off before, he'll do it again. You need to get your money."

"Shut up! I'll get paid. We'll be set. You'll see." Scorch closed his eyes for a moment as the room seemed to sway. When he opened them again, he was alone.

He stood up straight, ran his fingers through his hair, and took a deep breath. He walked back into the office, closing the bathroom door behind him to try to contain the smell.

***

"Please explain to me why you were helping a criminal organization launder money," Nick said.

Jeannie flushed slightly. "I didn't know I was laundering money. I did know it wasn't right, but I didn't see that much harm in it, and it felt really good to know that I was doing something that would piss off my dad so much."

"There could have been anything in those packages," Nick said. "It could have been drugs, or guns."

"I knew what it was. The first time they gave me one, I opened it to see what I was carrying. I wouldn't have done it if it was drugs. I'd just take the boat to Keelows once a week for a beer. While I was inside, someone would load the package onto the boat. Some weeks there'd be one, and some weeks, not. Once I got back to Boca Cheeca, I'd put the package in a locked storage box on the dock, and the next day it'd be gone."

"You had to know it was illegal. And dangerous."

"That was the fun. Though really, is it illegal to move money from one place to another? That was all I was doing."

"Yeah," Nick said. "If you're helping to launder money, I'm pretty sure it's illegal."

"Well, no harm done," Jeannie said. "I never got

caught and it's been over for a while."

"No harm? Two people are dead, and my fiancée –. Victoria is being held for a $37 million ransom. Some harm done, Jeannie! Some harm!"

Jeannie looked at Nick with wide eyes, and the color drained from her face. "This is my fault," she said. "You're right. They're dead because of me. Victoria's in danger, because of me." Tears pooled in her eyes and started to run down her face. "I never realized . . ."

"Hey," Nick said, and he wrapped his arms around her. "I didn't mean that. This isn't your fault. It would have happened anyway, your part was incidental." Nick could feel the warmth of her body through his shirt. He held her tighter. "This all happened because of the greed of Walter and Richard. We're all their victims."

"I'm so sorry, Nick."

Nick and Jeannie were still holding each other when they heard Scorch come back out of the bathroom.

They separated. Jeannie stood up straight and wiped her tears and Nick tried to look casual.

Scorch seemed a little steadier than before, but he was followed into the room by an invisible cloud of cologne mixed with the smell of decaying flesh.

Scorch hadn't noticed their embrace. He looked out the window to the pale gray line of light on the eastern horizon. "You almost done here?" he asked. "People are gonna start coming in to work soon."

"We need a little more time. We won't be too long."

Without another word, Scorch went back to his spot on the sofa and watched them with half an eye.

"So," Nick said. "Now we know that Richard had the funds in cash. What did he do with it? You can't carry around that much money in currency."

Nick went back to the computer screen and started sorting emails. After a moment, he pointed to a lengthy string of messages, all to the same client. "There's way more communication between Richard and this guy than can be explained by his importance as a client." He clicked over to Richard's calendar. "And look how many appointments there are. One every other week or so."

"That's how often the packages were being delivered." Jeannie wrote the name and address on Nick's pad. "South Florida Diamond Exchange. I guess we know what he did with the cash."

Nick pulled up the customer's account file. "Here. The owner is Ishkhan Bedrossian. Get his home address, too. I think we'll start there." Nick stood. "Hey, Scorch. You ready to go? We've got to go see a man about some diamonds."

TWENTY-FIVE

Don't complain about the pressures of the job. Without pressure, diamonds would just be lumps of coal.

From – *You Want to Be Successful? Read this Book!*

At exactly 6:00 am, Walter's cell phone rang.

"Good morning, Mr. Rohmer. I trust you have something new to report?"

"We're making progress," Nick said. "I think we've tracked the money back here to Miami. Right now, we're going to see someone who should be able to verify that."

"I'm glad that you are satisfying your intellectual curiosity, but are you any closer to actually finding my money?"

"Yes," Nick said without hesitation. "Is Victoria okay?"

"She's still fine. As long as you stay on track and find my money within the next twelve hours, everyone will be fine."

"I'll call you in three hours," Nick said and disconnected the call.

Walter turned to Victoria, who was bound to a chair and gagged. "Your boyfriend has become quite the hard worker now that I've found the proper motivation. If you live through this, you should be very proud of him."

***

The ride to Ishkhan Bedrossian's house took about thirty minutes. Nick was again in the front passenger seat, and Scorch was driving. Even with the windows down, Nick could still catch an occasional whiff of Scorch's cologne-soaked bandages. He was actually thankful the air conditioning was broken. He couldn't imagine what it would be like in a closed car.

Nick kept an eye on Scorch. Under his sunburn, he had turned a kind of pale gray, and there were beads of sweat on his forehead, even though it was not yet above eighty degrees. Once in a while, Scorch would close his eyes, and just as Nick was preparing to grab the wheel, afraid that Scorch had either fallen asleep or passed out, they would open again and focus on the road.

They pulled up to the Bedrossian house and found that it sat behind a high wall with an iron gate across the driveway.

"I guess this won't be as easy as just going up to the door and knocking," Nick said.

"Allow me." Jeannie jumped out of the car and stepped up to a small box set in the wall next to the gate. She pressed the button. She looked up at a camera mounted overhead and smiled pleasantly. After a moment, a voice came over the speaker.

"Who is it?"

"Hi, Mr. Bedrossian? I'm Jeannie from Burnham & Fields?" She said it like a question, with the inflection going up at the end. "I have a check for you, but you have to sign for it?"

"A check? What for?"

Jeannie giggled. "Oh, I don't know. They just asked me to bring this to you right away and get a signature. It has something to do with Richard Golden?"

"Richard's dead."

"Yeah, that's so sad. This was something of his that needed to get cleared up? Can I come in?"

By way of an answer, the iron gate blocking the driveway started to roll open.

Jeannie stepped through the opening and waited for Nick and Scorch to join her. The three of them walked up to the front of the house and she rang the bell.

Bedrossian opened the door. "Three people to deliver one check?" he said. Then he saw Scorch and tried to slam the door again.

Scorch got Thor into the opening, then used his good hand to force the door open the rest of the way. They stepped inside to find a clearly panicky Mr. Bedrossian.

"We need to speak with you about your dealings with Richard Golden," Nick said.

Bedrossian looked from one face to the other. "There isn't any check, is there."

"Sorry. Afraid not," Jeannie said. Then she turned to Scorch. "You look around and see if there's anyone else here, okay?"

"I don't work for you," he said.

"Fine. I'll do it and you can question our friend here," she said.

"Fuck you," Scorch said, then slouched down the hall to check the other rooms.

"Where can we talk?" Nick asked.

Bedrossian pointed to a dark room off the entry hall that was apparently his home office. There was a work desk, two guest chairs, and a small sofa. The entire wall opposite the desk was filled by an enormous salt water aquarium.

"Wow," Jeannie said. "This is huge." She stepped up to the fish tank and tapped on it.

"Please don't tap on the glass," Bedrossian said. "It scares the fish."

Jeannie turned back to face him. "I guess you and the fish have a lot in common right now."

"Have a seat," Nick said. "We just want to talk."

Bedrossian went to sit behind the desk, but Nick directed him to one of the guest chairs. "This would be better," he said.

Bedrossian sat and wiped nervous hands down his pant legs. "What do you want?"

"Just some information," Nick said. "About cash and diamonds."

"I conduct all that kind of business at my store," he said. "I have no diamonds or money here."

"I just need information," Nick said again. "This isn't a robbery."

"What do you want to know?"

"We're tracking a large sum of money that we believe Richard Golden helped to embezzle using his position at Burnham & Fields. We believe that he converted some or all of it to diamonds, through you."

"That's absurd," Bedrossian said. "I may have sold Richard the occasional piece of jewelry, but nothing like you're describing."

Nick smiled at the diamond merchant. "Why did you two meet every other week for the past eight months? Was Richard shopping for a special item?"

"We never met that often. Once or twice a year, at most."

"I have Richard's emails and calendar."

"I don't have to answer any of your questions," Bedrossian said.

"No, you don't," Nick said. "Jeannie, why don't you see if you can find Scorch? It seems Mr. Bedrossian will need to be encouraged to be more forthcoming."

Jeannie gave a mock salute and stepped into the hall.

"She'll be back in a moment with our hammer-handed colleague."

"Please, there's no need for violence," Bedrossian said.

"I agree," Nick said. "Let's just say that I have some hypothetical questions, then. Will you answer them?"

"If I can."

"If I were a criminal and wanted to convert, say, ten million dollars into diamonds, could that be done?"

"A cash transaction like that would need to be reported. It would be traceable."

"Let's assume," Nick said, "that the merchant didn't follow that rule, and didn't take all the cash to the bank, so it went unreported. What would ten million in diamonds look like?"

"Well, it could be just one very expensive stone. They exist, but they're easily traceable. Stones that expensive are very rare." Bedrossian seemed to be warming to his subject. "If you wanted them to be easily converted back to cash, and not be traced, you'd have to look at a lot of smaller diamonds, in the range of one to one-and-a-half carats. Good quality stones of that size, you'd need a pile about so big," he said, indicating a large handful.

"And where would a diamond merchant get such a pile of stones? Could that be done legitimately?"

"No. Diamonds are carefully tracked to make sure they're coming from legitimate sources. What you're asking about would have to be smuggled in from conflict areas. That trade is illegal."

"I see," Nick said.

Jeannie returned with Scorch. "No one else home," she said. "Looks like there's a wife, but she's not here."

Scorch turned his back to Nick and Bedrossian to examine the fish tank, but his presence in the room was both felt and smelled.

Bedrossian wrinkled his nose and looked at Nick with a question in his eyes.

Nick just shrugged in answer.

"How long would it take, theoretically, to put together enough diamonds of this size and type to equal about thirty million dollars?"

"I have no first-hand knowledge of this sort of thing, you understand," Bedrossian said.

"Of course not."

"But from what I've heard, I would guess about three to six months, but that would be almost every illegal diamond coming into Florida in that period. Someone would have to be very well-connected to pull that off."

"Someone like you?" Nick asked.

"I thought we were talking hypothetically."

"We were," Nick said, standing up, "but I have a friend whose life is in danger, and I can't afford to be chasing false leads. Did you do this for Richard? Did you help him convert thirty plus millions of dollars into untraceable diamonds? Do you have any idea what he did with them?"

Bedrossian smiled up at Nick. "You've got nothing on me," he said. "I'm certainly not going to sit here and admit to a felony. If you think I did this, then call the police."

"Sorry, no time. Scorch, can you see if you can persuade Mr. Bedrossian to cooperate?"

"Nice fuckin' fish," Scorch said, his forehead resting against the front of the fish tank. "Did you know there's a little shark in here?" He tapped the glass with his hammer, and Nick saw Bedrossian visibly flinch. "Salt water ain't easy. Takes a lot of work."

"Scorch," Nick said. "I need you to come over here and get Mr. Bedrossian to answer some questions."

Scorch ignored Nick and continued peering into the fish tank, occasionally tapping the glass with his hammer.

"Can you get him to stop doing that?" Bedrossian said.

"I saw this movie once," Scorch said. "This guy was hiding a fuckin' fortune in diamonds in a fish tank. In the water, you could barely see 'em. Just sittin' there like rocks."

"I assure you," Bedrossian said, "I don't have diamonds hidden in my fish tank. That's ridiculous."

"Yeah? You seem like that kind of guy. Smug fuckin' know-it-all rich asshole. And you're a crook, like me. I was you? I'd have diamonds in the tank." Scorch tapped the glass a little harder and the fish darted in all directions.

"Please!" Bedrossian said. "The glass can't take much of that."

"How about you answer Nick's questions, I stop banging on your fuckin' tank?"

"Fine! Fine. What was the question?"

"Did you help Richard convert thirty million dollars into untraceable diamonds?"

"You ever repeat this, I'll flat out deny it." Bedrossian paused for a moment. Scorch put his hammer up against the glass and drew a lazy figure eight with it. "Yes. Yes, I did. I put him together with a guy who was bringing in conflict diamonds, and they made a series of transactions. I don't know how much, but it was a lot."

"How many diamonds?" Nick asked.

"I don't know. Thousands. They were all high quality, too."

"How much space would that many diamonds fill?"

Bedrossian tried to formulate a space with his hands, then gave up. "I need my calculator," he said and pointed to the top of his desk. Nick handed it to him. After some calculation, he said, "About half a liter. Like one pint. It would weigh about three pounds."

"That's pretty compact," Nick said.

"That's the one of the beauties of diamonds," Bedrossian said. "So much value in such a small beautiful space."

Jeannie asked, "You have any idea what Richard was doing with all those diamonds?"

"No idea at all. I never asked."

"I think we got everything we can from this guy," Nick said to Jeannie. "Can you think of anything else you want to ask?"

Jeannie shook her head. "No. Looks like we have a treasure hunt now. Those diamonds could be anywhere."

"I think they're in this fuckin' fish tank," Scorch said,

and he drew back Thor and smashed it through the glass.

At first, only a small hole the size of the hammer's head opened, and water started to gush out.

"No!" Bedrossian screamed. He rushed to block the hole with his hands, futilely trying to hold back the water. Scorch aimed another blow at the glass, and this time, the whole front of the tank blew out and one thousand gallons of salt water cascaded into the room, bringing the fish, coral, and plants with it.

Scorch stood his ground as the water poured onto the floor around him. He reached into the tank and started raking through the gravel with his fingers, sifting the sand and coral in search of diamonds. Nick and Jeannie watched in fascination as he methodically worked across the bottom of the tank. Finally, he gave up and wiped his hand on his pants. "Shit," he said. "I guess not. Let's go."

Nick and Jeannie left Bedrossian kneeling on the floor of his study in an enormous pool of dead and dying fish.

***

Nick and Jeannie had their first fight in front of the Bedrossian residence.

"I am not going to sit in the back seat again," Jeannie said. "It's like riding around in a dumpster. It's your turn."

"But I'm almost a foot taller than you. I need the legroom."

"Don't 'legroom' me. Your knees bend." She shoved him out of the way and sat in the front passenger seat. It was almost as dirty, with old soda cans and fast food cast-offs on the floor. The smell was no better, either, but she felt she'd won a moral victory.

Nick climbed in the back seat and had to shift debris out of the way to make room for his legs. "This is really gross," he said.

"You can both shut the fuck up," Scorch said. "Where we goin'?"

"I don't know," Nick said, "but after what just happened inside, I don't think we should hang around. Drive until you find a park or someplace we can pull over and come up with a plan."

"Fine," Scorch said, and he hit the gas. The old Impala reluctantly started to roll, gradually picking up speed.

Nick shoved some of the junk on the back seat to the other side of the car. Then he dug into the garbage at his feet to see if he could make more room. He found a winter coat, a filthy beach towel, and a half-roll of paper towels. When he shifted all of that to the other side of the seat, he discovered a large, overstuffed, leather briefcase that was in surprisingly good shape. He pulled it up onto his lap and gasped.

"What is it?" Jeannie asked.

"Something I found on the floor."

"Nothing would surprise me," she said. "What is it?"

Nick held it up and turned it around to examine it from all sides. "It's Richard Golden's briefcase."

TWENTY-SIX

Learn to play golf. It can get you out of the office and it looks like you're conducting business.

From – *What, Me Work?*

Scorch slept in the car while Nick and Jeannie huddled over coffee and the contents of Richard Golden's briefcase in a booth of the Coral Café. At first, Scorch had insisted that he accompany them, but Jeannie convinced him that the smell he was generating would get them thrown out of any eating establishment. They brought him a take-out cup, which he threw in the back seat after he was finished.

They split the contents of the bag into two piles – one for documents, and the other for anything else. In the 'anything else' pile were: five ball point pens, two mechanical pencils, a broken cell phone, a broken iPad, nail clippers, two unmarked keys, two empty key chains, several rubber bands and an empty black velvet bag.

The documents they arranged into piles: accounting files, loose notebook paper, complete notebooks, business receipts, sales brochures, business cards, a passport, and a roundtrip airline ticket to the Maldives.

The passport had a recent picture of Richard Golden in it but was in the name of Patrick Elfman, the same name that was on the airline ticket. The ticket was for a flight that had left at 4:40 pm the previous day.

"It looks like Richard was ready to leave town for good," Nick said.

"It also looks like he never cleaned out his briefcase. Some of this junk is years old." She picked up the broken cell phone. "I haven't seen one of these since I was ten."

"Can you look up the Maldives on your phone? See if they have an extradition treaty with the U.S."

Jeannie surfed the internet on her phone while Nick went through the receipts, dividing them into separate piles.

"No extradition with the U.S.," she said. "I guess it's as good a place as any to hide out with money, but unless you like fishing and diving, there's not much there."

"These receipts are recent," Nick said. "Lots of gas, restaurants, parking and toll receipts. This one stands out, though." He held up a pale blue handwritten receipt. "It's from the pro shop at his country club for a new golf bag. It's dated last Saturday, two days before he died." He shuffled through some more. "Here's another one from the pro shop, for new golf club grips."

"So?"

"Why would he buy a bag and grips for clubs just days before he's leaving the country?"

"Maybe he was going to take them with him."

"Can you see how many golf courses there are in the Maldives?"

"Sure," Jeannie said and went back to her phone. "One, and it's a pitch and putt. I take it that's not a real golf course?"

"Not if you play golf like Richard did."

"Maybe the Maldives is only a stopping-off point," Jeannie said.

"Maybe."

Jeannie sipped her coffee and sorted through the business cards without really paying attention to them. "Can we discuss the elephant in the room?" she said.

Nick set down the receipts and focused his attention on Jeannie. "You mean how Richard's briefcase got to be in the back seat of Scorch's car?"

"Yeah, that elephant."

"I've been trying to come up with scenarios," Nick said, "but the only ones that I can think of that make sense involve Richard being killed by Scorch."

"Pretty hard to see how he'd end up with it otherwise. You think Walter hired Scorch to kill him?"

Nick shook his head. "I can't see how that makes sense, either. Maybe Scorch heard about the diamonds and was trying to strong-arm the money out of him?"

"I don't think Scorch knew about the diamonds until we did."

"Whatever his motives were, he had to be involved in Richard's death, and now Walter has him glued to us. Once we find the diamonds, they'll probably kill us, too. Until then, they need us and we need Scorch to make sure Walter doesn't hurt Victoria."

"It's an interesting balancing act," Jeannie said.

"It all falls apart if we don't find the diamonds."

"Or if we do. So what's our next move?"

"Do you think I'm dressed well enough to get into the pro shop at Richard's country club?"

"You stand a better chance than yesterday."

***

Scorch rested in the front seat of his car. He was dozing when Donna woke him up.

"If they find those diamonds, you can take them all for yourself," she said.

Scorch nodded. "As soon as they find them, they're dead."

"You don't owe anything to that Walter guy. He doesn't give a shit about you. And those two," Donna nodded toward the diner, "they're probably in there right now plotting how to get rid of you and keep the diamonds for themselves. Keep an eye on them, Scorch. You got to get paid."

"Fuck them," he said and fell back into a restless sleep.

***

From the front door of the diner, they could see Scorch in his car across the parking lot. A cloud of flies swarmed around him where he sat slumped in the driver's seat.

"They seem to prefer Scorch to the trash," Nick said.

"You think he's dead?"

"We should be so lucky."

The slamming of the car doors roused Scorch. "Where we goin' now?" he said.

"Camino Golf Club," Nick said, and handed him a piece of paper with the address. "It's on Miami Beach."

"I know where it is," Scorch said but took the paper anyway. "I got to buy gas, and I'm not payin' for it. One of you got a credit card?"

"I'll take care of it," Nick said.

"Big fuckin' man," Scorch said and put the car in drive.

***

Camino Golf Club was the second oldest country club in Miami-Dade County, and probably the most prestigious. The course was surrounded by the private homes of some of the area's wealthiest residents, and it was only through their efforts to preserve their golf course views that the land had not long ago been bought up and developed by someone like Andrew Keene.

Scorch's car was a blemish on the country club parking

lot that was otherwise filled with Bentleys, BMWs, and the occasional Jaguar. As usual, he parked under a tree, even though it was cloudy.

"We're going to the pro shop," Nick said. "You wait here."

"Fuck that, I'm coming with you."

Nick pointed to Scorch's bandaged arm. "You're going to have to cover Thor if you're going inside with us. One look at that, and they'll call the police, if they haven't already." He dug around for the beach towel he had uncovered earlier. "Here, wrap it in this," he said and passed it over the back of the seat.

The three of them entered the pro shop to the sound of a tinkling bell over the door. Two older club members were at the counter engaging the sole employee on duty, so they pretended to browse. Nick looked at the new golf bags, Jeannie checked out the hats, and Scorch was drawn to the display of bug repellant.

When he was free, the young man on duty came up to Nick. He was wearing a neatly ironed pair of khaki pants and a green golf shirt with 'Camino Golf Club' embroidered on the chest. He was also wearing a plastic name tag with 'Todd' engraved on it.

"Can I help you?" Todd asked.

"I hope so," Nick said. "I worked for Richard Golden, one of your members here –"

"We heard about what happened to Mr. Golden," Todd said. "Truly a tragedy."

Nick heard Scorch snort.

"Yes. Everyone at Burnham & Fields is pretty upset, too. But we were trying to tie up some of Mr. Golden's personal business, and we came across these receipts." Nick handed the receipts to Todd. "Mr. Golden bought a new golf bag last Saturday?"

Todd reviewed the receipts. "Yeah, I remember these transactions. It wasn't a golf bag, actually. This is written up wrong. It was a golf travel bag."

"Oh? How's that different?"

"You put your golf bag, with everything in it, inside the travel bag, and you can take it on vacation with you. It protects your equipment and has handles and wheels to make it easy to transport. You need it to fly with your bag."

Jeannie stepped over to join them. "So I guess he was planning to take a golf vacation."

"Oh, yes," Todd said. "He was very excited about it."

"So you knew about his trip?" Jeannie asked.

"Everyone did. He was really looking forward to playing some of those famous Scottish courses. St. Andrews, Royal Troon. You know."

Nick nodded. "Sure. Sounds exciting. And the new grips?" Nick asked, referring to the second receipt.

"Yeah, that was a little strange," Todd said. "He has a fantastic set of Callaways that he loves, but he brought in a cheap set of Spalding clubs for grips. The weird thing was that the shafts were short and stiff, and I know that Mr. Golden likes a longer whippy club."

"And that was weird?" Jeannie said.

"Yeah. The shafts had been cut down. I asked him about it, and he said he was trying something new. Anyway, the grips were completed and he picked them up on Saturday when he bought the travel bag."

"Did Mr. Golden keep his clubs here?"

"Oh, sure. He kept all his golf stuff here. Why?"

"We'd really like to take a look at his clubs, and his locker, if possible," Nick said.

"I can show you his clubs. One second." Todd went back to his counter and pulled out a sign that said 'Back in 5 minutes,' then he led them out through the rear of the shop.

"All the clubs are kept together back here," he said, "where the head caddy can get to them." He led them into a cramped space that was doing the work of a much larger room. There were racks against every wall, and several freestanding down the middle of the floor, each filled with golf bags. The room smelled strongly of cut grass and wet leather.

"Richard's are over here." He led them to a well-worn maroon and white bag, with a full set of clubs. The woods were sheathed in knitted caps with a number and pom-pom on it.

Nick pulled number three out of the bag. "These are the new clubs?"

"Oh, no. These are his trusty old Callaways. The new clubs aren't here. He put those in the travel bag he bought and took them with him." Todd took the club from Nick and replaced it in the bag. "I thought that was odd. I can't believe that he'd take those clubs on his trip with him. They're not very good. He'd do better with rentals."

"What about a locker? Did he have a locker here?" Nick asked.

"We don't have enough lockers, so the members just get the use of the locker for the day, and they have to empty it when they leave. There've been some grumblings about that, but there just isn't room right now."

"Thanks," Nick said. "You've been a big help."

"No problem," Todd said, and he led them back into the pro shop. He handed the receipts back to Nick. "Is there anything else I can help you with?"

"You got any bug spray?" Scorch asked.

Todd turned his full attention to Scorch for the first time. He stared at the arm wrapped in the dirty beach towel for a moment, then said, "I beg your pardon?"

Scorch waved his hand at the display. "All you got here is mosquito repellant. I'm looking for something that kills flies."

"We don't sell that here," Todd said. "Just what you see there."

"Not much of a fuckin' store," Scorch said.

"Thanks again," Nick said, and he and Jeannie led Scorch outside and back to the car.

"We need to find those clubs," Jeannie said.

"Apparently they're not here," Nick said, "and they weren't in his office. We need to check his car and his townhouse."

"They're in the townhouse," Scorch said.

"What?" Jeannie said.

"I seen 'em. They're in a closet next to the front door."

Nick and Jeannie exchanged a look.

"Yeah?" Nick said.

"Next to the vacuum cleaner."

***

"Now, baby," Donna said into Scorch's ear. "You can ditch 'em now. You know where the diamonds are – they're in the golf clubs at the condo."

Scorch looked first at Nick, then at Jeannie. "I don't need you assholes anymore." He got in the car and started the engine.

Nick leaned on the driver's door. "What're you doing?"

"I'm getting me some diamonds," Scorch said and put the car in gear.

"You still need us, Scorch. If you leave us here, we'll call Walter and we'll tell him you're coming for him. If you kill us, when Walter doesn't hear from us at our regular check-in, he'll know you're coming for him. Either way, he's ready for you."

"Yeah? You got a better idea?" he asked Donna. She shook her head, but Nick answered him.

"We'll help you. We can make sure you get the diamonds. All I want is Victoria, and Jeannie's already rich. All we want is the girl and Walter Hughes. We'll help you get everything else."

Scorch looked at Donna, now in his passenger seat.

"He's got a point, babe," she said. "You might need them just a little bit longer, at least until they check in with Walter."

Scorch turned to Nick. "So, what're you saying? Now we're partners?"

"No," Nick said. "Not partners. We work for you. Our job is to make you rich so you can give us Victoria. Deal?"

Donna nodded. "For now," she said.

"Okay. For now," Scorch said. "First trouble from either of you, you'll deal with Thor."

"That's all we ask," Nick said. He and Jeannie climbed into the car.

TWENTY-SEVEN

Don't let yourself get shackled to a job. It may not be the best use of your time.

From – *The Fastest Rat in the Race*

Scorch drove them back to Dinner Key in silence, his arm out the window to limit the smell. Nick and Jeannie were absorbed in their own thoughts and plans. Nick was concerned with what Scorch might be planning, but so far, had not seen much evidence of any thought process at all.

Once at the marina, they quickly got underway. Nick again helped to cast off the lines, being careful to bring them aboard. The wind was still strong and was now coming out of the southeast. It created a heavy chop in the bay, but it didn't seem to affect Jeannie. Once beyond the channel, she turned the boat to the southeast, directly into the wind.

As their speed picked up, they caught increasing amounts of spray coming over the bow. Within minutes, they were all soaked.

Nick yelled to Jeannie over the sound of the wind and the engine, "It's time to call Walter again."

"What're you going to tell him?"

"The truth, mostly. Can I have the phone?"

***

"Hello, Nicholas. Making progress?"

"Yes."

"Oh my goodness," Walter said. "An unequivocal answer. That's a first. You're sure you don't want to hedge your answer?"

"We have the money."

"What?"

"We have the money. It's in the form of diamonds, so I can't say exactly how much it is, but it should be in the range of thirty million dollars."

Walter was silent for a moment. "Don't toy with me, Mr. Rohmer. If you're lying, it will not go well for you or Victoria."

Nick ignored the threat. "We have it, and if you want it, I need to have Victoria first."

Walter chuckled. "Don't be so demanding. You're in no position to demand."

"I think I am. I'm pretty sure you want this money a lot more than you want to hurt Victoria. So I'll be calling you with instructions on how we're going to make this exchange. Wait for my call."

"One moment," Walter said. "I want to talk to Scorch first."

"Okay, but he doesn't know where the money is. He only knows that we found it. He thinks we're on the way to pick it up."

"Are we having trust issues?"

"We thought it might be safer for everyone if we kept the details to ourselves."

"Where is Scorch now?"

"Out of earshot. I'd like to keep the details of this between us for now."

"I understand your caution. Please let me speak to him."

Nick held onto the phone for a moment, then passed it to Scorch.

"What." Scorch said. "Yeah, that's what they say."

***

Scorch disconnected the call.

Donna whispered in his ear, "Now."

He stood up, fighting to maintain his footing in the bucking boat. He moved close to Nick and handed him the phone. He stood there a moment, and while Nick was leaning forward to hand the phone back to Jeannie, he made a quick slash with his left arm and tried to bring Thor down on Nick's head.

With the motion of the boat and his overall lack of balance, his swing was off-target and landed on Nick's shoulder with a thud. Nick cursed, and rolled with the blow, onto the deck. He jumped to his feet and faced Scorch, who was coming after him, his hammer raised.

"What're you doing?" Nick said. "We're working together, remember?"

Jeannie watched the standoff from the wheel but said nothing.

"I don't fuckin' need you!"

"You tell him, babe!" Donna said.

"You just talked to Walter," Scorch said, "and he doesn't suspect a thing. I got three hours before he starts to wonder what happened to you."

"You're not thinking this through," Nick said, dodging a clumsy swing from Scorch.

"What about me?" Jeannie asked.

"She's next," Donna said.

"You're next," he said, without looking at her, and he took another swing at Nick. As his arm was coming down, Jeannie goosed the throttle and turned the wheel hard to the left. Scorch lost his balance completely and fell face first on the deck. Nick dropped hard onto his back and sat on him.

Jeannie slowed the engine to idle and grabbed a short piece of rope. She quickly bound Scorch's hands behind his back. She cinched them tight, then placed her foot on his head. "What the hell is wrong with you?" she asked.

"We're going to help you get your money," Nick said. "Don't go crazy on us. You still need us and we need you. Pull it together."

"You don't need them," Donna said.

"I don't need nobody!" Scorch shouted. "I never have."

"Yeah?" Nick said. "How's that been working for you?"

***

By the time they were docked in one of the Keene's private slips on Boca Cheeca, it was raining again, but they were already so soaked that they barely noticed. After the boat was tied up, Nick sat next to Scorch, whose hands were still bound behind his back.

"So, how was your ride?" Nick asked.

"Fuck you."

"Have it your way. We'll do this without you." Nick turned to Jeannie. "Where can we stash him?"

Jeannie surveyed their situation. "I think he'll fit nicely in one of the dock boxes," she said. "The same place I used to hide the cash."

Nick eyed the storage box up on the dock, a short ten feet away, but an impossibly long ten feet with a resisting Scorch. "How're we going to get him in there?"

Jeannie stood in front of Scorch, just out of the range of his feet. "We can knock him out and drag him, or he can cooperate and possibly not get a concussion. What works for you, Scorch?"

Scorch mumbled something unintelligible.

"What was that?" Jeannie said. "Was that an answer or another 'fuck you'?"

"Fuck you." Scorch stared fiercely at Jeannie.

"You just keep making bad choices, don't you?" she said. Jeannie grabbed a fire extinguisher that was mounted near the wheel. "This should do it. Nick, you're the one he tried to kill. You want the honors?"

Nick thought about hitting Scorch in the head, hard enough to render him unconscious. He was able to imagine the feel of cracking his skull, and he was repulsed by it.

Jeannie was able to read Nick's hesitation. "Okay," she said. "I guess it's up to me." She got next to Scorch and raised the fire extinguisher over her head.

"I'll walk," Scorch said.

Jeannie still had her arms raised. "What did you say?"

"I'll fuckin' walk there, alright? Don't hit me with that thing."

"Look at that," Jeannie said. "Cooperation."

She set the fire extinguisher down, and she and Nick guided Scorch up onto the dock and got him tucked into the storage box in a fetal crouch.

"Nighty-night," Jeannie said as she closed and latched the lid.

"Were you really going to bash him in the head with that thing?" Nick asked.

"He tried to kill you."

"Yeah, but he's crazy."

"And he's deadly, so, yeah, I was going to hit him," she said. "Does that bother you?"

Nick thought about it a moment. "No," he said. "I guess it bothers me that I couldn't do it."

Jeannie put a hand on his shoulder. "You just don't have the killer instinct," she said. "I think that's one of the things I like about you."

"Let's hope I at least have a strong instinct for survival, because it's time to call Walter. You ready?"

"Just like we planned it," Jeannie said.

Nick dialed Walter's phone and waited.

***

Walter's phone rang. He was sitting in the bedroom of Richard's townhouse with the still bound, but no longer gagged, Victoria.

"This should be interesting," he said to Victoria, then he answered his phone.

"So, what is your plan, Nicholas? I can't wait to hear."

"First I have to know that Victoria is still okay."

"I thought you might say that. Here she is." Walter held the phone up to Victoria's ear. "Say something, darling, your knight in shining armor awaits."

"Oh, Nick," she said and started to cry. "I'm so sorry, Nick."

"Don't worry, Victoria. We're going to get you, okay? This is almost over."

"I love you, Nick," Victoria shouted as Walter took the phone back.

"Very touching," Walter said. "So what is your plan, since you are now calling the shots?"

"We do the exchange in public," Nick said.

"Of course. And what public place have you chosen on this godforsaken island?"

"The plaza by the ferry. At the foot of the boarding ramp."

"You do know that the ferry isn't running today, correct?"

"It isn't?" Nick asked.

"The wind is too high for safe operation, so the ferry service has been temporarily suspended. Your public place is going to be very deserted on this rainy morning." Walter could hear Nick whispering something to Jeannie on the other end of the line.

"That's fine," Nick said. "It's probably as good a place

as any. We'll be there in ten minutes. Bring Victoria. If I don't see her, you'll get nothing."

"Fine. Ten minutes. Please put Scorch on the line."

After a slight hesitation, Nick said, "Scorch isn't here."

"Well that's unacceptable," Walter said. "Scorch is my eyes and ears. What have you done with him?"

"He got a little out of control and we had to tie him up. I don't think it's safe to have him as part of the exchange."

"Mr. Rohmer, you impress me! You took Scorch down? Oh, wait. That's much more the Keene girl's style. She probably knocked him out and tied him up while you cowered somewhere. Regardless, I need to see Scorch there when we make the exchange, or it's no deal."

"Why? The guy's crazy."

"Precisely," Walter said. "He's unpredictable, and if I don't see him, I can't know what he might be up to. I would hate to collect my money only to be jumped in some ambush by Scorch. Bring him, or no deal."

"Okay, we'll bring him."

"I'm not leaving here until I know he's alive, so I suggest you have him call me." Walter hung up the phone and turned to Victoria. "Your boy is turning out to be full of surprises," he said. "I hate that."

***

Nick gave the phone back to Jeannie. "He insists on Scorch being there, or no deal."

Jeannie opened the dock box, releasing the foul smell that had accumulated in the short time that it was closed. "Good God!" she said. "It's a good thing Walter wants to see you. You could have died from your own stench." She reached into the box and grabbed Scorch by the rope binding his arms, and pulled him to his feet. "You feel like playing nice?"

"Sure."

"I don't believe him," Jeannie said.

"Me, neither," Nick said, "but we have to work with him for now. And we can't march him into town with his hands tied behind his back."

Jeannie jumped back in the boat and grabbed a gaff.

"What the hell is that?" Nick asked.

"It's the proverbial ten-foot pole. It's used to land big fish, or grab mooring buoys." She showed him the sharp hook on the end. "You untie him, and I'll stand over here, just in case."

Nick stepped behind Scorch and said, "I wouldn't piss her off. That hook looks nasty." He fumbled at the knot binding Scorch's hands, trying to figure out how to release it. It was a complicated nest of loops.

After a moment, Jeannie came over and handed the gaff to Nick. "I'll get that," she said.

Nick took the pole and stood at a safe distance and watched Jeannie release the rope with two quick flicks of her wrist. "There," she said. "Free again."

"All right," Nick said. "Let's do this."

TWENTY-EIGHT

The best way to enter a negotiation is to not care about the outcome. If you care, you've probably already lost.

From –*Zen and the Art of Negotiation*

The small plaza at the foot of the boarding ramp was wet, windblown, and deserted. Scorch sat down at a plastic table near the closed snack bar. It was under the eaves of the building and mostly out of the rain.

Donna sat next to him. "Here's the plan," she said.

"I'm not listening to you anymore," Scorch said. "You got me locked in a fuckin' dock box."

"Okay, so here's a new approach," Donna said. "We'll wait until Walter has the money and the others are out of the picture. Then you can jump that prick Walter and get what you deserve."

Scorch just nodded.

***

Nick and Jeannie stood together near the foot of the ramp so they could have a clear view of anyone coming into or out of the plaza. Nick held Richard Golden's briefcase, and Jeannie held the gaff.

Within a minute, Nick spotted Walter Hughes and Victoria coming down the main street toward them. Walter was wearing his hat but had otherwise made no concession to the weather. Victoria had a rumpled men's raincoat draped over her, covering her head and shoulders, and not coincidentally, concealing the fact that her hands were still bound behind her back. Walter had his hand under the raincoat as though he was holding Victoria's arm. Nick assumed that was the hand with the gun.

Walter led Victoria to Scorch's table and sat her down, taking a seat to her right, so that she was between the two men. He signaled to Nick. "Don't be shy. We're all friends here, right?"

Jeannie laid the gaff on the ground, and she and Nick walked to the table.

"Are you okay?" Nick said to Victoria.

She nodded.

"She's fine," Walter said. "And why wouldn't she be? You've done such a good job of doing everything that was asked of you. I'm sure that poor dead Richard would be proud of you." Walter still had his hand under Victoria's raincoat. "I'd like to get this done quickly, if possible. Did you bring the diamonds?"

Nick put the briefcase on the table, and Walter reached for it eagerly with his free hand.

"They're not in there," Scorch said.

Walter looked at Nick. "They're not?"

Nick shook his head.

"Well, that wasn't very clever of you, Mr. Rohmer. Did you think I wouldn't notice?"

"They're not in the bag," Nick said, "but I can have them here in five minutes."

"The deal was you would bring the diamonds and I would bring the girl. I did my part." Walter stood and pulled Victoria to her feet next to him. "You failed to do yours. Scorch, make sure that they don't follow us."

"Wait!" Nick said. "This isn't a trick. I couldn't get the diamonds until you were here."

"Now you're talking nonsense," Walter said.

"They're in the fucking townhouse," Scorch said. "He had to get you out of the townhouse to get his hands on 'em."

"That's absurd. I searched that townhouse from top to bottom. There are no diamonds there."

"They're hidden," Scorch said. "They've been there the whole fuckin' time, ten feet from us."

"Is this true?" Walter asked Nick.

"Yes. I'll bring them to you," Nick said. "You stay here, and I'll be back in five minutes with the diamonds, and then you can leave with the money and take me as your hostage. Once you're clear away, you can let me go. No one will say anything until I've been released."

"I've got a better idea," Walter said. "Let's all go to the townhouse together to get the diamonds."

Nick shook his head. "No way. Once you have them, there's no reason to keep us alive. That's why I want to do the exchange in public. I don't trust you."

"And you shouldn't," Walter said. He thought for a moment. "Fine. We'll do this your way, but I'm not going to sit around here with two hostages while we wait for you. Go get the money. Call me when you have it."

"Two hostages?"

"Why, yes. Now I have both Victoria and Miss Keene. So don't dawdle. Scorch, you'll help me corral the ladies."

"Is the townhouse locked?" Nick asked.

"Yes."

Nick held out his hand to Walter. "Give me the key."

Walter fished in his pocket with his free hand and dropped a key marked "Golden" into Nick's palm.

Nick grasped the key so hard, his fingers turned white. He stood there, with a mixture of indecision and anger running through him.

"You heard the man, Nick," Jeannie said. "Here's my phone. Now go get the money and call. We'll be all right. He knows he won't get the money if he kills us."

Nick looked first at Victoria's frightened face, and then at Jeannie. "I'll get you out of this," he said.

"Not by standing there. Go!" Jeannie said, and he went.

***

Without looking back, he ran. He ran out of the plaza, and down Keene Boulevard. He splashed across the cobbled street until he found Number 15. He pounded up the steps to the door and shoved the key in the lock.

Once inside, he tore open the door to the closet and pulled out the golf clubs. They were in a golf bag within the travel bag. He yanked a club from the bag and examined it. It looked just like a regular golf club to him. He grasped it with one hand at each end, and with a quick motion, broke it over his bent leg.

He expected a stream of diamonds to pour out of the club, but was disappointed. He looked in the end of the broken shaft. There was nothing. It was hollow and empty.

He grabbed another club and repeated the procedure, with the same results. Nothing.

"No, no, no!" he yelled. "They have to be here!" He took two more clubs and broke them each in turn. He took another, a three-iron, and swinging it like a bat, punched a hole in a wall of the hallway. He swung it again and put a hole in the other wall. He smashed it down on the tile floor and cracked the marble. He smashed it into the floor again, and this time, the club broke in his hands and the head flew off.

He stared at the hollow, broken shaft in his hand, then threw it away across the living room.

Next he attacked the golf bag, but with less rage and more purpose. First, he went through all the pockets, and there were a lot of them. He pulled out golf gloves, tees, scorecards, pencils, a hat, a poncho, a rain cover, multiple golf balls, a pair of golf shoes, and a towel.

He discarded the smaller items and examined everything else in detail. The golf balls in particular looked promising, but they appeared to be solid, with no seams, and they bounced across the marble floor like regular golf balls. The shoes held no surprises, either.

He went to the kitchen in search of a knife. With the bag now empty, he cut through the lining looking for hidden compartments. He sliced open the shoulder strap and pulled out the padding. Within a few minutes, the bag was a shredded mess, with most of the nylon cut away from the frame.

Nick sat back on his heels and looked at the shambles he'd made. The only part of the bag still intact was the thick plastic base. He examined it carefully, probing it with the tip of the knife. He held it up and shook it, but the silence told him nothing.

He reached into what was left of the bag and felt to see if there was a compartment in the base. With his left hand on the outside and his right on the inside, he estimated his hands were at least four inches apart. That was plenty of space. That's why Golden had the clubs cut down, so they would fit in the bag on top of the false bottom.

He went back into the closet and pulled out the golden shovel he had seen there. Gripping it with both hands, he brought the sharp tip down hard onto the base of the golf bag. Once, twice, and on the third blow, the base split open, spilling a dozen little black velvet bags across the floor of the hallway.

***

Once Nick ran from the plaza, Walter hustled Jeannie and Victoria out in the opposite direction, north toward the Keene house. Walter maintained his grip on Victoria and Scorch stayed close to Jeannie.

He whispered in her ear, "You gonna cooperate, or do I got to give you a concussion?"

Jeannie said nothing and just walked.

"You ain't such a hotshot when my hands aren't tied, are you?" He prodded her in the ribs with Thor.

She whipped around to face him. "You touch me with the fucking hammer one more time, I'm going to rip it off your arm and shove it down your throat."

Despite the size and strength differential, Scorch was momentarily intimidated by the ferocious way she delivered her threat. He pulled himself together and raised his arm to strike her when Walter yelled at him to stop.

"We don't need a display of violence, Scorch. Control her. She's half your size."

"Yeah, well, she's fuckin' mean."

"Quiet," Walter said. They were now at the crest of the little bridge. He looked north toward the Keene house, and then surveyed the private marina. "Let's get out of the rain, shall we?"

***

Nick sat on the floor of Richard's hallway surrounded by the mangled remains of the golf bag, and in his hand, he held a couple of million dollars' worth of diamonds.

He poured the stones back into their black bag, then went to the kitchen in search of something he could use to hold them all. He scrounged up a plastic shopping bag from Publix and dumped all twelve bags of diamonds inside.

He pulled Jeannie's phone from his pocket and called Walter.

"That took longer than five minutes. I was beginning to think you had abandoned your women."

"I ran into some complications," Nick said. "We're good now. See you in the plaza again?"

"I think not. This time, I'm making the arrangements.

Yours didn't turn out so well."

"Okay, what do you have in mind?"

"Walk to the crest of the bridge by the Keene house," Walter said, then disconnected the call.

Nick stood and looked around at the chaos he had caused. He picked up the knife that he had used to destroy the golf bag and slipped it into one of the pockets of his cargo shorts. He grabbed the Publix bag and walked out into the rain.

***

Nick stopped at the top of the little bridge. There was no one there. From this vantage point, he had a good view of the Keene's private residence, both marinas, and several townhouses. He stood in the rain, the plastic bag of diamonds at his side, looking for some sign of Walter and the hostages.

His phone rang.

"Walk toward the Keene's private marina," Walter said. "I'll tell you when to stop."

Nick continued down the bridge and retraced the path that he and Jeannie had recently taken on the way to their first rendezvous. He held the phone to his ear, waiting for his next instructions.

When Nick reached the first slip, he heard Walter's voice say, "Stop there." After a moment, he said, "Go aboard *Andy's Dream* and wait."

"No," Nick said. "I'll only do the exchange in public. We already talked about this."

"Fine," Walter said, and again disconnected the call.

As Nick stood there waiting for Walter to emerge, he heard the loud bang of a gunshot, coming from the big sailboat.

"No!" Nick yelled, and sprinted toward the boat as fast as he could over the rain-slick dock. He jumped on board just as Walter emerged, the smoking gun in his hand.

"I'm glad you decided to see it my way," Walter said.

Nick shoved past him to the open hatch and jumped down into the cabin, calling "Victoria! Jeannie!" The air in the poorly ventilated cabin was hazy with smoke and reeked of both gunpowder and Scorch's festering wound. Through the haze, he saw that Scorch was standing guard over Jeannie and Victoria, and neither of them appeared to be injured. He rushed toward the women and tried to take both into his embrace at the same time. "I thought he killed one of you," he said.

"Not yet," Jeannie said.

Walter came down the steps into the main cabin. "I guess I know how to get your attention," he said. He held out his hand. "Now give me the bag."

Nick handed it over and Walter emptied the contents onto the table. He grabbed one of the small velvet bags and poured the contents into his hand. Even in the dim light of the boat cabin, the diamonds sparkled.

"My retirement fund," Walter said. "I was beginning to think I might never see it, and I have you to thank, Mr. Rohmer. You have turned out to be extraordinarily resourceful, for a bean counter. I must admit that you have surprised me."

"Okay," Nick said. "You have what you wanted. Now let's get out of here. Victoria and Jeannie won't say a thing as long as you have me as a hostage."

"That is very gallant of you, Mr. Rohmer, but unfortunately, you aren't of any further use to me. I do, however, have need of a boat captain since the ferry is not running. Turn around."

"We had a deal," Nick said.

"No, we didn't. Be happy I don't shoot you on the spot. Now turn around before I change my mind." Nick turned his back to Walter. "Miss Keene, I need you to tie Mr. Rohmer's hands and feet. I'll be checking the knots."

Jeannie pulled some rope from a storage bin and tied Nick's hands behind his back. She then had him sit on the settee and bound his feet. "Sorry, Nick," she said.

"Please do the same to Victoria's feet," Walter said. "We don't want her running around and getting hurt."

When she was finished, Walter checked all the knots and found them to his satisfaction. Next he went to the forward cabin. He returned a moment later with a large black knob in his hand. "This opens the forward hatch," he said. "I'll be taking this with me. I'll also be locking the main hatch. Once I get where I'm going, I'll let Miss Keene go and she can notify someone to release you. Does that sound fair?"

"It's more than you did for Andrew," Nick said. "You must have really hated him to strangle him in cold blood like that."

"You're a clever boy, Nicholas, but you're misinformed."

"So I guess it was just a coincidence that he died right after ordering a complete audit of the books that would have uncovered your embezzlement?"

"That was no embezzlement. That was getting back what was taken from us. Andrew stole the company from Richard and me, forcing us to sell out far below fair value, then hiring us as lackeys to work for him. That was our money we got back. Now it's my retirement fund, and believe me, I earned it."

"And you completed your revenge by strangling Andrew," Nick said.

"Believe what you wish. I haven't time to argue. Miss Keene, you're in the lead. Come on, Scorch."

Jeannie climbed the three steps to the deck, followed by Scorch.

Walter lingered a moment after they passed, then he stepped up to the electrical panel and flipped a few switches. "This one," he said, "turns off the power to the galley." He flipped the switch, then walked to the range and turned on a burner. He then carefully removed the burner's control knob. "With no power, there's no pilot light," he said, and he turned on the second burner, also removing the knob. "So the gas will just settle in the bilge." He turned on the last two burners, taking the knobs off in the process. "When the bilge pump comes on, they'll be a small electrical spark, and the boat will explode. But, if you're lucky, the gas might suffocate you first."

Victoria started to cry.

"Why're you doing this?" Nick asked. "You got your money."

"Loose ends, Mr. Rohmer. I hate loose ends."

Walter climbed to the deck. Once topside, he closed the hatch and Nick heard the lock click into place.

"Shit!" Nick said.

TWENTY-NINE

When you're the boss, you have control over a lot of lives. If you let that be a burden, you'll sink under the weight.

From – *It May be Lonely, But There's a Hell of a View – Conversations from the Top*

"Shit!" Nick said again.

Victoria was crying so hard that she was having trouble catching her breath. To Nick, it looked like she was approaching full-blown panic. He couldn't blame her.

"Victoria. Victoria!" The second time he shouted to get her attention.

She looked at him.

"I can get us out of this. You have to be calm."

"How? We're trussed up in here like lambs for the slaughter!" She was yelling.

Rather than answer, Nick rolled from his sitting position onto his back and crunched his knees up to his chest as tight as he could. He worked his bound hands down his back and around his butt then squeezing slowly, painfully, he forced his feet between his arms, getting his hands in front of him.

Victoria watched in astonishment as Nick transformed into a contortionist before her eyes.

He now sat upright and bent to his feet, quickly untying the rope around his ankles. He was grateful that he was now familiar with Jeannie's knots.

"Turn around, Vic," he said. "Let me untie you."

She turned and presented her bound hands, and within a few seconds, she was loose.

"Now me," he said, and he extended his hands toward her. She struggled with the knot, uncertain how to untie it. "Never mind. There's a knife in my pocket." Nick thrust his hip pocket toward her, the one that held the knife he had taken from Richard's townhouse.

She reached in his pocket and in five seconds had the rope cut from his wrists.

He ran to the galley to try to turn off the gas, but with the knobs gone there was nothing he could do. The smell of gas was strong.

He looked around for something, anything he could use to break the hatch. Like Jeannie earlier, he grabbed a fire extinguisher. Using it as a battering ram, he smashed it into the hatch that led to the deck. The wood was resilient, built to resist the pounding of heavy seas, and it appeared that Nick's attack was doing little damage. He kept at it, concentrating his blows on the area around the lock, and after a few powerful hits, the wood began to splinter.

Two more blows of the extinguisher separated the hatch from the frame, and Nick was able to slide it open. He turned to Victoria and offered her his hand. She took it and the two of them climbed up to the deck.

They immediately jumped to the dock and put as much distance between themselves and the boat as possible.

Once clear, he stopped and took a deep breath. Victoria threw her arms around his neck and gave him such a powerful hug she almost choked him.

"Thank you, Nick," she said. "I was sure we were going to die in there."

He pulled her off of him. "No time. You need to get up to the Keene house and tell them what's going on. Call the Coast Guard. He's going to kill her once they get to land."

She nodded. "Okay. What about you?"

"I want to see what boat they took. I'll join you."

"Okay," she said and turned to run for help.

Nick looked around the little marina to see what boat Walter had chosen for his getaway. The bigger boats all still seemed to be in their slips. He looked for the small center console boat that he and Jeannie had been using for the last two days, but it was gone. Nick peered out into the windswept bay toward Miami but saw no sign of it.

He looked closer inshore, and thought he saw a glimpse of something moving into the little channel between the two islands, but it disappeared behind the seawall before he could be sure.

Nick ran up to the road, and as he neared the bridge, he saw the boat coming through the channel, headed east into the Atlantic. He broke into a run.

He reached the crest of the little bridge just as the boat was passing under. Without pausing to check speed or angles, he jumped up and over the railing, and down toward the canal fifteen feet below.

He landed hard on the deck toward the bow and he heard something pop in his right leg. He fell heavily on his side and rolled to a stop at the feet of Walter Hughes.

Walter had his gun out, pointed directly at him. "Another surprise from the indomitable Mr. Rohmer. Do you have a plan? Did you give this any thought before you hurled yourself off the bridge?"

Before Nick could answer, the rumble of an explosion overtook them. He looked back toward the marina and saw a cloud a black smoke being whipped by the wind.

"What the hell was that?" Jeannie asked.

"That was *Andy's Dream*," Nick said. "Walter expected that Victoria and I would still be on it."

"You tried to kill them?" Jeannie said.

"Guilty as charged," Walter said. He continued to point the gun at Nick. "Sit right there and don't make any trouble, and I might still decide not to kill you both."

"You may as well give up," Nick said. "Victoria's already called the Coast Guard."

"It's a big ocean," Walter said. "On a day like this, a boat this size is hard to spot. I think I'll take my chances." He stepped over to the console next to Jeannie and ripped the microphone from the marine radio. "We can't have you giving any hints to the Coast Guard, can we?"

As the little boat left the channel and made its way into the Atlantic, it started to be tossed around by the waves. Walter seated himself so that he didn't fall over. Jeannie gave the boat more throttle, and they headed east for a while, before she made a slow turn to the north, per Walter's instructions.

***

A half hour out from Boca Cheeca, they sailed into another squall. The wind increased suddenly and they were lashed by hard rain. Visibility dropped to near zero, but Jeannie held course. There was no boat traffic or land for miles.

Scorch had been in a half sleep, but the rain roused him. Donna was next to him again, her floppy hat undisturbed by the powerful wind of the storm.

"You need to get paid, babe," she said. "All that money is right here, waiting for you to take it. It's time you took it."

Scorch stood and stared out at the sea. "I need to fucking get paid!" he shouted.

"That's right, babe!" Donna yelled.

"I need to get fucking paid now!"

"Sit down, Scorch," Walter said. "No one knows what you're talking about."

Scorch turned to Walter with fever-red eyes. "I need my fucking money, man."

"This is neither the time nor the –"

"Pay me!" Scorch yelled, and he hurled himself at Walter.

"Kill him!" Donna yelled.

Scorch's ferocious attack caught Walter unprepared. Scorch landed on him, pinning the gun between them. He raised Thor and brought it down with a sickening crunch onto Walter's head. "Pay me, motherfucker!" he shouted.

***

Nick and Jeannie watched in stunned silence as Scorch smashed his hammer into Walter's head again and again, shouting, "Pay me!" with each blow.

After thirty seconds of this, Scorch went limp. His body slumped and he rolled slowly off of Walter, revealing a red mass of exposed brain and shattered bone where a head once was.

The rain continued to pour, with streams of blood-red water flowing down Walter's body and onto the deck.

Scorch's eyes were closed, and he appeared to be unconscious. Nick stood carefully on his good leg and tried to quietly approach Walter's body and the gun that was still clutched in his dead hand. He took one limping step, and Scorch opened his eyes.

"No you don't," he said. He grabbed the gun and pointed it at Nick.

Nick stopped where he was and put his hands up. "What now, Scorch?"

Scorch looked over at Walter's corpse and then at the blood-soaked hammer and arm that had done the damage. "He needed to fuckin' pay me," he said, without force this time.

"You're paid," Jeannie said. "The money's all yours. We'll take you to shore – anywhere you want to go."

"I hate both of you," he said. "So fuckin' smug. And you," he pointed the gun at Jeannie. "You're just a mean bitch."

The rain had begun to let up, and it was possible to see land again to the west. Scorch sat and looked out at the horizon. After a moment, Scorch's gun hand started to weave unsteadily. The barrel dipped and was pointed at the deck. Scorch's eyes closed.

Jeannie made a lunge for the gun.

She wasn't quick enough.

Scorch felt her coming and snapped to attention. He swung Thor at Jeannie as she grabbed for the gun, but she was inside the arc of his swing and blocked the blow with her arm. She cried out in pain.

Nick tried to come to her aid, but he didn't get far on his injured leg before Scorch had them both at gunpoint again.

Jeannie stood there rubbing her arm and giving Scorch her fiercest stare. "What now, asshole?" she said. "Are we just going to wait for you to pass out?"

"Fuck that. You get in the water."

"Sure," Jeannie said. In one fluid motion, she stepped back to the wheel, killed the engine, and took the key from the ignition. She stood near the gunwale dangling the key from her hand. "I go for a swim, the key comes with me."

There was an explosion as Scorch fired the gun at Jeannie. The bullet hit her, spinning her around. She fell over the side, into the water, dropping the key on the deck.

For an instant, Nick was frozen. Then he scrambled across the boat and peered over the side where Jeannie had just disappeared. Other than a faint trail of red in the water, there was no sign of her.

"What did you do?" he screamed at Scorch. "You killed her!"

"You're next," he said.

Nick ignored Scorch behind him and continued to scan the water, looking for any sign of Jeannie, but there was nothing. He looked astern, thinking their forward momentum might have carried them away from the body. There was no trace.

Nick bent down and picked up the key. He looked at Scorch.

"That didn't help her, it ain't gonna help you."

"Catch," Nick said, and he tossed the key to Scorch.

With one dead hand taped to a hammer, and the other holding a gun, Scorch was momentarily at a loss. Nick took advantage of his indecision, and launched himself across the boat, pushing off with his good leg, aiming for the gun.

He came up short, hitting Scorch in the legs, knocking him over. They landed in a heap on the deck, Scorch trying to beat at Nick with Thor, while getting the gun clear of their tangled bodies.

He landed only weak blows on Nick's back but won the skirmish when he pressed the barrel of the gun to Nick's head. "Get the fuck off me," he said.

Nick stopped struggling, and backed away, still on his knees.

Scorch stood. He spotted the key on the deck, and placed his foot over it while keeping Nick covered with the gun. "Get in the fuckin' water," he said, "or I'll shoot you and throw you in."

"Okay," Nick said. He stood slowly and limped backward toward the stern. When he reached the transom, he stopped and looked behind him at the gray water of the Atlantic. He looked back at Scorch. "You sure about this?" he asked.

Scorch's answer was to raise the gun and take aim.

"Fine," Nick said. He turned to face the water and balanced himself with a hand on the transom, next to the cleat with the dock line attached. Nick sat and swung his legs over the side, putting one hand on the rope.

"Don't be such a goddamn wimp, and jump," Scorch yelled.

Without another word, Nick slid into the ocean, the dock line still in his hands. He treaded water and pulled the rest of the line over after him, then carefully wrapped it around the shaft of the propeller and backed away.

He swam along the side of the boat, staying up close. An observer on deck would have to lean far over the water to see him, snug up against the hull. He waited for Scorch to start the engine.

Something touched his shoulder, and he spun around to find Jeannie, her finger to her lips, a bleeding wound on her arm, and a smile on her face.

Nick grabbed her and pulled her to him, and she grunted. "Arm," she said. "Bullet."

"Sorry," Nick said, trying to keep his voice low despite his excitement. "I thought you were dead. I couldn't find you."

"My mom used to say I could hold my breath for a week."

"Even with a bullet wound?

"It's a small one." She showed him the wound in her shoulder. It was more than a graze. It looked like it took a chunk of skin and muscle, but had missed the bone. "I'll be okay." She pointed to the back of the boat. "I saw what you did with the line," she whispered. "Brilliant."

"If he can figure out how to start the engine."

At that moment, they heard the first sounds of the engine turning over. It roared to life, and Jeannie and Nick drifted back from the boat, unsure of what might happen next.

***

Scorch revved the engine, then let it settle back to idle, the way he had seen Jeannie do it. When the speed was constant, he pressed the button on the throttle that engaged the propeller, and he heard the distinct "clunk" as the prop was engaged. He pushed the throttle forward.

There was a terrible shudder that pulsed through the boat as the propeller seized up from the rope tied around it, stripping the prop hub. With the connection between the engine's drive shaft and the propeller severed, the engine was a useless hunk of iron that was good for little more than making noise and burning fuel.

"Why aren't we moving?" Donna asked.

"We're not?" Scorch looked again at the throttle and pushed it all the way forward.

"That bitch did something to the boat," Donna said.

Scorch let the engine rev at full speed for another minute. Finally, he throttled back down and went aft to examine the engine. He saw the dock line wrapped around the prop.

"It wasn't her, it was him." He uttered a monumental string of expletives, even by his standards, and concluded by slamming Thor into the top of the gunwale, punching a hammer-sized hole in the fiberglass. It took him some effort to extract the hammer.

He finally sat in the captain's chair and shut the engine off. "What now?" he asked, but Donna was gone.

With the engine silenced, Scorch heard a voice calling him from the water. He shook his head to rid himself of this new delusion, but there it was again. Calling his name.

***

"Scorch," Jeannie yelled. "Scorch, over here." She was treading water about ten feet from the boat. "Yoo-hoo, Scorch."

Scorch finally stood and came to the side of the boat. He looked at Jeannie. "You're dead. I fuckin' shot you," he said.

"Missed me," she said. She ducked her head underwater and swam under the boat. She reappeared on the other side of the boat, ten feet beyond his reach.

"Over here!" she yelled.

Scorch walked across the deck to the other side of the boat, picking up the gun on his way. "You're dead," he said again and took aim with the gun.

Before he could fire, Jeannie ducked underwater again and swam back under the boat once more, surfacing where she had started.

"Behind you," she shouted.

Scorch ran back across the deck, trying to aim as he moved. Jeannie ducked underwater again, and this time surfaced up against the hull, out of his line of sight, next to Nick.

They could hear him on deck, moving from side to side, trying to find her again. She reached up the side of the boat and grabbed the gunwale. She briefly pulled herself up to the level of the deck. "Over here," she said and dropped back in the water.

Scorch came to the side and leaned over. He spotted Jeannie up against the hull.

"Boo!" she said.

Scorch reached over the side with his gun hand, and tried to take aim at Jeannie, but before he could, Nick burst to the surface and grabbed his arm. He yanked with everything he had and pulled Scorch over the side of the boat and into the water.

One moment he was on the surface, staring into the faces of Nick and Jeannie, and the next he was gone. Scorch sank quickly and seemingly without a struggle, dragged down by the weight of a hammer taped to one hand, and a Beretta clutched in the other.

THIRTY

Being right means never having to say you're sorry. To anyone. Ever.

From – *Business Ethics: Hard Choices*

Nick and Jeannie were huddled together in their little boat in the middle of a big ocean. The rain had stopped hours ago, and now the clouds were breaking up, making for a spectacular sunset.

Nick's ankle had been the size of a cantaloupe but was now down to grapefruit size. Jeannie's shoulder had stiffened up once they were out of the water, and was bandaged in whatever they could find in the boat's first aid kit. The body of Walter Hughes was just where Scorch had left it, since neither of them wanted to touch it. They both tried not to look at it.

They had been keeping careful watch for other boats, signal flares at the ready. They had seen two commercial freighters and were disappointed two times when neither had seen their flare. They were down to their last one.

Jeannie flipped on the boat's running lights. "We should have enough battery for tonight," she said.

"I see a boat." Nick pointed. "Over there."

Jeannie looked where he was pointing and saw a boat approaching fast, bouncing over the chop. "Give me the flare," she said, and he did. She sparked it up and started waving it frantically. The approaching boat sounded its horn to let them know they had been seen. Nick grabbed Jeannie around the waist and picked her up, spinning her around. She continued to wave her flare, but as a victory salute instead of an emergency signal.

When the approaching vessel was close enough to see, Jeannie said, "I know that boat."

As it pulled up beside them, Jeannie threw them a line and shouted, "Hey Biggie! What the hell are you doing out here?"

Biggie Johnson stood on the deck of his forty-two-foot cigarette boat. "Looking for you, Jean-bean. The whole world's looking for you. You want a tow?"

Jeannie nodded and rigged the boat for towing. When she and Nick were on Biggie's boat, Jeannie gave him a hug and stood up on her toes to kiss him. Nick shook his hand.

"How'd you find us?" she asked.

Biggie grinned. "I've been known to monitor the Coast Guard frequencies, just to see what they're up to. When we heard you were missing, the whole club got out and helped in the search. We have thirty boats searching between here and Key Largo. A Coast Guard plane spotted you about an hour ago, and we were the closest, so . . ."

***

Two days later, the Keene family hosted a party as a thank-you to Nick. Victoria was there, as was Paul Gonzalez-Smith, perpetually at the side of Charlotte Keene. The Boca Cheeca police department was invited, as well as Alex Sotolongo of the FDLE.

A buffet was laid out in the same dining room where

Nick had first met the Keene family, but this time, a room air conditioner hummed in the corner, chilling the air to a frosty seventy degrees. "It's just temporary," Skip said. "We have a central air system going in next week."

The dinner was extraordinary. With Philip no longer constrained by Andrew, he outdid himself. The buffet featured fresh Florida lobster, shrimp, and oysters. For the non-seafood lovers, there was filet mignon, roast duck, and mango salad. The desserts were many and varied, with the homemade key lime pie a favorite.

The crowd overflowed the small room, and despite the availability of the air conditioning, the party spilled out onto the screened patio. Nick was sitting by himself, a plate balanced on his knee when Victoria came up to him.

Nick stood and kissed her on the cheek and she took his hand. "I just wanted to thank you again for everything you did, and to say I'm sorry I was so unsupportive. I never realized . . . I mean, you never showed . . ."

"I know, Victoria. That's okay."

"I was wondering if, maybe, now that all this is over, you might want to give us another try?"

Nick looked into her beautiful blue eyes. "I think you were right about us, Vic. We're not a good fit. I love you, but I don't think I'll ever be the guy you're looking for."

She pulled his face to hers and kissed him. "I love you, too, Nick. Don't ever forget that," she said. "You take care of yourself. And don't forget to vote!"

"I'll be thinking of you when I do. See you, Vic." Nick watched as she walked away to join Paul and Charlotte by the dining room.

Jeannie came over and took Nick's arm. "What was that about?" she asked.

"Just saying goodbye," Nick said. He removed Jeannie's arm from his and took a step back to look at her. "No ponytail tonight? And a dress! Who are you?"

She gave a quick spin. "I wanted to impress someone tonight."

Nick gave a low whistle. "Whoever it is, he's very lucky." He looked around. "Is he here?"

Jeannie punched him in the arm.

"Ow," he said and rubbed the spot. "That's going to leave a mark."

"You're such a baby."

Nick looked over the group gathered on the patio. "Is your mom here? I wanted to talk to her."

Jeannie shook her head. "My mom's getting a new psych evaluation. The doctor thinks she could be out of Colonial Pines by the end of the week. Nelson's there with her. They're seeing what kind of help they can give him."

"I'm sure he'll be fine."

"With a little luck, we might have the family back together in a few days," she said.

Nick sat again. "Sit with me?" he said.

She sat next to him and then lay back on the lounge. "Come here," she said, pulling Nick down next to her. She turned toward him and their faces were only inches apart. She drew him close and kissed him. After a moment, she pulled back. "What's the matter?"

Nick sat up. "Nothing. I just keep thinking . . ."

"About what?"

"Your dad's murder."

"No!" Jeannie said. "I don't want to talk about that anymore. Not tonight, anyway. Let's talk about us."

He brushed a stray hair back from her face. "What about us?"

"I think we should take a vacation. A little trip to put all this behind us, just the two of us."

Nick smiled. "That sounds really nice. You have something in mind?"

"How about a cruise?"

"No boats," Nick said. "I've had enough boats for a while."

Jeannie laughed. "Okay. How about Paris? Ever been to Paris?"

"Sure. Paris, Ohio."

"I'm sure it's nice," she said, "but I meant the Paris in France."

"There's one in France, too?"

"Or how about Rome? Or London? They speak English there, sort of."

Before Nick could weigh in on his preference, Skip came out on the patio, banging his wine glass with a fork. "Attention everyone. I want to propose a toast." He waited until the group focused their attention on him. He raised his glass. "To my sister, the bravest, toughest person I know." He raised his glass again. "To Jeannie."

"To Jeannie," the group echoed.

"To me!" Jeannie said.

"And here's to Nick Rohmer," Skip said. "He uncovered Walter's fraud, found the money, saved my sister, and solved a murder."

"Don't forget he saved me, too," Victoria added.

"And saved Victoria. Here's to Nick." He raised his glass to drink and everyone joined him again. Nick blushed.

"How about a reward?" Jeannie said. "Isn't ten percent a standard recovery fee?"

Skip choked on his wine. "A finder's fee for the money his company stole? I don't think –"

"That's a great idea," Charlotte said. "We should do something nice for Nick."

Carolyn just stood with her arms crossed and looked at Nick with her usual disapproval.

"We'll talk about it," Skip said. "In the meantime," he turned to Nick. "I think we need a speech."

"Speech!" Jeannie echoed, and various voices in the crowd joined in.

After a moment of this, Skip said. "It looks like you have no choice. Let's hear it, Nick."

"I don't really have anything to say," Nick said, to a chorus of boos. "Ok. Fine. But you'll be sorry." He cleared his throat and scanned the faces all turned toward him. "First, I want to thank you for this dinner. It's a little different from the last one I had here." He raised his glass. "Well done, Philip."

There were scattered calls of "to Philip."

"Second, I should apologize on behalf of my former company. Now that I'm no longer employed by them I think I can safely say that they sucked, and you should seriously consider suing them for financial malpractice." That got a loud laugh from the Keenes.

"And third, I'm happy to take credit for finding the money and saving Victoria, but as to solving the murder, I'm pretty sure that the case is still open. Right, Special Agent Sotolongo?" Nick looked over at Alex standing by the French doors.

She nodded. "It's still under investigation."

"What do you mean?" Skip said. "Walter did it, didn't he?" He looked first at Alex, then at Nick.

Nick looked at Alex for guidance, but she just said, "It's your party and you have the floor."

"Walter did it, right?" Skip said to Nick. "He stole all that money and killed my dad when he heard there was going to be an audit. It makes perfect sense."

"Well," Nick said, "he did steal from the company, with Richard's help, but I don't think he killed your dad. He didn't need to."

"What about the audit?" Skip said.

"That would have taken weeks to find anything, and Walter's plan was to find the money and get out of town long before that. Your dad's death just complicated things for him. Also, he told me he didn't do it."

"And we're just going to take his word for it?" Skip said.

"He didn't deny anything else. He admitted to the theft, to the kidnapping, and he even told me he was going to kill me. It doesn't make sense that he would lie about that one thing."

"So, who did it?" Skip looked from Alex to Nick and back again. "Do you know?"

Alex held her hand out to Nick, in a "be my guest" gesture. "You're doing well so far," she said.

"I don't know for sure who did it," Nick said, "but I've given this a lot of thought the last couple of days. There's no shortage of suspects. Everyone that was here that night had a reason to kill Andrew Keene."

"Well, I certainly didn't," Skip said.

"Sure you did." Nick hesitated. "Are you sure you want to do this here? You're not going to like some of this."

"Of course I want to hear this," Skip said. "I think we would all like to know who you think killed my father."

"Okay, if you say so," Nick said. "Let's start with you, Skip. First, there's the money that you would be inheriting. That's a motive for everyone in the Keene family. Also, you're a natural suspect just based on your physical size. You were one of only three people that probably could have overpowered your father. And, the timing with the audit looks bad for you since you're stealing from the company."

"I certainly am not!" Skip said.

"Yes, you are. I spent a lot of time digging through the company records when I was trying to figure out Walter's scam. I know about the bogus subcontractor you set up and the fake bills you were paying to yourself, and I'm sure that Richard knew it too and was either getting a cut or was blackmailing you."

"I . . . We . . ."

"It's okay, Skip. For what it's worth, I don't think you did it. First, the theft was pretty small potatoes, and I doubt you'd kill to cover it up. And second, I saw your reaction when you found me over your dad's body. You were genuinely shocked. If you'd done it, you would have stood there and blustered, like you're doing now, instead of screaming like a girl."

"I never screamed like a girl," Skip said.

"Yes, you did," Charlotte said. "We all heard you."

Nick continued. "So, if we look at the question of who else was capable of physically confronting your dad, another possibility was Scorch. He was also in the office that night. He's the one that cut the screen and broke in. He sneaked into Andrew's office and stole some of his gold-plated souvenirs. They were found in the closet of Richard Golden's townhouse with the golf clubs. There was a gold shovel, an earth mover of some sort, and a plaque that appeared to have had a hammer mounted on it. Jeannie and I became very familiar with that hammer." He looked at Jeannie and she nodded. "But I think he took those things after Andrew was killed and that he didn't see the body behind the desk. If Scorch had killed him, he would have smashed his head in, or kicked him to death. Strangulation with a necktie wasn't his style. Too subtle."

"And that leaves Nelson as the only other person with the necessary physical capability to take on Andrew," Nick said. "Andrew had decided to have Nelson committed. I think Nelson found out and lost his temper. He shoved his father. He saw him fall and hit his head. He left a footprint in the blood from the head wound. When he later heard Andrew was dead, he just assumed he'd killed him. That's what he told the police when he confessed, right Chief?"

Buddy Grinnell just nodded.

"He didn't know about the necktie, and since that's what killed Andrew, it seems pretty likely that Nelson didn't do it. But, by knocking Andrew unconscious, he made it possible for anyone who found him lying there to strangle him. Not a lot of strength was needed at that point, so that opens the field of suspects further."

"Let's see," Nick said. "There's Betty Keene. No question she hated Andrew, and she was dedicated to harassing him, but in all these years, she's never done anything more violent than throwing eggs. She also tried to confess, to protect Nelson. She got the crime wrong, too. Right, Chief?

Buddy Grinnell nodded again. "She couldn't describe the tie."

"If she'd done it, she would have known what the murder weapon looked like," Nick said. "So it wasn't Betty, either."

"That brings us to Carolyn and Charlotte. Carolyn, your little scheme with the fake employees would have come to light in an audit."

Carolyn's face turned scarlet and she started to stammer. "I . . . I never . . . "

Nick held up his hand to preempt her objection. "I have the bogus employee names. None of them exist in South Florida. Also, their banking information is all the same. Their pay was going into an account controlled by you. But, like Skip's theft, it wasn't big enough to kill for. At least, I don't think it was. And Skip said that you were already in bed by the time Andrew was killed. I thought that eliminated you as a suspect until I found out you two have separate bedrooms. His sleep apnea machine is too loud, or something. That means he didn't really know if you were in bed or not. As it turns out, you were, but you weren't alone. You were with Charlotte."

This revelation started a loud hum of voices on the patio, as Carolyn found her voice and objected. "That's a lie! You have no idea what you're talking about!"

"How do you know that?" Charlotte asked, her voice as calm and even as ever. "I thought we were very discreet."

"She's lying!" Carolyn shouted. She turned to Skip. "Don't listen to her."

Nick ignored Carolyn and responded to Charlotte. "Nelson was taking pictures of your trysts. There's actually a series of photos of the two of you in an upstairs guest room that were shot shortly before Nelson had his fight with Andrew. It doesn't appear that either of you were in a position to murder anyone at that moment."

"He just happened to be taking our picture at the time

someone was killing Andrew?" Charlotte said. "That seems like quite the coincidence."

"Technically, it was about ten minutes before someone killed Andrew, but it's not as much of a coincidence as you might think. It looks like it was a regular evening activity of his. Nelson has pictures of the two of you almost every night going back months. He seems to have been a little obsessed."

"Who can blame him?" someone mumbled.

"So that eliminates both of us from suspicion?" Charlotte asked.

"It appears to, yes," Nick said. "You were . . . otherwise engaged at the time of the murder."

"So who does that leave?" Charlotte said. "Philip?"

"No," Nick said. "I don't think so. In this case, the butler didn't do it." He looked at Jeannie, and she shook her head.

"Don't," she said.

"When Jeannie and I picked Nelson up at the ice cream warehouse, he tried to confess to us." He turned to Jeannie again and spoke directly to her. "He told you he did it, but you didn't believe him."

"Well, he didn't do it," she said. "We know that now."

"You were so sure," Nick said. "It made an impression on me just how certain you were that your brother hadn't done it. Even he thought he did it. When he shoved your dad and caused the head injury, Nelson could have easily killed him accidentally."

"But he didn't," Jeannie said.

"You didn't even want him to think he might have done it. You're a good sister."

"He's got enough problems. He doesn't have to add that to the list."

Nick continued. "Later, when I tackled Scorch on the boat, right after we figured out where the diamonds were, you tied him up while I sat on him. You remember?"

Jeannie nodded.

"When I went to untie him later, I couldn't do it. You had to. It was some sort of crazy sailing knot that you use on the boat, I guess."

"What are you doing?" Jeannie said. "Everything's perfect the way it is. It's a perfect ending." She stepped in front of Nick and stared up into his eyes. "Don't you see how good we are together? What a great team we make? We got the money back. We saved everyone."

Nick met her gaze and was silent for a moment. "You're right," he said. "It was like nothing else I've ever experienced. For the first time, I felt like I was doing something real, something important, not just playing with numbers. And you, you're the icing. Beautiful, smart, rich. And you like me."

She grabbed his shirt, bunching it up in her two fists. "I love you," she said. She shook him hard, and then released him. "It may have been the fear, but I've never wanted someone so much in my life."

"Me too," said Nick. "But I can't leave it. Not like this."

Jeannie's eyes pleaded. "Please don't," she said.

"I couldn't untie that knot on Scorch, remember? You had to do it."

Jeannie said nothing.

"I've seen you use that knot two or three times since then. It's a go-to for you. I've never seen anyone else use it."

"It's a common enough knot."

"If you're a boater or climber, maybe. Anyway, I didn't realize it at the time, but there was one other place that I'd seen that knot."

Jeannie said, "Think about what you're saying."

Nick continued quietly, so that his voice carried only a few feet. "This is what I think happened, Jeannie. I think you saw your brother's fight with your dad, or maybe you saw your brother leaving the office agitated, and you went in there to see what was going on. You saw your opportunity. All the years of bullying - the psychological abuse of you, your mom, your brother - all that could end. You just had to be strong. You grabbed the first thing you found. You tied it around his throat and you choked the life out of him."

"Goddamn it, Nick!" she shouted. "You don't know what he was like! Someone had to do it! He was a monster. He destroyed my family. He had my mom committed, he drove my brother insane. He was doing the same thing to me! He had to be stopped! I had to stop him!" Jeannie began to sob. "I had to do it," she said.

Nick pulled her close, enfolding her in his arms, and she collapsed into him, sobbing. He held her and stroked her hair, her hot tears soaking into his shirt.

"He was a monster," she whispered. "You can't know what it was like."

The guests on the patio opened a way for Alex and Buddy as they approached. Alex stepped forward and gently removed Jeannie from Nick's arms.

"I'm sorry, Miss Keene, but you have to come with me now," she said.

Nick released Jeannie, still sobbing, and she turned and leaned on Alex. Buddy stood on her other side and held her by the elbow, and the three of them walked slowly from the house.

The End

About the author

T.A. Clark was born and raised in Pittsburgh, Pennsylvania and realized a lifelong dream of permanently avoiding winter by moving to South Florida after college. Following a spiritually unfulfilling career in credit and financial services, he is now writing full-time. He is the author of two other Bean Counter mysteries: *Old Flame*, and *Magna Finesse*, as well as the stand-alone mystery *Dead Loss.*

For more information, or if you would like to be notified about T.A. Clark's new and upcoming releases, please sign up for his email newsletter at: https://taclark.net/

Novels by T.A. Clark

Bean Counter Mysteries:
- Bean Counter
- Magna Finesse
- Old Flame

Adria Hill Mystery:
- Dead Loss

Fantasy (middle grade):
- Uncertain Magic

Made in the USA
Middletown, DE
18 May 2020